ACCLAIM

"Will remind readers what chattering teeth sound like."
—*Kirkus Reviews*

"Voracious readers of horror will delightfully consume the contents of Bates's World's Scariest Places books."
—*Publishers Weekly*

"Creatively creepy and sure to scare." —*The Japan Times*

"Jeremy Bates writes like a deviant angel I'm glad doesn't live on my shoulder."
—Christian Galacar, author of GILCHRIST

"Thriller fans and readers of Stephen King, Joe Lansdale, and other masters of the art will find much to love."
—*Midwest Book Review*

"An ice-cold thriller full of mystery, suspense, fear."
—David Moody, author of HATER and AUTUMN

"A page-turner in the true sense of the word."
—*HorrorAddicts*

"Will make your skin crawl." —*Scream Magazine*

"Told with an authoritative voice full of heart and insight."
—Richard Thomas, Bram Stoker nominated author

"Grabs and doesn't let go until the end." —*Writer's Digest*

I

BY JEREMY BATES

The No-End House ♦ Suicide Forest ♦ The Catacombs ♦ Helltown ♦ Island of the Dolls ♦ Mountain of the Dead ♦ Hotel Chelsea ♦ Congo ♦ Mosquito Man ♦ The Sleep Experiment ♦ The Man from Taured ♦ Merfolk ♦ The Dancing Plague 1 & 2 ♦ Denisovans ♦ White Lies ♦ Black Canyon ♦ Run ♦ Rewind ♦ Neighbors ♦ Six Bullets ♦ Box of Bones ♦ The Mailman ♦ Re-Roll ♦ New World ♦ Unpremeditated ♦ Once Upon a Halloween Night ♦ Dark Hearts ♦ Bad People

DENISOVANS
World's Scariest Legends 7

JEREMY BATES

Copyright © 2025 Jeremy Bates

All rights reserved

The characters and events portrayed in this book are fictitious. Any similarity to real persons, living or dead, is coincidental and not intended by the author.

No part of this book may be reproduced, or stored in a retrieval system, or transmitted in any form or by any means, electronic, mechanical, photocopying, recording, or otherwise, without express written permission of the publisher.

ISBN-13: 978-1-988091-85-3

ALSO BY JEREMY BATES

THE NO-END HOUSE

A stand-alone thriller novel from Kensington Publishing.

In the tradition of Stephen King, Alma Katsu, and Christopher Golden's evil supernatural twists, two strangers unwittingly volunteer for the ultimate haunted house challenge in Barcelona's Gothic Quarter.

Nine rooms. Nine tests. One chance to get out alive. No one makes it to the end of The No-End House.

Claim Your Free Horror Novella

Join the mailing list (jeremybatesbooks.com) for exclusive bonus content and a free copy of *Black Canyon*, winner of the prestigious Lou Allin Memorial Award.

A NIGHTMARE'S DREAM

I see my mind's mumblings, broken by its mirror

Thinking that it's you, drawing me nearer

Is it me, or is it you?

I hang by a string, a nauseous, vertigo view

A nightmare's dream, strangling my sleep

Its blanket of thorns bleeds me deep

It cuts my overheated heart,

That pleads for a cooler light within the heavy dark

                              -Tyler Cavell

PURPLE-HEARTED VEINS

I'm a son, a brother, a mother and a daughter

Lead us not to the slaughter, father

I'm still an unmarked, universal soldier

Take me to another place

Nurse stole my weed, she's diseased

knocked my brain to its knees

Wailing, "Psilocybin for the ward

psilocybin for the morgue!"

                              -Tyler Cavell

PROLOGUE
FOREST PEOPLE

The village was dead.

Or so it seemed to Lana Dao as she got out of the car and shaded her eyes with her hand. The dirt road she had driven in on bisected maybe two dozen shanty buildings. They were nearly identical, each composed of one or two rooms with thatched roofs. Most featured an adjacent vegetable patch, an outhouse, and a water well. Several water buffalo grazed on the parched grass that stretched away to a muddy brown river to the east and flooded rice paddies to the north. Chickens clucked about, scratching and pecking the ground, and a single pony stood listlessly inside a fenced corral. There were no power lines overhead; the village didn't have electricity. Lana didn't see a single person anywhere.

Two doors slammed shut, loud in the humid stillness, as her graduate students got out of the car.

"Wow," said Taylor Lane sarcastically, shuffling in a circle. He wore his blond hair in a messy bun, designer sunglasses, an oversized zebra-striped shirt beneath a zip-up black hoodie, and black pants tucked into black Doc Martins. His questionable fashion sense wasn't why Lana chose him to accompany her on the seven-day expedition; he was an exceptionally bright student who seemed serious about pursuing a career in zoology.

"Where is everyone?" asked Karen Zhang. She was dressed more appropriately in a wide-brimmed hat, long-sleeved nylon shirt, khaki pants, and sturdy hiking boots. Her auburn-dyed hair was braided into a single ponytail that reached halfway down her back. She was in three of Lana's courses, and her attendance record was spotless. She was a textbook teacher's pet: the first student to raise her hand and the last to leave the class, often so she could pepper Lana with questions about the lecture.

"Over there," said **Taylor**, pointing to the rice paddies.

Lana squinted against the glaring sun. For the first time she saw several lines of villagers bent over, planting rice seedlings. Their skin was sun-darkened and their clothing muddy. Conical hats obscured their faces. The bright reflection from the shin-high water in which they worked had made them difficult to spot. They would certainly have heard the car approach, but none of them looked Lana's way, let alone waved or called out.

"Not exactly a welcoming bunch, are they?" she said.

"Who cares?" said Taylor. "We're not hanging around. Let's roll."

"Just a sec, Tee," Lana said. "I'd like to speak to someone here first..."

"How about him?" Karen pointed toward the river. A man stood in the shade of a tree on the riverbank. He was looking directly at them. Like the others in the rice paddies, he didn't acknowledge their presence.

Lana waved. He didn't return the gesture.

"Weird," said Karen, and there was a note of unease in her voice.

"Guess they're just not used to visitors," Lana said. "You guys wait here. I'll be right back."

Lana started toward the river, feeling like an intruder on private land who had ignored all the KEEP OUT and TRESPASSERS WILL BE PROSECUTED signs.

The door to one of the shanties on her right stood open. As she passed it, she saw no one inside. In the next ramshackle building, however, a man was dozing in a hammock with a hat over his face, and in the shadows on the porch a woman sat on top of a wooden crate, breastfeeding an infant.

"*Xin chào!*" Lana said, smiling.

The woman didn't respond, and Lana wondered what the hell was going on. Was it Taylor Lane? Because he was white? Some Vietnamese who'd lived through the Vietnam War still held prejudices. They remembered the air raids and Napalm and Agent Orange. They lived through an era where everything from the West—music, jeans, dancing, books—was evil by official decree. But those attitudes were rare these days thanks to a booming economy bolstered by foreign investment and a government with Western-friendly policies. In Lana's more than ten years living in Hanoi, she could count on her fingers the number of times she'd encountered anybody openly hostile toward an American. For an entire village to hold such a view was unheard of.

Even so, Lana couldn't deny the vibes she was getting: these people didn't want her there.

A thin mutt appeared from behind the breast-feeding woman's shack. It growled and raised its tail in aggression.

Lana froze.

The mutt trotted to the edge of the road and paced back and forth, never taking its eyes off her. One was blue, the other amber. It stopped to scratch its side with its rear leg. Then it began to bark.

"It's okay," Lana said. "Good dog. You're a good dog…"

The mutt stopped barking.

She crouched and held out her arms. "That's a good boy. Aren't you a good boy? Come here."

Suddenly its demeanor changed. It loped toward her, its tail now wagging. It pressed its muzzle against her face and licked her cheek. Laughing, she cupped its head in her hands and scratched behind its ears.

And then recoiled in disgust.

It was covered in ticks. They swarmed over its fur and along its hairless belly, both tiny nymphs and fat, blood-engorged adults.

Lana shot to her feet and stumbled backward a step. But the mutt had found a friend in her. It rubbed up against her thigh and pushed its snout into her crotch, yipping and wagging its tail with such enthusiasm that its entire backside swayed from side to side. It likely wanted her to give its tick-infested pelt a good scratch.

Lana nearly retched. "Stop it!" she said, shoving its snout away. "Go!"

"Professor?" called Karen apprehensively. "Are you okay?"

"I'm fine!" she called back. "It's harmless." Then to the mutt again: *"Stop it!"*

The mutt stopped wagging its tail and cocked its head at her. It had likely never been spoken to in English before, but it could recognize tone, and hers was stern and angry. Perhaps it associated such a tone with a swift kick in its ribs by an annoyed villager or a beating with a stick. In any event it remained in the middle of the road for a few moments with something almost resembling betrayal in its differently colored eyes. Then with a reedy whine it lowered its snout to the ground and sulked away, disappearing behind the shack.

The breastfeeding woman was still watching Lana without expression, and Lana had the strangest premonition. *It's dead. The baby's dead. She's holding a dead infant to her breast.*

Averting her eyes, Lana continued toward the man standing beneath the tree. She stopped a dozen feet from him. He was elderly with skin like cracked leather and a thin, unruly mop of white hair. He wore loose-fitting black trousers and a white cotton tunic. In one hand he held a large knife and in the other a block of wood. It appeared he had been carving some sort of bird.

Lana bowed slightly. "*Chào anh,*" she greeted respectfully. She didn't expect an answer and didn't get one. She continued in Vietnamese, "Can we speak for a moment?"

He said nothing.

"My name is Lana Dao. I'm a professor at Hanoi University. I study primates and other mammals. I'm also interested in the myths surrounding the Nguoi Rung."

Something shifted in the old man's eyes, or at least Lana thought something did. His face remained inscrutable.

The Montagnard, along with other indigenous tribal peoples in the central and southern regions of Vietnam, have long held beliefs in the existence of a mysterious ape-like creature, often referred to as the Batutut or Nguoi Rung. The cryptid, described as a non-hominin hominid, is said to inhabit the remote mountains and dense jungles of the area. In 1947 a French colonist allegedly spotted the elusive creature (which he referred to as a *l'homme sauvage* or "wild man"), but it wasn't until the Vietnam War that Vietnam's Bigfoot went mainstream. Several U.S. patrols in remote locations reported encounters with ape-like creatures that were human-sized, bipedal, well-muscled, and agile. The soldiers nicknamed them Rock Apes because they threw rocks at the soldiers (usually in response to the soldiers throwing rocks at them first).

Such encounters weren't limited to American troops. The North Vietnamese Army and the Viet Cong reported their own sightings of the Nguoi Rung. There were enough reports to pique the interest of a North Vietnamese general who approved an expedition into the Central Highlands to capture one of the creatures. Although that proved unsuccessful, a professor from Hanoi University returned with a cast of a footprint that was wider than a human's at the inset but too large to be an ape's. The discovery spurred scientific debate within the country's academia, from anthropologists to cryptozoologists, and over the years other expeditions were mounted. They yielded no evidence of the Nguoi Rung, only more eyewitness reports, which ranged from the credible to the fantastical. Eventually interest in the mystery ape waned.

Lana had heard about the Nguoi Rung even before she relocated to Vietnam from California in 2010. Her field of interest was mammal morphology, and she'd always had an interest in cryptids. It was a hobby and nothing more, but she wasn't one to immediately dismiss the possibility that an elusive creature existed somewhere in the wild simply because it hadn't yet been substantiated by science. Many well-known animals today were once nothing but anecdotal stories rejected by the scientific community. A hairy, terrifying giant from the jungles of Africa: the gorilla. A hybrid of a donkey and a zebra in the Congo: the okapi. A venomous mammal in Australia with the feet of an otter, the tail of a beaver, and the bill of a duck that laid eggs: the platypus. Later discoveries included the Komodo dragon, the giant panda, the giant squid, and the oarfish, to name only a few—all famous cryptids until they weren't.

Lana was convinced the trend of myth becoming reality in the animal kingdom would continue. More new species were being found today than in any other time since the beginning of scientific classification in the mid-1700s, prompting naturalists to coin the 21st century "a new age of discovery." Within the last two decades hundreds of species of mammals had been classified, including a slew of marsupials and primates.

This was why Lana always kept an open mind when she learned about the sighting of a previously unknown and novel creature, even the tabloid-magazine variety. It was also why she didn't hesitate to fly to Bin Durong last week to hear first-hand from a young boy who claimed to have been attacked by a Nguoi Rung. The two-paragraph article she read in the *Hanoi Times* had been sparse on details, so she hadn't been sure what to expect when she met the kid at a hospital in Thủ Dầu Một; the world of cryptids was rife with profiteers and hoaxers. But the boy's injuries–several cracked ribs, a broken wrist, and a dislocated collarbone—were real, and he seemed genuine.

He told Lana that he and his sister were in the jungle north of their village when a Nguoi Rung attacked them and then carried away his sister. Lana questioned him for half an hour but couldn't find fault in his story. Yet what preoccupied her on the flight back to Hanoi—and what led her to organize the impromptu expedition to the jungle where the attack allegedly happened—was the reason for the children venturing so deeply into the jungle in the first place. The boy told her that the adults in the village sent them to leave sugar and salt and other ritualistic offerings for the Nguoi Rung. And if that proved true, it meant the existence of the creatures was not simply in one child's imagination.

An entire village worshipped them.

The old man finally spoke: "What do you want here?" His voice was scratchy and frail.

Lana said, "A boy from this village claims that he and his sister were attacked by a Nguoi Rung. I have spoken with him. He told me that the attacker resembled an ape but wasn't an ape. He said it was as large as a man, and there are no known primates in Vietnam that large."

The old man didn't reply.

"What of the boy's sister? Is she still missing? Has anybody gone looking for her?"

Nothing.

"What do you know?" Lana pressed, tamping down on her anger at his obfuscation. "Why do you send children to leave offerings for the Nguoi Rung? Clearly you must believe—"

"*There are no Nguoi Rung.*"

"Then what attacked the children?"

"You must leave."

"Tell me."

"You must—"

"*Tell me.*"

His jaw trembled. His black eyes blazed.

And then he told her.

\#

Back at the car Lana said, "He doesn't believe a Nguoi Rung attacked the children. He says it was a *ma quỷ*."

Karen gasped.

Taylor frowned. "What's a makwi?"

"A ghost," said Karen, her eyes wide.

"Or devil," Lana said.

Taylor laughed. "You don't believe in that shit, do you, professor? Come on, don't tell me you believe in that shit?"

"Of course I don't, Tee." She opened the car's trunk and heaved their three rucksacks onto the dirt road. "Gear up. We're not learning anything more here."

#

They sprayed each other with insect repellent, slathered on sunscreen, and slung their rucksacks over their shoulders. Then they set off north along the bank of the muddy, slow-moving river. Lana's plan for the expedition was simple. They would hike north for three days, remain at camp for the fourth to recuperate, and then hike back to the village. Her reasoning was that as long as they kept the river in sight, they couldn't get lost, a very real possibility in the disorienting jungle.

Moreover, every animal required water, and the **Nguoi Rung** would be no different. Hence the best place they might encounter one of the creatures, or at least evidence of one—footprints, scat, hair snagged in the bark of a tree—would be in the vicinity of the river.

They reached the spot where the field touched the edge of the jungle just before ten o'clock. The morning was already hot and muggy, and all three of them were sweating freely. Lana glanced at the villagers toiling away in the rice paddies to the west. They remained singularly focused on planting rice seedlings. Their fabricated effort to not see Lana and the students might have been comical if it wasn't so disturbing. It was a see-no-evil mentality, as though they saw something bad in the cards for the interlopers and wanted no part of it.

Lana knew she and the students were not in danger. She had been on countless field expeditions before, the majority in

Vietnam and Sumatra, but also in North and Central America while she was a professor at UC Berkeley. She had learned many lessons over the years, but the one she always shared with her students (and sometimes with her uninitiated colleagues) who joined her on an expedition was this: wild animals aren't out to get you, even the ones that are large enough to eat you.

Big cats are the boogeymen that most people fear. Jaguars and pumas in Central America, mountain lions in North America, lions and leopards in Africa, and tigers in Asia. However, in all the time that Lana had spent trekking through remote forests and jungles, sometimes for up to ten hours a day, she had never encountered a single big cat. She saw evidence of them, of course, and she didn't doubt one or two had stalked her from the shadows out of curiosity. But she wasn't a natural food source, and they had never bothered her, let alone tried to eat her.

So what happened to the two unfortunate village children? Why were they the exception to the rule? It was difficult to say without knowing for certain what attacked them. But supposing it was an elusive Nguoi Rung, Lana assumed they had done something stupid to provoke the creature. What this might have been, who knew? But when dealing with wild animals, respect and common sense went a long way—two traits that children didn't always have in great supply.

Lana produced a machete from the sheath on her belt and led the way into the jungle.

#

It was cooler beneath the trees. They filtered out most of the sun except for the odd spear of light that penetrated the lush canopy and vines and creepers to reach the tangled, shrub-covered ground. It was dark, too, and Lana found it difficult to see more than five or six meters in any direction. She removed her sunglasses and hooked them onto the neck of her safari jacket. Flies buzzed around her head, and it wasn't long before mosquitos began biting her despite the insect repellent.

Aside from the nearly constant drone of cicadas, the shadowy jungle world was preternaturally quiet. Lana heard the occasional caw of a distant bird, but that was all. She and the students were the ones making most of the noise. Deadfall snapping beneath their feet, palm fronds and tree branches swishing, a curse when one of them stumbled over the unreliable ground, heavy breathing. It all made Lana acutely aware of how ill-suited modern humans were to virgin, primordial environments. Without the supplies in their rucksacks, they wouldn't survive two weeks.

Progress was slow, and the hours slogged by. With no path to follow Lana had to pioneer her own through the thick underbrush. She did this on autopilot, barely thinking about where the machete was landing. When her shoulder began to burn from the effort, she switched the knife to her other hand. At one point she lost her boonie hat while crouching to get below a nest of low-hanging vines. When she retrieved it from the mud and looked back, she realized that she couldn't see Taylor or Karen. She heard them chatting though. You might not be able to see far in the jungle, but sound carried exceptionally well. It was deceptive, too. Although the students sounded as if they were just out of sight, nearly a full minute passed before they came into view.

"How you guys doing?" Lana called.

"Fine!" replied Karen.

"Bugs are driving me crazy!" said Taylor, swatting at the cloud of insects circling his head.

"They like his sweat better than mine," said Karen.

They stopped next to Lana and slumped down with aggrieved sighs on a moss-covered log.

"How much farther?" asked Taylor.

Lana checked her wristwatch. "I'd like to put in another couple of hours."

Groans.

"You guys can do it," she said. "You're doing great so far."

Just then a butterfly painted the bluest blue that Lana had ever seen alighted atop Taylor's head.

"Oh!" said Karen. "Don't move!"

Taylor frowned. "Huh?"

"Something's on your head."

He sat ramrod straight. "What is it?"

"Just don't move." She took her phone from her pocket and snapped a picture of him.

"*What is it?*"

"You don't want to know—"

Taylor leaped to his feet and ran his hands through his hair, shouting.

The butterfly flew away.

Lana smiled. "It's all right, Tee. It's gone now."

Karen was busting a gut laughing. Taylor snatched her phone from her hand and looked at the photo she'd taken.

"Aw, you fucker," he said, blushing.

"Language," Lana said.

On that note, they resumed the trek deeper into the jungle.

#

An hour later they came across the ruins of an abandoned village. The jungle had almost completely overgrown dozens of rickety bamboo huts. Plants tumbled out of windows and doorways, trees pushed through gaps in what remained of the thatched roofs, and vines teased their way between cracks in the foundations and walls.

The aerial roots of a banyan tree framed the doorway to a shack directly in front of Lana. She stuck her head inside. The walls were rotten and crumbling from decades of monsoons and humidity. Fallen leaves and branches littered the floor, which curiously had been dug down five or six feet into the earth.

"Careful, professor," said Karen.

"I'm not going inside," Lana said, stepping away.

"Wonder why this village was abandoned," said Taylor.

"I don't think it was a village. It could have been an NVA base..." Fists planted on her hips, Lana surveyed the other derelict structures. "You know what, guys? We've done enough hiking for today. Why don't we camp here tonight?"

"Thank God!" said Taylor, immediately slipping out from beneath the weight of his rucksack and dumping it to the ground. And then he began coughing. "Bug," he rasped, slapping a hand against his chest. "Just swallowed a bug."

"Couldn't wait for dinner?" said Karen. "And speaking of that, I'm starving. I'll collect some kindling for the fire."

Forty minutes later they had pitched their tents and had a fire blazing. Karen went about preparing dinner, and Taylor fished in the nearby river in the hopes of catching something to complement their meager rations. Lana set up a few mist nets to snag bats during the night so she could collect samples to study when she returned to Hanoi. While doing this she discovered an uncovered trapdoor in the ground at the bottom of a pit, confirming her suspicion that this was no village but rather an NVA or Viet Cong military base left over from the war.

By the time they finished dinner, twilight was fading quickly to night. They were all tired from the long day, and they had another full day of hiking tomorrow, so after cleaning up they said goodnight and retired to their tents. Lana was asleep within minutes of lying down on top of her sleeping bag.

She woke some time later to a scream.

She thought it had been part of her dream, but another scream followed: female, sharp, terror-stricken.

Karen.

Lana jolted upright and rolled forward onto her knees. She grabbed the zipper to the tent's door flap.

The scream stopped abruptly.

Lana hesitated.

"Karen...?" she called, fear in her voice. "Taylor...?"

Did she hear somebody moan?

She tugged the zipper down—and saw a large shadow dash past outside.

That wasn't Karen or Taylor—

The tent shook violently.

With a startled cry Lana fell back into the center of the groundsheet. The aluminum poles rattled. The polyester fabric flapped. Glancing around desperately in the dark, she gasped.

Pressed against one of the mesh windows was a gargoyleish face. The eyes peering in at her from beneath a bulging, ape-like forehead gleamed with malice.

Lana screamed, but all that escaped her throat was a whimper. The creature continued to savage the tent until its claws split the thin fabric. A muscular arm reached through the slit.

Lana scrambled on her hands and knees toward the door flap. Before she could get through it, the tent crashed down on top of her. So did the creature. It pinned her beneath its body, a weight so crushing she couldn't breathe. Powerful hands gripped her head and slammed it into the ground. Stars scattered behind her eyes. She heard a primitive, fiendish howl a moment before her head slammed against the ground a second time and everything went black.

PART 1
SAN FRANCISCO

CHAPTER 1

BAD NEWS

Ernest Campbell disliked waiting rooms more than just about anywhere else. Everybody sitting politely in their chairs and pretending to mind their own business, which was almost impossible when it was quiet enough you could hear the tick of the wall clock, fingers tapping on a mobile phone, or the whisper of paper as a frail hand turned the page of a People or Consumer Reports magazine. Even young children seemed to appreciate the held-breath reverence of waiting rooms; they were places where raised voices, whiny demands, and rambunctious behavior were Not Allowed.

And the doctor's waiting room was the worst of the bunch. Worse even than the dentist's. Because while a needle in your gums or a shrieking drill poking around your mouth was hellish, you can grin and bear that sort of stuff. It paled in comparison to facing whitewashed mortality. Like your doctor telling you, "Have a seat, Steve, I've got some bad news..." Or, "Well, Sally, it was nice having you as a patient..."

Doctors were not only purveyors of bad news but also experts on such matters. What they told you was gospel, and what they usually told you (unless you were a fourteen-year-old kid popping in for your yearly physical) was more often than not a diagnosis you didn't want to hear. *That looks like melanoma to me, all right. 'Fraid you got Type 2 diabetes. Might be a tapeworm.*

No, I agree, your eyes shouldn't be that color of yellow. Et cetera, et cetera, et al.

Ernest sighed silently to himself and shifted on the hard plastic chair. He glanced at his wristwatch (*twenty minutes now*, he thought, annoyed, *and I arrived early*), then around the waiting room. He might be pretending to mind his own business like everyone else, but that didn't stop him from taking a guess or two at some of these other folks' ailments. The Asian mother and her sniffling kid were probably just getting a flu shot. The twenty-something with the brim of his Red Sox cap pulled low might have gotten himself an STD on his last big night out. And all the geriatrics? Who knew? Your health was a crapshoot when you reached the Golden Years.

Ernest was very much aware of this. He was seventy-one years old, and he seemed to be seeing the good doctor three, maybe four times a year for one reason or another.

Getting old wasn't fun, the internal plumbing wasn't what it used to be...but that was life, so to hell with worrying about it.

An elderly woman with a cane resting between her legs glanced his way. She smiled as if to say, *I ain't dying today, sonny, what do you think about that?*

Ernest smiled back. It was little more than a tight press of his lips. Then he folded his hands on his lap, closed his eyes, and tried to doze off.

A few minutes later Dr. Gilsdorf emerged from a hallway adjacent to the reception counter. He chatted with the receptionist, laughed (doctors and receptionists seemed to be the only ones with a sense of humor in a medical clinic), and peered over her shoulder at her computer monitor. Most of the waiting patients looked expectantly at him. Ignoring the attention, Gilsdorf said something to the receptionist and returned the way he'd come. The receptionist fussed around a little longer before standing up and saying, "Mr. Campbell?"

Thank God.

Ernest went to the counter. Rebecca, the regular receptionist, must have called in sick because he didn't recognize the burly woman with the shocking hair. The roots were black, the mid-lengths blonde, the tips mauve.

"Hi," she said, picking up a clipboard. The questionnaire he'd filled out was on the top page. "Follow me, please."

She led him through a maze of little rooms, far too many for a clinic with only two general physicians and a urologist. She stopped before an open door and stuck the clipboard in a plastic sleeve attached to it. "Have a seat. Dr. Gilsdorf will see you shortly."

"Thank you…"

"Pearl. I'm just in on Thursdays."

Ernest entered the examination room. He sat in a chair opposite Gilsdorf's workspace. The only other place was the patient's bed, and he didn't want to disturb the disposable tissue-like paper that draped it. He wasn't there for a physical exam; the Z-Pak of antibiotics that he was taking for his cough, mild yet frustratingly persistent, wasn't doing the job, and he needed something stronger.

On the wall opposite Ernest was Gilsdorf's black-framed medical school diploma, as well as several other certificates representing postgraduate endeavors. Medical supplies lined two shelves along another wall. Space had been made for three framed photographs: Gilsdorf's daughter, Lisa; his son, Luke; and an overweight golden retriever. No wife. Gilsdorf had been divorced since before he became Ernest's GP ten years earlier (when Ernest's previous GP retired early and moved to the Bahamas).

Surprisingly, Dr. Gilsdorf arrived within a few minutes. He was short and bald with trendy tortoiseshell eyeglasses. His beefy paunch filled out his white coat. He always wore attention-getting running shoes, and today's flavor was a pair of fluorescent-green Adidas.

"Hi, Ernie," he said, scooping the clipboard from the plastic sleeve. His German accent was faint enough that you had to listen for it. "Appreciate you coming back in."

"You wanted to see me, and I was out of apples."

Gilsdorf smiled slightly, and Ernest felt a twang of unease in his gut. Gilsdorf loved bad jokes, and Ernest had been expecting a hearty laugh.

Ernest flashed back to the phone call he received two days ago from Rebecca. *Dr. Gilsdorf would like to schedule an appointment later this week to follow up on the bloodwork you had done. You can discuss the antibiotics with him then.* Innocent enough, Ernest thought. But on reflection Rebecca had been rather stoic. No chirpy chatter. No singsong *toodle-oo!* her usual sign-off.

Gilsdorf sat in the chair at his workstation and set aside the clipboard without looking at it. "So I've been reviewing your blood test reports," he said, foregoing the usual small talk. "I'm not sure how to break this to you, Ernie..."

The words were an invisible slap. Ernest blinked, thinking inanely, *Have a seat, Steve, I've got some bad news...* Only he wasn't a Steve, and this wasn't bored, internal dialogue. *I'm not sure how to break this to you...* Jesus Christ, this was real and happening. He was the chump in the meme, and it wasn't funny at all.

Ernest swallowed. "Break what, doc?"

"Good news first. You don't have high cholesterol."

Ernest didn't smile.

Gilsdorf sighed. "That cough of yours was bothering me, especially when you're otherwise fit as a fiddle. So I ran tests for tumor markers in your blood."

Tumor, Ernest thought with a hot wave of nausea. "I have

cancer?" he said flatly. He was too shocked to be surprised or afraid.

"The tests suggest the presence of cancer somewhere in your body, yes."

Now the coldness of fear flushed through him. "Lung cancer?" he said.

"I'm not an oncologist, Ernie. You're going to need more tests to—"

"But the cough...?"

"Might be related."

"Might? Be straight with me, doc."

"You're just coughing up green gunk?"

"Just?"

"No blood?"

"No."

"Well, that's good..."

"Shit," Ernest said quietly. He felt suddenly exhausted. And old. Very old. "Shit," he said again. "Wasn't expecting this."

"We might have caught it early."

"And if we didn't?"

"One step at a time," said Gilsdorf and swiveled his chair to face his computer. "I'm going to order you a chest X-ray for today, and we'll take it from there..."

#

Ernest had both an X-ray and a CT scan at a nearby lab. Shortly after he arrived home his phone rang. The radiologist had discovered a mass in his lungs that she believed was a carcinoma. The following morning a pulmonologist performed a diagnostic bronchoscopy. Ernest spent a restless weekend waiting for the pathology results, and at five o'clock on Tuesday he learned that he did indeed have lung cancer...but not only that, it was Stage 4 lung cancer.

Two weeks and many more tests and scans later, he was delivered a second and even worse diagnosis.

The cancer had spread to his spine and brain.

He likely had less than six months to live.

CHAPTER 2
FIRST DATE

I'm just a small girl in a big world trying to find someone to love, Nika Campbell thought as she took a moment to steel her nerves while standing beneath the green canopy of Harris' Restaurant on San Francisco's Pacific Avenue. Unlike Marilyn Monroe who'd coined that playful phrase, Nika had dark hair and dark eyes, thanks to her Indian and Spanish heritage. And also unlike Marilyn, Nika had yet to find love. Not once in her twenty-seven years on the planet. She might have thought she'd been in love once or twice in high school, but looking back she no longer believed that. Teenagers couldn't fall in love. They could fall into infatuations, maybe. But love? Real love? Nika didn't think so. Love was complex. Love was difficult. Love was painful. Love was an adult thing.

So says the woman who's just copped to never having found love. What do you know about it?

Not much admittedly. But she knew one thing for certain: it wasn't easy to find.

And you think you're going to find it tonight?

Only one way to know.

Nika entered the steakhouse.

\#

The classy interior smelled of beer, citrus fruits used in cocktails, and beneath that, faintly, cooked red meat. The button-tufted leather booths were large and comfortable looking. Moody pastoral artwork adorned the walls. Spotlighting illuminated vibrant-green palms in clay pots. All the tables were set, but only a few were occupied. Ditto for the stools that fronted the bar, which featured intricate dark woodwork and stacked crystal glassware. One of those stools was occupied by the man Nika believed was her date. She couldn't see his face, but his neatly trimmed brown hair looked like the photographs of Lee Jordon she'd seen on Tinder (where he'd described himself as an "adventurous soul" and "fitness enthusiast" who was "seeking a genuine connection"). Also, the only other person seated at the bar was in his late fifties or sixties.

Nika slipped onto a stool two down from her possible date in case she was wrong. He was drinking a gin and tonic. His phone rested on the polished bar top, and he was absently swiping the screen with a finger. He glanced at her, then at the phone... and then at her again, this time with his eyebrows raised inquisitively.

"Nika?" he said, and she was relieved to see that he looked the same in person as he did online. He might not be a Hollywood leading man, but he was handsome with a good complexion and pleasant brown eyes. Definitely a step up from her previous Tinder date, a bore named Travis something who had been a decade older than his profile pics suggested and had lost half his hair in the years between.

"Do we know each other?" she asked coyly.

"We do if you're the Nika I've been texting with."

"Do I look like her?"

His smile was lopsided but charming. "You do."

She mock-curtsied. "Then I am she."

"Great!" He stood and stuck out his hand. "I'm—well, you know who I am. I'm Lee."

Nika stood, shook, and moved one stool closer, leaving a lonely stool between them. They were still strangers, after all.

"What can I get you to drink?" Lee asked her.

"A white wine would be great, something dry."

When Lee caught the bartender's attention, he said, "One of your Napa Valley Chardonnays, Francis, thanks."

Nika chalked up a mental checkmark. Lee Jordon wasn't a cheapskate. Travis of the Missing Years, on the other hand, had ordered her a watery house Sauvignon Blanc on their date, which had been at a Thai restaurant where most people were picking up their food rather than dining in.

Nika gave Lee a discreet up-and-down glance. His black jeans and black turtleneck were safe but stylish. However, she chalked up another mental checkmark for his blue loafers, which appeared to be genuine crocodile leather.

Two checkmarks within the first two minutes of meeting each other? Slow down, NC, or you're going to be making out with him before the bill arrives.

And what's wrong with that? she shot back at her nagging doppelgänger. *Five long years in prison—during my prime, no less—so I think I'm entitled to a fun night out, don't you? I'm just a small girl in a big world—*

Yeah, yeah. Zip it, Blondie.

The bartender set a wine glass on a napkin bearing the restaurant's namesake and showed Nika the bottle's label: The Prisoner.

With a straight face Nika said, "Looks good to me."

"I'm not much of a wine drinker," said the bartender, a plump, pretty brunette in a white dress shirt and black vest. "But this is a good one. Medium-bodied."

"Vanilla and peach on the nose," said Lee. "Traces of apple, pear, and oak."

Nika was impressed. "You know wine."

He raised his gin and tonic. "I prefer these. But my brother sells wine. Every dinner he brings something fancy and forces everybody to drink it. Correction: he forces everybody to *taste* it. And then he'll tell everyone how it tastes."

"Are you two close?"

Lee nodded. "We get together most weekends, in fact. We have the same friends."

"Lee's a good catch, sweetie," said the bartender, tipping her a wink. "And he didn't tell me to say that."

"And he's rich, too!" the old guy down the bar said loudly. He was wearing a pressed pink dress shirt with silver cufflinks and drinking Scotch on the rocks. "But that don't mean he ever buys me a round!"

Pinkie and Francis the bartender shared a laugh, and then Francis went over to chat with him.

"You're popular around here," Nika said.

Lee shrugged. "I come by once a month or so. The food is good. And sometimes there's live music."

Come by with your brother? she wanted to ask. *Or with other girls you meet on Tinder like me?*

Jealously nipped at her heart, and although the emotion surprised her, it didn't bother her. Rather, it excited her. She had, she realized, been locked up for way too long.

Nika raised her glass. "To peaches and cream or whatever you said."

They clinked and sipped.

"So, Nika," said Lee, turning on his stool to face her. "Tell me something about yourself."

Why, funny you ask, Lee, because oh my do I have a whopper of a story to tell you…

It began in the spring of 2016. She was studying finance at Stanford University and life was good. She had fun friends, partied most days while still making all (or most) of her classes, and was looking forward to a bright future as a financial advisor or manager.

Then Ari Schwartz came along and ruined everything.

He was ten years older than her, handsome as an Arabian prince, and unquestionably the smartest (and shrewdest) person in any room. They met at a fancy piano lounge. She was there for a friend's birthday, he was dining in a private room, and they crossed paths on the back patio where they'd both gone for a cigarette. She was impressed by the conversation he made, and even more impressed when, later that night, he drove her in a Maserati to a club that was guest-list only.

Fast forward two weeks and they were seeing each other almost every day. A week after that he convinced her to drop out of school and join his tech startup, AS Solutions, which created tools for video game developers. He had a staff of ten, but they were all techies. He wanted an in-house accountant. Did she accept? She sure did, and that was the beginning of the end of her ordinary, simple life, she just didn't know it then.

Ari was a brilliant visionary and an equally brilliant CEO, and within a year, the little-known startup had raised over twenty million dollars from hundreds of individual and corporate investors.

At first everything was on the up and up, but then Ari got greedy. To secure larger investments, he made her falsely overstate the company's financial performance. The inflations to the monthly revenues inevitably led to the fabrication of entire corporate business relationships. It was a vicious circle necessary to support the increasingly audacious bogus statements. It got so out of control near the end that Nika began creating fake email accounts for prominent investors to convince investment firms to invest more and more money into AS Solutions.

Looking back, Nika didn't know what had possessed her to go along with the fraud—she had never participated in anything remotely criminal in her life before that—but she had been under Ari's spell. It wasn't love. More like awe...awe of his wealth, his power, and his intelligence. And surely her own insecurities played a part. Every day she wondered why someone like him was with someone like her, and when you live with a mindset like that, you're pretty much living with Stockholm syndrome.

In any event, Nika never took a penny for herself from the ill-gotten investor funds. Unlike Ari, who diverted massive amounts of money to his personal bank accounts which he used for everything from lavish weekend getaways on private jets to premium seats at sporting events to down payments on a mansion in Oakland and a fishing lodge in Colorado. This diversion of company assets surely hastened in no small part the sudden and spectacular collapse of AS Solutions.

In the summer of 2018 federal prosecutors charged Ari and Nika in a 19-count indictment. Ari pleaded not guilty and wanted her to do the same. She couldn't. The blinders were finally off. Ari was an emotionless, unrepentant sociopath. He cared about nobody but himself. The hundreds of investors they fleeced meant nothing to him. Nika, on the other hand, hated herself. She had been in a dark depression for months by then, and in a strange way she welcomed getting caught. She wanted nothing more than to right the wrongs they'd committed, or at least make amends for them, so she was more than happy to sign a cooperation agreement with the government.

A day before she was set to testify in court as a star witness against Ari, she was nearly run over by a car. She avoided it by a matter of inches, and only because a mother pushing her child in a stroller cried out when she saw the speeding vehicle barreling toward Nika. Ari had been behind the botched hit-and-run, she had no doubt about that. She saw the truth in his eyes the next day in court. He wanted her dead. And throughout her nearly eight-hour testimony, he accompanied his death stares with nasty laughs, scoffs, and a lot of head shaking.

His defense lawyer tried to discredit Nika by playing up her drug use (the truth was that Ari was a cokehead and she'd only tried the stuff on a couple of occasions at his insistence), but the cross-examination went nowhere. Ultimately a judge for the Northern District of California sentenced Ari to 145 months, or 12 years, in federal prison, while Nika received less than half of that time. She was released from the minimum-security prison camp that she had called home for the last five years just over three weeks ago. And the previous Monday she began a new "felon-friendly" job which didn't require a criminal background check as a sales associate in a mobile phone store.

Nika wasn't going to tell Lee all of this, of course. She couldn't think of a faster way to tank a first date than admitting to being a convicted felon. If they ever became serious, she knew she would have to tell him the whole saga. But that was a matter for another time, and so for now she simply replied to his question with, "I'm in sales. It's a terribly boring job and even more boring to talk about. So why don't we jump to you, Lee? What do you do?"

"I'm a doctor," he said.

"A doctor!" she said, surprised. "In a hospital?"

"No, a small clinic in Parnassus Heights."

"You know, I can sort of see you in a white coat. Stethoscope around your neck."

"He ain't your ordinary doc!" said Pinky from down the bar. His Scotch had been topped up. "He's a brain surgeon!"

Nika looked at Lee. "You're a brain surgeon?"

"They call us neurologists these days."

She grinned. "That's something you left off your Tinder profile."

"I don't want to date somebody who only wants to date me because I'm a doctor."

"You reel them in with your looks, huh?"

Now he grinned. "You're here, aren't you?"

"I liked the 'adventurous soul' stuff." She sipped her wine, and was she starting to feel a tingle in her fingers and toes? She was, and she didn't think that it was due solely to the alcohol. "So why's a brain surgeon on Tinder? I'm sure you have all sorts of other ways to meet women."

"Not really, no. I don't think I've ever approached a woman in a bar. I'm not comfortable doing that sort of thing."

"That's not what I mean. You know, friends of friends? People from work?"

"My circle of friends is rather small. Not to mention, they're all married, so that's that. And people from work—no thanks. I like my private life to be separate from my professional one."

"Why aren't you married?"

"Why aren't you?"

Oh, I don't know. Maybe because it's kinda hard to find a good man while locked up in a cage in an all-women's prison. What she said was, "I'm only twenty-seven. I'm still looking. You must be closer to…thirty-five? And speaking of that, you're awfully young to be a brain surgeon, aren't you?"

"I completed my residency at UCSF when I was thirty-two. So I'm young, yes. But I have a couple years of patient care under my belt."

"So..." she said, circling back, "too busy to get married?"

"I was married," he said and rattled the ice in his drink. "For nearly ten years. We separated earlier this year."

"Oh, jeez." Nika shook her head. "Sorry. I shouldn't have—"

"You should have." He smiled. "You're curious, and I like that. I feel like you might have a thousand more questions you want to ask, and I like that, too. I've only been on a couple of dates since the divorce was finalized, and they were rather boring compared to this one."

She smiled back. "Well, *I* like that you like that I'm nosey. But now I feel all this pressure to ask interesting questions." She raised her wine. "Cheers."

"Cheers again," he said, clinking. "Do you want to get a table and have a look at the menu?"

"I would love that." They stood. "I'll meet you there. I need to detour to the ladies'..."

"That way," he said, pointing. "I'll get a booth by a window."

Leaving her empty wine glass on the bar, Nika entered the hallway that led to the bathrooms. She didn't see the man in the beige trench coat until she turned to find him almost on top of her. He was huge and bald. His wide-spaced eyes were pressed like two onyx marbles into a face cratered with old acne scars.

Before she could say anything, he jabbed something into her belly and said in a thick voice, "Make a sound and I'll gut you right here." He had an Italian accent that reminded her of the thugs in mafia movies.

Nika looked down and saw a serrated hunting knife in his hand. Alarm shrieked inside her head. This kind of thing was supposed to happen in a dark alleyway, not in an expensive steakhouse.

"That way," said the thug, spinning her around roughly. The

blade pressed into the small of her back, sharp even through her thin leather jacket. "The kitchen." He pushed her. "Go."

The kitchen? she thought, stumbling a few steps before finding her feet. When they stepped through a pair of aluminum saloon doors, two cooks chopping vegetables at a prep station frowned at them.

"She's sick!" the bald man bellowed from behind her. "Where's the back exit?"

A chef wearing a pleated hat, a double-breasted white coat, and a folded red scarf around his neck snapped his fingers regally and told them to follow him. He strode toward a large metal door and pulled it open with a flourish. The goon shoved Nika toward it, sticking close enough to her backside to conceal the knife.

Nika felt as though she were in a dream. *I'm being kidnapped! Kidnapped in public, no less!* How was that possible? She was on a date, and it had been going so well. Now when she didn't return from the bathroom, handsome Lee Jordan would think she stood him up, and he was so nice, he was *a brain surgeon*, and he would likely never want to see her again—

See you again? Damn, NC! Who knows if you're even going to be alive tomorrow morning!

A part of her mind told her she had to stop this madness right now before it went any further, so she came to an abrupt halt, locking her knees. The bald man simply shoved her forward, forcing her to either fall over on her face or take a step. She took a step. And another one. She wanted to scream, plead for help. But then she was moving past the chef, stepping outside onto a busy street.

\#

The metal door clanged shut behind them. The sky was dark and starless. Cars tooled past on Van Ness Avenue, but there weren't any people on the sidewalk. Parked ominously at the curb, lit up in a pool of yellow light from an old-fashioned sodium vapor streetlamp, was a white SUV with tinted windows. Nika's mind screamed, *Time's almost up! Do something!*

She tried yanking her shoulder free of the bald man's grip (*it's going to leave a bruise, you know*, she thought stupidly), but he just squeezed harder.

She thrashed from side to side. "Let...me...go..."

The knife pressed harder into the small of her back. "Your old fling wants you dead," Craterface grunted in her ear. "He wants it filmed. But mostly he wants you dead. So get moving or I'm gonna unzip you from crotch to tits and leave you on a pile of your guts right here. *Capisci che?*"

Ari! Nika thought angrily. *Ari Schwartz, you asshole! You're behind this—*

The back door to the SUV opened. An ugly man with a head that was almost square peered out at them from beneath bushy black eyebrows. Craterface shoved her forward. She locked her knees again.

"I'll—I'll pay you double," she stammered.

Another shove, harder. She resisted.

"Get in the—"

His words died midsentence. He saw what Nika saw. Three uniformed police officers on mountain bikes had turned the corner of Pacific and Van Ness. One of them pulled a wheelie, raising his front tire a good three feet in the air. His buddies laughed.

The bald man stiffened against her.

"Don't say a—"

"No means NO!" Nika shouted, pulling away from him. "Now leave me ALONE!"

The cops braked to a stop on the other side of the SUV. The one who had done the wheelie pushed his helmet up his forehead a little and said, "Everything okay, miss?"

"Not really." She pointed a finger at the goon who was suddenly looking bored with his hands thrust into the deep pockets of his trench coat. She could tell the police the truth, but where would that lead? Blockhead in the back seat of the SUV leaping out with a shotgun and mowing everyone down? She added, "This creep won't take no for an answer."

"You bothering this lady, sir?"

Craterface raised his hands innocently. No serrated hunting knife in sight. "Hey, I know when I'm not wanted, officer. I'm going, I'm going." He walked past Nika without looking at her and slid into the back of the SUV. The door slammed shut, and the vehicle pulled away from the curb, vanishing into a strange dark tunnel…

The cop was wheeling his bike toward Nika, asking if she was okay, saying she didn't look very well—

She fainted.

CHAPTER 3
THE UNEXPECTED GUEST

The study was Ernest's favorite room in his Victorian mansion, and he sat there now, in a leather wing chair, staring at nothing, his mind on other times.

Much of his life had been lived out within the study's four walls. In the 1980s he installed an Apple II on the big antique desk, and it was there he wrote the code for his early microcomputer software. In the early 2000s, after he sold the company for more money than he would ever need, he spent his days in the captain's chair behind the desk writing articles for *Wired* magazine, tech journals, and numerous national newspapers, usually espousing the wonders of the emerging internet.

After Neeti, his wife of more than twenty-five years of marriage, died from ovarian cancer a few years later, he spent most days on the Chesterfield sofa reading histories and literature that he'd been too busy to read when he was younger. The cabinets on either side of the fireplace were still filled with the likes of Churchill, Herodotus, Shakespeare, Dickens, and his favorite author, Tolkien.

These days Ernest neglected the study for the most part, but he came back this evening. He'd had a lot on his mind since his cancer diagnosis, and this was where he did his best thinking.

He lifted his eyes to the portrait of Neeti, which hung on the oak-paneled wall next to equally opulent and rather haunting portraits of his parents. It was obscured in shadows, and he realized he hadn't noticed dusk come and go. He turned on the Tiffany-style lamp on the small table next to him and looked again at the portrait. Neeti had posed for the painting with her lush black hair pulled forward over her left shoulder. Her eyes —large, dark, and intense—stared out from a face that was as smooth and sweet as butterscotch. His heart ached as it did every time he thought of her.

"What are the chances," he said to himself, "that both of us would get the unfortunate opportunity to see our deaths coming…"

Ernest never had any illusions that he would live forever, of course. But he was still robust enough that he'd thought of his expiry date not in weeks or months but years. He was in better shape than most people his age. He walked five miles each day. He played tennis at his club on weekends. He ate healthily.

He wasn't supposed to die before his seventy-second birthday.

He certainly wasn't supposed to know *when* and *how* he was going to die.

People who suffered fatal heart attacks were lucky. A heart attack, at least, didn't announce its coming, and it was over before you knew it.

According to one of the oncologists Ernest had seen, his cancer had metastasized to the point that treatment would likely only extend his life by two months, maybe three. No thanks, he thought. Chemo and all that shit wasn't worth the privilege of dying in March instead of December.

So six months, give or take.

And maybe only half that time of relatively *good* days before the symptoms began to reveal themselves. He'd seen it all with Neeti: bedsores, bone fractures, vomiting, cracked lips, culminating with him bed-ridden in a hospital, breathing canned oxygen through a nasal cannula, feeling as though he was being strangled while begging for one last drip of morphine.

Ernest had two options, he knew. He could do what they do in those bucket-list movies and live what little time he had left to the fullest. He could go on a road trip across Canada. Eat shark in Iceland. Hike to Machu Picchu. Take a luxury cruise somewhere. He could do any of that, sure, but it wouldn't be like it was in the movies. He wouldn't find happiness or love or some deep insight into the human condition in his waning days. He would find only more sadness. Because eating at the back of his mind every hour of every day (just as vociferous as the cancer eating at him from the inside out) would be the thought that he was one hour closer to Death's doorstep.

That left the second option, and that was to never think about the ticking clock again, and the only way to do that was...

In a fit of rage, he threw the crystal tumbler in his hand across the room. It shattered against the broad front panel of his desk. Whiskey splashed across the Khorasan carpet, a sixtieth-birthday gift from an Iranian business associate.

"Fuck it," Ernest said, snatching the .45 caliber pistol from the small table with the Tiffany lamp. He went upstairs.

\#

The master bathroom was the only modern room in the old house, which his grandfather had rebuilt after it was largely destroyed in the earthquake and fire of 1906. Ernest had gutted the bathroom about a decade earlier, replacing the wallpaper and gilded mirrors and other fuss with clean lines, polished black marble, and accents of gold and bamboo. One wall featured a surrealist oil painting that had once been on display in the lobby of a chic London hotel.

Ernest sat on the edge of the bathtub so he was facing the painting. He had purchased it at an auction for more money than most people make in a year. He liked collecting expensive things. Not only artwork but luxury timepieces, Chinese porcelain, fine wine he didn't drink. These accouterments made him happy. Looking at them made him happy. Knowing how much they cost made him happy.

He was an idiot, he decided. All the things meant nothing. They held no value...no *real* value. Anyone who thought otherwise was also an idiot. Just as anyone who bought a house because it was the biggest on the street was an idiot. Or a yacht that required a crew to pilot. Or more cars than there were days in the week.

Christ, he thought, darkly amused. *I've known a lot of idiots in my life...*

Maybe monks had it right. Move to a monastery and renounce your worldly possessions. Devote your days to prayer, meditation, study. Concern yourself with nothing more stressful than cooking, cleaning, gardening, and perhaps old-fashioned cheese-making.

And never mind that pesky vow of chastity...?

Yes, that would have been a problem for Ernest. Not just abstaining from sex but also saying no to romantic relationships as a whole. That wasn't natural. Men and women were meant to live in union. He couldn't imagine never having shared his life with Neeti.

Okay, you're no monk, that much is clear...so how about you stop with all the navel-gazing and get to what's gotta be done?

Ernest looked at the Colt in his hand. Blowing one's brains out was a messy affair, which was why he came to the bathroom. No need to make things more difficult than necessary for the clean-up crew. He could have downed a bottle of sleeping pills with a liter of whiskey, he knew. But that seemed like the equivalent of slipping out the back door of a party. Lame, in other words. He'd considered hanging himself, and that would have been an acceptable way to go…if it worked. Because what if the chandelier tore free from the ceiling, or the rope snapped, or something else equally embarrassing happened? He might end up bedridden in a hospital—the very fate he was trying to avoid.

After an hour or two of morose contemplations, Ernest had decided there were only a couple of surefire ways to kill yourself. Jumping off something really high was one of them, and he had access to one of the most popular places in the country to do just that with the Golden Gate Bridge a forty-five-minute drive away. But they'd put up those suicide nets on the underside, which would make things tricky. Besides, why bother with all that jazz when he had the Colt 1911? Not only was it the champ of two World Wars, but it was also the standard-issue sidearm of the US military in 'Nam, and he had seen firsthand what a 230-grain ball could do to a human head at fifteen yards. With the barrel pressed snugly against his temple, his chances of survival would be zero.

"Shit," Ernest mumbled, turning the pistol over in his hand, which was clammy with sweat against the scalloped grips. He wasn't kidding around here, was he? His mind was made up. He was really going to do this.

So get to it and stop dicking around.

He pulled the slide back, loading a round into the chamber. *Clack-rack!* He thumbed down the manual safety. He cocked the hammer. With a slow and underwater sensation, he raised the barrel to his right temple. He closed his eyes.

Primed and ready to go, chief. You either do it, or you chicken out, and you're no chicken, are you?

No, he wasn't.

He squeezed the trigger.

#

The report of the gunshot deafened him. He cried out but didn't hear himself. A monkey was slamming cymbals inside his head, and his ears throbbed like a sonofabitch, especially the right one.

Standing, he wobbled unsteadily to the vanity, dropped the Colt onto the marble countertop with a heavy clatter of metal, and braced both hands against the polished stone to keep himself upright. His heart was racing, and he didn't yet trust his legs, which felt about as sturdy as matchsticks.

His reflection in the mirror was ghost-white and pained, but his skull was still intact. He'd flinched at the last moment, tilting the gun away from his temple. Looking up at the ceiling, he saw a silver-dollar-sized hole in the plasterboard.

The cymbals inside his head seemed to be getting louder, and it took Ernest a confused moment to realize what he was really hearing: the alarm.

Grabbing the Colt, he left the bathroom and hurried downstairs. He poked his head into the parlor and study and drawing room on his way to the front door; they all appeared secure.

It was in the foyer that he found the culprit.

A good-sized stone sat on the hardwood floor amidst a colorful splash of broken glass. It had come through one of the stained-glass sidelights that bordered the front door.

Ernest peered through the now glassless window and saw nobody outside.

Kids?

The neighborhood was upscale, and he'd never had problems before. But regardless of whoever the vandal or vandals were, they would have likely been frightened away by the gunshot.

He went to the wall-mounted alarm panel and punched in the

code to turn off the racket.

The abrupt silence was nearly as jarring as the wailing siren had been. He glanced again at the stone, which was almost certainly from his front garden, and then went to check the back door in the kitchen.

He tugged aside the curtain that covered the little window and started in surprise.

Somebody was looking in at him.

He raised the pistol.

"Don't shoot!" said the woman. "It's me!"

Ernest squinted. "Scooter...?" He opened the door that led to the backyard.

His granddaughter was scowling at him, her arms folded across her chest. "What the hell is going on here?"

"You tell me," he said, baffled by her posture. "Did you throw a stone through my window?"

"I heard a gunshot! I thought someone was attacking you. I figured the alarm might scare them off."

"Oh," he said, a little awkwardly. "That was nothing."

"Nothing? It was a gunshot!"

"I was cleaning an old revolver. It went off accidentally."

"Jeez, Papi! You scared me half to death." She shook her head, and in her anger, she was the spitting image of her late, fiery mother. "Well? Can I come inside?"

"What are you doing here, Scooter?"

"I'm not that little girl anymore..."

"No, you're not. How long has it been?"

"Do you mean since I lived here with you? Or since you stopped talking to me?"

Ernest sighed. "Come in...Nika. And welcome home."

CHAPTER 4
COMING HOME

Nika was leaning with the small of her back against the stone countertop. Her eyes roamed the kitchen, which was just how she remembered it: the scuffed hardwood floors from over a century of wear (where she used to play with her dolls while her grandmother busied herself preparing dinner); the open cabinetry showcasing the beautiful dishware and glassware (no sign of the big Peter Pan glass, her favorite, which she got from a gas station promotion one year); pots and pans hanging from a wrought-iron ceiling-mounted rack; the walls and moldings painted in deep jewel tones; and the checkerboard backsplash where Papi once told her he played chess but only when no one was around to see him (God, had she really believed he'd played chess on a vertical surface? How old had she been? Six? Seven? And did it really matter?).

No, it did not. But the memories were warm and nostalgic. The years she'd spent in this house had been good ones.

"So what's going on, Nika?" asked her grandfather now. He stood next to the oversized refrigerator, and Nika realized the fridge, at least, was relatively new. In fact, all the appliances were modern—and black. Her grandmother would never have approved of that, she thought. "This is…well, a surprise, to say the least."

"A pleasant surprise?" she asked.

He shrugged. "Sure."

"Thanks, Papi. But don't sound so excited to see me. It's only been five years."

"I didn't go anywhere."

"A visit would have been nice."

"You were in Texas…"

"That's hardly the dark side of the moon."

He shifted his weight from one foot to the other, folded his arms across his chest. With his silvery hair and tanned skin, his chinos and collared shirt beneath a lime-green V-neck sweater, he looked like he could have been straight out of a Ralph Lauren ad.

Same old Popeye, she thought.

He wasn't Nika's biological grandfather, so to avoid having three "Grandpas," her parents told her to call him "Papi," which was the word for grandfather in Spanish, her father's nationality. One morning when she was four, not long after her parents died and her grandparents took custody of her, Nika had been watching TV and came across a *Popeye the Sailor* episode. She thought the old sailor kind of looked like Papi with his strong chin and cheeky smile. But more, Popeye sounded phonetically like Papi (at least in her young mind it did)—and he had been Popeye to her ever since.

"Listen, Nika," said her grandfather, clearing his throat. "The last five years…"

She waved a hand. "I'm not here to talk about that. It's behind me, okay?"

He appeared relieved. "So…?"

She hesitated. "I was on a date earlier tonight."

He raised his eyebrows. "Don't tell me you came here for dating advice?"

"Please, Papi."

"So why did you come to see me?"

"I didn't come to see you. I just—I need a place to stay for a few days."

"What's going on?"

"Someone tried to kidnap me tonight."

His face hardened. "Your date tried to *kidnap* you?" He managed to sound both concerned and incredulous.

She shook her head. "Can I make tea? This is all a little…crazy."

"I only have Earl Grey," he said, going to a cupboard.

Nika filled the kettle with water and put it on the stove to boil. Her grandfather set two mugs on the counter alongside a jar of sugar. He dumped a teabag in each. She took a carton of cream from the refrigerator, which was nearly empty.

"Don't you eat these days?" she asked him, setting the cream next to the sugar.

"Usually at the club," he said. "It's rather lonely eating by oneself in a large house. So this date of yours…?"

She leaned against the counter again. "He's a brain surgeon, you know."

"No, I didn't know that. But congratulations. A brain surgeon and a kidnapper rolled into one."

She studied Popeye for a long moment. His craggy, handsome face was unreadable, but she could tell he was worried for her. "He wasn't the kidnapper, Papi. When I went to the bathroom in the restaurant, some goon stuck a knife in my back and told me to go with him."

"And you went with him?"

"I didn't know what else to do. He said if I didn't, he would gut me right there."

"Those were his words?"

"Pretty much. And he looked like the kind of guy who would do it. He forced me out of the back of the restaurant through the kitchen. A car was waiting at the curb. But before he could make me get into it, some cops came down the street. They asked if I was all right, and the man got in the car and drove off."

"The cops let him drive off?"

"They didn't know he was trying to kidnap me. He hid the knife in his pocket, and I didn't say anything…"

Now the emotion on his face was clear as day: he was furious. "Why the hell not?"

"What could they do, Papi? They didn't see the knife. I was just standing on the sidewalk with some dude. My word versus his. And if I *did* say something, I'd probably be sitting in a police station right now."

"At least the police could learn who the guy was. They might even learn why he was trying to kidnap you."

The kettle whistled. Nika filled the two mugs with steaming water, adding a dollop of cream and a spoonful of sugar into hers. She left her grandfather's black, which was how he drank it. She sipped and said, "I know why he was trying to kidnap me. Ari Schwartz wanted—"

"Ari Schwartz!"

"That's who was behind it."

Popeye balled his hands into fists. "That jackass? He's in prison!"

"The kidnapper told me Ari wanted me dead. He wanted to film me dying. That's why they were taking me somewhere. So they could kill me and film it and show it to Ari…"

That did it. That broke the ice.

"Ah, Scooter…" said Popeye, wrapping his arms around her.

The gesture was so unexpected that Nika stood stiff as a board in his embrace. But the awkwardness lasted only a moment. He smelled like he always had, like spicy sandalwood and wool, and that brought back a flood of so many memories she couldn't process any of them. She simply felt safe and good—and then she was crying into his shoulder. She had remained strong all night, but now she couldn't help herself.

Eventually she took a deep breath and stepped away. She rubbed the wetness from her cheeks with the back of her hand. She couldn't seem to look her grandfather in the eyes. Instead she went to the kitchen table. She sat in a chair, rested her elbows on the tabletop, and massaged her temples.

Popeye sat in a chair opposite her.

"Sorry," she said, still not looking at him. "I don't know where that came from. I guess tonight's just been a bit overwhelming…"

"Ari Schwartz," he said, shaking his head. "He's just a computer nerd like me. How does he go about hiring a kidnapper while he's locked up in prison?"

"Before he founded his video game company he was working on an app to connect people with private investigators. If you heard him talk about it, it was supposed to be the next big thing, the next Uber."

Popeye scoffed. "How many people are looking for private investigators?"

"You'd be surprised," she said. "And the thing is, most people don't know how to get one. They think you have to go on the Dark Web or something even though you can just use Google. Anyway, Ari said he had a lot of investors. He said the app was going to be huge, but it was never published. He never said why. I didn't really care. But knowing him, I suspect he was playing funny with the money and the investors pulled out."

Popeye grunted but said nothing.

"My point is, Ari would have met a lot of private investigators while working on the app. He also would have met the kinds of people looking for private investigators—some of whom would be super shady."

"Not likely upstanding citizens, no. Still—he could organize all this from prison?"

"You have a lot of time to think about things in prison. Also, Ari had millions of dollars stashed in offshore bank accounts. I'm sure he still has money somewhere that nobody knows about except for his guy on the outside who gets things done for him."

Popeye nodded silently. Then he said, "You have to go to the police, Nika."

She rolled her eyes. "And what are they going to do? Ari's already in prison."

"The asshole put a hit on you! He'll no doubt try again."

"Yes, well, I know what he's up to now. I'll be more careful."

"You need to take this seriously."

"I am! Trust me, I am. But right now—right now, I'm fine. He can't possibly know where I am."

"You can't stay here forever." He waved dismissively. "What I mean is, I would like the company…but you're a young woman. You can't spend your days cooped up in your grandfather's house—"

"I'm *not* staying here forever. It's just for a few days until I sort things out."

"And what does 'sort things out' entail?"

"I don't know! Getting a new apartment—"

"He found you already. That's how the kidnapper ended up at the restaurant, isn't it? He must have followed you there. So what's to say he's not going to find you at a new apartment?"

"I don't know. I guess I'll rent it under a false name."

"That's fraud, Nika," he said disapprovingly. "I thought you would have put that kind of behavior behind you?"

Nika glowered at him. "This is nothing like *that*. Would you prefer I get kidnapped and murdered?"

"I'd prefer that you went to the police. I don't know how it works, but I'd suspect they'd contact the prison, and the guards there would monitor Ari's communications, his visitors, et cetera. At the very least, he won't be able to operate so brazenly."

She shook her head. "I don't know…" She sighed. "Maybe, okay? But right now I just want to go to bed. I'm exhausted."

He studied her for a few moments—judgingly and disapprovingly, it seemed to her—before saying, "Come with me then, Scooter," he said, getting up. "The guest bedroom is where it's always been."

Nika almost reprimanded him for calling her that again, but then her grandfather glanced back and said, "Are you coming?" And in that moment he appeared uncharacteristically old and tired. Moreover, in that moment she also saw the man who had raised her from four years of age, who had once bought her a Barbie Playhouse for Christmas, and years after that, four tickets to a Bon Jovi concert for her sixteenth birthday. Who had taught her how to read while she sat on his lap in his study, and who had taught her how to drive in his vintage MGB. Who had sent her to one of the finest boarding schools in the San Francisco Bay area, and who had paid for her tuition at Stanford University. Who had been the best father she'd never had.

"Yes, I'm coming," she said, getting to her feet.

#

The guest bedroom was like the rest of the house: old, grand, haunting…lonely. A large four-poster queen bed dominated the antique-cluttered space. It looked as though it belonged in a fairytale and featured a gold-and-princess-blue canopy as well as matching curtains that could be pulled closed to create a cozy, private space. Nika didn't remember ever seeing it when she lived in the house. She mentioned that.

"It's from a villa in Italy," Popeye told her. "Your grandmother and I were staying there, she fell in love with it, and I made the owner an offer. Half of this house is filled with crap she shipped back from overseas."

"But it never used to be in this room…"

He shrugged. "It was in the attic. After your grandmother passed, I got rid of a lot of clutter in the house. But I couldn't get rid of this. That villa is where we spent much of our honeymoon. So I moved it down here. You were boarding at The Athenian School then."

"This room used to be Nana's study."

Popeye nodded. "She spent hours in here knitting."

"That's right… She had a big sewing machine, too. She used it to make my Halloween costume every year. You sold it?"

"Gave it to a church. Did you want it?"

"No, but I mean…it was Nana's…"

"Yes, it was. It was also a *sewing machine*. I kept the bed, didn't I? Wait here. I'll be right back."

He returned downstairs, and Nika explored the room. On the dresser were numerous silver-framed photographs. Most were of her grandmother, but there was one of Nika that had been taken on picture day at school when she was nine or ten. She had a short bob then and braces. She smiled faintly. Not nine: she'd been ten. Because that was the year she'd developed a crush on a boy in her grade named Daniel Philips, but she'd been too embarrassed to talk to him until she'd gotten rid of the braces in the summer of that year. When school returned in September, they began dating...which consisted of spending recess talking to each other and walking home together every so often.

When Popeye returned, he held a pair of folded silk pajamas in his arms. "These are mine, but I've never worn them. Crimson was your grandmother's favorite color. I can't stand it."

"You can't stand crimson?"

"It's the color of blood."

"So why did you buy crimson pajamas?"

"I didn't, Nika. Your grandmother bought them for me." He set them on the bed. "I'm not too much bigger than you, so they should fit well enough."

"Thanks...Popeye."

"Popeye." He smiled at her. "Right. Get some sleep. I'll see you in the morning." He left, and Nika listened to the stairs creak as he returned downstairs. She changed out of her leather jacket and slinky date dress into the pajamas. The bottoms had a drawstring, so they fit, but she felt as though she was swimming inside the top. Her grandfather wasn't a large man, but she wasn't a large woman. "Petite" probably described her best. She was self-conscious about her height, hence the three-inch heels she'd picked up at an outlet store specifically for her evening with Lee Jordon, which were now standing neatly next to the back door.

She fastened the final button, sat on the bed, and bounced a couple of times. She laid down on her back and stared up at the gold-and-blue canopy. She felt as though she were inside a tent. She got up and went to the door, where the light switch was located. She flicked it off but didn't return to bed. She left the room and went down the hallway, passing two closed doors before stopping at a third. It was also closed.

It's going to be just another guestroom, she thought. *Popeye wouldn't have kept my stuff. He would have tossed it all out, just as he had done with Nana's things...*

Nika opened the door and hit the light switch. The last time she had slept in the bedroom had been the winter before she'd met Ari Schwartz, when she'd returned from Stanford to spend Christmas with Popeye. But the last time she'd considered the bedroom *her* bedroom had been when she was twelve before she went to live at The Athenian School, and the room was as it had been then. Pastel pink walls plastered with posters of boybands; beaded curtains made from colorful glass; fairy lights wrapped around the ornate wrought-iron headboard of the neatly made twin bed; bookcase crammed with young adult novels, a purple lava lamp, and a CD player; and her desk with an old and yellowed Dell computer, which she'd begged Papi to buy for her (although she'd told him she needed it to type up her school reports, she really wanted it to chat with her friends on AOL Instant Messenger).

"Weird," Nika said to herself, taking it all in. It might have only been fifteen years since she'd last called the room her room, but it felt like a lifetime ago. She went to the bookcase and scanned the spines of the novels. She plucked out *The Sisterhood of the Traveling Pants*. The book had been one of her favorites, and she'd spent many fond hours reading it by flashlight late into the night. She thumbed through the pages, holding them to her nose to smell the foxed paper. She put it back in its place and went to the closet.

The shelves were stuffed with toys, but it was the back wall that interested her. It resembled a graffitied toilet stall door in a public bathroom in the wrong part of town. Scribbled in colorful pencil crayons and markers were bad schoolyard jokes, cartoonish doodles of characters and creatures from Harry Potter, random musings, and lists. One of those lists was the names of boys who had been in her grade. She'd ranked them in cuteness. Daniel Philips, of course, was #1. She couldn't believe she used to drag her desk chair in here, close the door, and content herself in the little space for hours at a time with just her thoughts. Kids were strange indeed...

Nika frowned. A black gap extended along the right side of the back wall. Curious, she stuck her fingers into the space and pulled. The wall whined open on hidden hinges just like a door.

Revealing a secret passageway.

\#

"What the...?" she said. The false wall had never been there when she was a kid.

Or had it? she wondered. Had she simply never known about it?

Just inside the cramped passageway, on a short shelf, was a red candle in a ceramic holder and an old box of Swan Vestas safety matchsticks.

She lit a match on the strike strip and touched it to the candlewick. Narrow and steep steps twisted away down into the darkness. They were finished in the same mahogany as the wainscotting that decorated the walls of so many rooms in the house. There was even a handrail with intricately carved balusters.

Nika started down, her mind burning with questions. The most pressing were: *Where does this lead?* And, *What am I going to find there?*

She wasn't entirely sure she *wanted* to know what she would find...but she knew she couldn't simply retreat back to the guest room. Sleep would be impossible with the secret passage on her mind.

You could ask Popeye about it tomorrow morning. It's his house, after all, and what you're doing is snooping, and nobody likes a snoop...

And nobody likes discovering a secret passage leading to their old bedroom.

While Nika descended, she tried to figure out which walls within the house she might be passing behind, but she had no idea. She was already disorientated.

And then the mahogany paneling changed to stone and mortar, and the stairs ended not at another false wall but a stone archway.

Holding the candle before her, the flickering flame barely keeping the blackness at bay, she went forward.

#

She emerged in a low-ceilinged room crowded with…stuff. Directly before her was some sort of large display case of the sort you would find in a museum. And just next to it—

She jumped with fright before realizing what she'd believed was a person was in fact a mannequin. It was dressed like a soldier in a green uniform, black boots, a belt heavy with ammunition pouches, and a helmet with what looked like a bullet hole near the crown. US ARMY was written in yellow letters above the right shirt pocket.

And then she saw that all the "stuff" in the room was actually war paraphernalia: miniature-scale military vehicles, replica weapons, a velvet-lined case filled with medals, another case with rank insignia badges. An entire wall was dedicated to framed documents. One was the front page of the *Washington Post* newspaper with the headline: "Saigon Surrenders to Vietcong; Withdrawal Ends Role of US." Another was a photograph of five soldiers posing with their weapons—and the guy in the middle, she was quite certain, was a very young Popeye. Next to it, two dog tags on a chain dangled from a peg. They were embossed with Popeye's name, his blood type, and CATH, presumably shorthand for Catholic.

He served in the Vietnam War? she thought. He was the right age, so it shouldn't have come as a surprise, but it *was* a surprise simply because he had never mentioned it to her.

She went to the display case in the center of the room. It was the size and shape of a large dining room table and came up to her chest. Inside it was a diorama of a jungle. Placed within the abundant lifelike foliage were very detailed American G.I.s in green uniforms fighting North Vietnamese soldiers in black pajamalike clothing. There were also peasants, a small village, and tanks and motorcycles and jeeps and other vehicles. Everything was impressively realistic, from the plumber's hemp used for the thatched-hut roofs to the sheets of balsa wood scored with a blunt knife to mimic planking.

The diorama sat on about a foot of brown Styrofoam. Looking through the glass wall, she could see all sorts of tunnels burrowing through it. There were subterranean rooms, too: a barracks, a command station, a kitchen, and some sort of arms factory—

She thought she heard a noise and stiffened. Yes, it sounded like somebody coming down a set of stairs...but not the stairs she had come down. And then, across the room, she saw another arched stone door. The darkness there lessened.

Nika blew out her candle. It was instinctual and stupid. Now she couldn't find her way back to her staircase without bumping into something.

She stood, frozen, unsure what to do.

A few moments later Popeye appeared, holding a candle just like hers. He was carrying a small black lacquered box. He set it on a nearby shelf, sat in a rocking chair, and then lit a cigarette. He sighed as he exhaled smoke.

Nika knew she couldn't remain hidden in the dark, and so she said, "I didn't know you smoked, Papi."

CHAPTER 5
SECRETS

Ernest started at the sound of Nika's voice. He peered into the shadows. "Nika?" he said, standing.

She stepped forward into the light from his candle. She wore his crimson pajamas with the cuffs at the ankles and wrists rolled up. Her feet were bare on the stone floor. Her expression was sheepish. "Funny meeting you down here," she said.

"What in God's name…?" But he suddenly understood. "You went to your old bedroom?"

"There was a secret passage in the closet. I couldn't exactly ignore it."

Ernest looked for somewhere to put out his cigarette; he hadn't thought to bring an ashtray with him. He didn't see anything suitable and stubbed it out on the stone wall.

"Seriously, Papi," Nika said. "I didn't know you smoked."

"I don't," he told her. "I did—years ago. I started again recently."

"Why? It's a filthy habit."

"Yes, well…" he said, trailing off as he thought, *Smoking's not what's going to kill me, kid*. He swept his arm around the room. "What do you think?"

"You fought in the Vietnam War? I didn't know that about you either."

Ernest was conscripted into the US Army in 1966. He trained with the 25th Infantry Division—nicknamed Tropic Lightning—in Hawaii and then was dumped right into the thick of things in Vietnam. He'd been expecting the kind of fighting seen in Korea, essentially mowing down wave after wave of rushing Chinese cannon fodder. But after the 25th set up base in Cu Chi, they quickly discovered they were sitting on top of a massive underground network of tunnels, and the enemy was stealthy, nearly invisible moles that would pop out of the ground, attack, and disappear again just as quickly.

Gradually the brass decided the best way to counter this new kind of warfare was to send G.I.s down into the tunnels. The 25th originally called the grunts who volunteered to do this tunnel runners. The Australians called them ferrets. In the end everyone settled on "tunnel rats." It wasn't a derogatory term; the tunnel rats held a special spot in the army hierarchy. They were the guys who did what nobody else had the guts to do. They took such pride in their work they made their own special cloth badge. A gray rat holding a pistol and a flashlight with a dog Latin motto: *Non Gratum Anus Rodentum* (Not worth a rat's ass).

Some rats volunteered for what was generally considered to be the most dangerous job in the war to prove their manhood. Some because they believed it was their duty. And some volunteered simply because they were crazy motherfuckers. Ernest supposed his motivation was a bit of all of those.

After his first few descents into the tunnels, after he became familiar and even comfortable in the sweaty darkness, he began to not only look forward to going down a hot hole but also to encountering Charlie. Because there was no air or artillery support underground. No personal armor or hi-tech weaponry. Just old-fashioned hand-to-hand combat, where your wits and strength were all that mattered. That for him was the ultimate rush. He became addicted to the primal thrill of the hunt, the longing for blood that exists in the pit of every man's soul whether they know it's there or not.

Quite simply, Ernest became a killer. And after he killed once, he never hesitated to kill again. He lost count of how many VC he killed, and their deaths never seemed to bother him.

His Army Commendation Medal citation was an apt example of his apathy. It was written as a glowing testament to a man with nerves of steel who—despite two rats already being gravely wounded in a hot tunnel, and despite his squad already contaminating the hole with CS riot gas—nevertheless volunteered to go down to retrieve documents and blow the complex with explosive charges. What the officer who penned the citation *didn't* mention—because Ernest never told him—was that Ernest had found a nearly unconscious Viet Cong guerilla at the end of a communication tunnel. And while the policy at the top was to take prisoners when possible—and in this case it certainly was—Ernest had never taken a prisoner and never would. Instead he set a forty-pound charge next to the prone solider and crawled back to the surface on his own. He detonated the blast, smoked a cigarette, and didn't think much more about it.

Looking back on the war, he didn't recognize the young man he had been. That man scared him. What he did—it seemed incomprehensible and reprehensible. It seemed nearly impossible to believe it had been him and not somebody else with all that blood on his hands. These days he tried to rationalize his actions. He would tell himself he'd simply been following orders. He'd been fighting the good fight against Communism. He'd been fighting for the flag or for his platoon. He'd just been doing his part to make the world a better place. It was all bullshit, of course. The truth was much darker. He had been a monster, an uncaring animal. Certainly he had not been human; a human being didn't do the things he did.

Which was why he never spoke about the war to anybody, not even to Neeti.

To Nika he said simply, "I fought in the war, yes." He hooked a thumb at the staircase behind him. "That leads to the closet in the master bedroom on the first floor." He pointed past her. "That one, as you've discovered, leads to your old bedroom on the second floor. And that one there"—he indicated a third stone archway, which was almost completely concealed in the darkness of the far wall—"leads to a room on the third floor, which I've been using for storage."

Nika was frowning. "But why? What are they for? What's this room for—originally?"

"That's a good question," he said. "My guess: stockpiling booze during the Prohibition era. It's not connected to the rest of the cellar, and it's only accessible by the three hidden staircases. Did you know this house burned down after the earthquake in 1906?"

"No," she said. "But I remember you telling me that your grandfather built it."

Ernest nodded. "He built it twice. The first time in the late nineteenth century and then again in the years following the quake and fire. The Volstead Act didn't go into effect until 1920, but the consumption of alcohol had been a touchy topic in this country ever since the colonial period. It had already been banned in certain states, and I think Gilbert—that was my grandfather's name: Gilbert Gallegos Cameron Campbell—was planning ahead when he rebuilt the house in the event of a nationwide ban. A lot of upper-class families stockpiled alcohol in their cellars before Prohibition began. They'd buy up the inventories of liquor retailers, saloons, club storerooms. I'm guessing old Gilbert did the same. Unfortunately, I didn't find any booze down here when I discovered the room."

"When was that?"

"A couple of years after your grandmother died. She had a gaudy bronze wall-standing mirror in the back of our walk-in closet that she used to change in front of. Christ, that woman would sometimes try on three or four different outfits before settling on one. When I dragged the mirror out of there, the wall behind it sprang open a few inches."

"And nothing was down here? Nothing at all?"

"Completely empty. Of course, after Prohibition ended, Gilbert wouldn't have needed a secret spot for his alcohol any longer, would he?"

"What's that?" Nika asked him, pointing to the black box he'd placed on a shelf.

"The gun I was cleaning," he said. "It's why I came down here. To put it away." *But for how long, chief?* he wondered. *After Nika finds somewhere else to stay, are you going to come down and get it again? Are you going to go back up to the bathroom with it? Are you going to have the balls to pull the trigger without flinching the next time?*

"Papi?"

"Huh?" He looked at Nika. "What did you ask?"

"All this stuff. If you didn't know about this room when I lived here, where was all this stuff? In the attic with Nana's bed?"

He shook his head. "During the Covid lockdown I needed something to do. I used to have a model train set when I was a kid. I liked it, but I spent most of my time creating the world around the tracks. The trees, tunnels, bridges. Those memories inspired me to build that." He waved at the display case. "I began working on it in my study for a few hours each day. I guess it brought the war back to me. I sorted through some boxes in the attic and brought anything from my deployments that I had saved down to my study. The rest of this stuff? I bought a few things on eBay. Then I bought a few more. You know how it goes."

"And you moved everything down here?"

"I don't socialize much these days, but I have friends over

sometimes. Having my study resemble a cross between a flea market and a war museum..." He shrugged. "I'm eccentric, but I don't want to be *the* eccentric. Gossip's a permanent member at the club."

"What about those medals? Are they yours? Or are they from eBay?"

Ernest glanced at the velvet-lined box that held his Silver Star, Bronze Star, Army Commendation Medal, and four Purple Hearts. "They're mine," he told her. "I wouldn't buy somebody else's medals."

She studied him, her expression enigmatic in the dim light. "So you're a war hero, huh?"

"If you want my honest answer, I think everyone who fought a single day in that war is a hero. Now, why don't we finish this talk tomorrow? It's getting late."

She gave the room a last look over. "Sure, Papi. Tomorrow," she said, and there was a hint of either weariness or irritation in her voice. She shook her head. "A Vietnam War hero. Are there any more secrets that you've been keeping from me?"

There's the little matter that I have less than six months to live, Scooter. That's one hell of a secret if I say so myself. But it's private, as secrets should be. No need to inconvenience you with it.

"No, Nika," he said, giving her shoulder a small squeeze. "No more secrets."

#

After Nika returned to her room, Ernest lit another cigarette and wandered about the room, moving from one memento of the 'Nam to another until he found himself standing in front of the photograph of his tunnel rat squad. It was taken in March 1969, about two weeks before a catastrophic search-and-destroy mission behind enemy lines. The five of them were goofing around, striking macho poses with their weapons on display and bandoleers of ammunition draped over their shoulders like they were the goddamn A-Team.

Ernest stood centermost with De Niro's "You talking to me?" eyes, a cigarette dangling from his lips, and his hand on the grip of his holstered .22 pistol. The NCO in charge of the squad, a Puerto Rican named Mario Mercado whom they called Rat Six, had a cigar clenched in a grin and his German Luger raised in his right hand. When he got close enough to engage in combat, he preferred the four-gauge riot shotgun that hung from a strap on his shoulder. It blew your eardrums in the confines of a tunnel, but the pellet scatter didn't miss targets even in the pitch black. Staff Sergeant Ricky Lynn, a red-headed kid from Minnesota, had one eye squeezed shut while aiming his .38 revolver at the camera. It was equipped with a silencer that doubled the barrel's length and made a quick draw awkward. That was why it never left his hand—his left one. His reasoning had been that if Charlie got the jump on him and sliced off his hand with a knife, he'd still have his good one with which to write, wipe his ass, and do other things. Looming tall above the rest of them was PFC Sam Lewis aka Pig. He was a six-foot-four Black guy from Kentucky who'd played defensive tackle in high school football. He was the platoon's machine gunner, and the big M-60 rested across his beefy neck like a shoulder yoke. It was useless in the tunnels, but that didn't matter because Pig was far too large to fit into them in the first place. His role was simply to stand guard duty at the entrance and pass supplies down or haul out an injured rat.

Finally there was SP4 Dick Hamilton who had donned his beloved leather Stetson for the occasion. The big brim shaded much of his face, but you couldn't miss his lanky blond handlebar mustache. He was a Texan whom Ernest had nicknamed Cowboy. In his right hand he held his old-fashioned Colt Peacemaker that he bought from a dust-off pilot for twenty bucks because his hero was John Wayne; in the other was a backup .25 Beretta pocket pistol he kept in an ankle holster. What wasn't in the photo was a captured AK-47 he sometimes brought down into a tunnel to confuse Charlie.

Although each of the tunnel rats had become like a brother to Ernest throughout their service, he shared the longest and strongest bond with Cowboy. They both arrived in Vietnam on the same Philippines Airlines flight, and they took the same chopper to their small patrol base in the north of **Tây Ninh Province**. Cowboy and the five other FNGs on board had been cool and collected as though zipping fast and low over a jungle halfway across the world from home was no big deal. But Ernest had been gripping his seat tightly; he hated heights. After they landed they ran, hunched over beneath their rucksacks and the spinning helicopter blades, to the company command post.

A sergeant with an impressive aura of authority for a kid all of twenty-two years old said, "Welcome to Vietnam, boys. I'm Sergeant Little, your Platoon Sergeant. You're at Fire Support Base Swag in an area of operations called War Zone C. Victor Charlie uses the jungle over yonder to infiltrate South Vietnam from Cambodia." He pointed his M-16 rifle north at the emerald-green vegetation that stretched as far as the eye could see. "What we do here is run patrols all day and ambushes all night to catch the commie bastards. So if you're itching to kill communists, you've come to the right place, and we're damn happy for the fresh blood. If you don't know already, you're in A Company, 2nd Battalion, 27th Infantry. They call us the Wolfhounds."

Cowboy and Ernest were ordered to spend their first night in Vietnam in a listening post on wire guard. As soon as it was dark they scurried over the base's defensive perimeter berm, crawled down a narrow ditch that ran fifty feet out to the first wall of concertina wire, crawled beneath that, and then continued along the ditch until they reached a small foxhole. As instructed, they checked it for snakes and scorpions before settling in for the night. Their job was simple: keep their eyes and ears open and radio in anything suspicious.

Ernest, then nineteen, had never been outside the US before his deployment to Vietnam, and the exotic noises he heard coming from the eerie, black woods sent shivers down his spine. He and Cowboy must have sat there staring out at the dark for an hour, their eyes wide and unblinking, before either of them spoke. Ernest cracked that he should have moved to Canada; Cowboy, who had volunteered for the draft lottery, said he must be as stupid as his teachers always told him he was.

Eventually they decided on two-hour shifts. Ernest took the first one. The heat of the day was gone, and the sweat dripping down his forehead and back was cold and uncomfortable. He imagined every sound he heard was Charlie coming to kill him, and he almost radioed the base on two occasions before convincing himself that what he heard was a rodent or bird.

There was no moon, and the darkness was so absolute he started to hallucinate, turning shadows into things they were not and even seeing lights that weren't there. He checked his wristwatch every ten minutes until his shift was up. He figured he would be asleep in seconds due to all his spent nervous energy, but it turned out he couldn't sleep at all. He gave up trying and stayed on watch with Cowboy. The company was good, and they made small talk to ease the tension. They talked about where they were from, school, girls, cars. What they were going to do when they got back home.

They figured since everybody had nicknames in the army, they may as well think up ones for themselves before they got stuck with something derogative like "Shrimp" or "Shortstop" due to their relatively short statures. Ernest settled on "Cowboy" for Dick because he walked and talked like one; Dick picked "Soup" for Ernest since his last name was Campbell. By the time dawn finally broke they were already well on their way to becoming the closest of friends, and over the next three years they would go on to save each other's asses more times than either of them cared to count.

"I always liked that photo."

Startled, Ernest turned around. Cowboy stepped out from the shadows on the other side of the room. Just like in the photograph he wore his leather Stetson, which clashed with his olive-green jungle fatigues. They were covered with mud as if he'd just crawled out of his grave.

"What the fuck?" Ernest said.

Cowboy smiled beneath his mustache. "Howdy, pal. Nice to see you, too."

"You're back."

"Got nothing better to do. Being dead ain't all the fun they make it out to be."

Ernest closed his eyes and pinched the bridge of his nose between his fingers. When he opened his eyes Cowboy was still there. He wasn't surprised. This was the third time in the last two weeks that the ghost of his friend had visited him. Doc Gilsdorf agreed that the hallucinations could be side effects of the cocktail of meds he was on. He said they could also be from the psychological weight of dealing with "existential distress." The bottom line was that at this late stage there wasn't really anything that could be done about them.

Ernest lit another cigarette.

Cowboy came over and bent close to the photograph pinned to the wall. "Hot damn, I was a handsome young buck. Do I still look that good?"

"You look just the same."

"Can't say the same for you, Soup. You're a fuckin' old man."

He said, "An old man who talks to himself."

Cowboy said, "You ain't talking to yourself, pal. You're talking to old Cowboy! Still got the cancer?"

"It's not going anywhere. It's going to kill me."

"Aw, shee-it. But, hey, it's a better way to go than getting a bamboo spear through your chest." He looked down at himself. The front of his shirt was bloodied and torn. "Wish we never went down that hole." His expression darkened. "I'm *still* down in that hole."

"I'm sorry, Cowboy."

"You said you wouldn't leave me there, man. You promised me."

"I know I did—"

"My wife never had a grave to visit, no *real* grave. Just a headstone and no fuckin' body beneath it. What's the point in that?"

"What do you want me to say?"

"Remember my last words? My last dying fuckin' words? 'Don't leave me down here, Soup. Promise me you won't leave me down here. I don't wanna be buried in no Charlie-made anthill.'

And you said, 'I won't, Cowboy. I promise. You're going home.'"

Ernest shook his head in frustration. "I tried to come back for you, but Top said we'd already lost too many men. He didn't want to risk more on a recovery op. Same bullshit all the way up to the Sergeant Major. And I was short. Two weeks left. They wouldn't let me re-up. They said I did my time and more and sent me home. What else could I do…?"

#

Ernest jerked awake in the rocking chair and dropped his cigarette on the ground. It had burned to the filter and scorched his fingers.

He looked around in the flickering candlelight.

He was alone.

Muttering to himself, he stood, stepped on the cigarette, and went upstairs to bed. He remained awake for a long time, thinking about a lot of things...and eventually making up his mind about one of them.

CHAPTER 6
A CHANGE OF PLANS

Nika woke at six o'clock the next morning. She had slept straight through the night, but her sleep had been filled with strange dreams. In one she'd been with Lee Jordon on Pier 39. They'd been having a great time, just walking and talking, enjoying the views of the harbor, laughing at the barking sea lions. All the while she had been pretending to ignore Craterface who had been following them. She didn't want to tell Lee about the goon; so far they hadn't spoken about their previous date. Lee seemed to have forgotten that she'd skipped out on it, and she didn't want to remind him. So she led the way through the crowds of tourists, gift shops, Chinatown, and a restaurant selling clam chowder (exiting through the back kitchen door) in an attempt to give the goon the slip. But he always remained stubbornly behind them, trying so hard to act inconspicuous it was almost comical.

And then they were in Alcatraz. The abandoned prison was dark and quiet except for their footsteps. Lee kept asking her why they were there. She thought they were still trying to get away from Craterface (the dream logic was fuzzy), but she realized she also wanted to show him her old cell. It had never been in Alcatraz, of course, but it was now.

What do you think? she asked him when they arrived, stepping inside the tiny space that she'd called home for far too long, waving at the narrow bed and wall-mounted desk, the stainless-steel toilet and the single window. *It's nice*, he said, clearly lying. *You live in a prison?* She shook her head. *Not anymore. I used to. There's something I need to tell you, Lee—*

Before she could finish her confession she sensed a dark shadow above them and looked up. A scream caught in her throat. Craterface was flattened against the ceiling, suspended like a ghoul in a horror movie, leering down at them with a devious, toothy grimace.

That was when Nika had woken, the scream still in her throat. She sat up quickly, disorientated. But the red silk pajamas she wore reminded her where she was. As her eyes adjusted to the dark, she made out the familiar shapes of the stuffy guest bedroom.

With a sigh she threw aside the bedcover and went to the window. She pulled back the heavy maroon curtains, revealing a drab, gray morning. She changed into her cocktail dress and leather jacket, left the pajamas folded on the bed, and went downstairs. Some of the lights were on, but she didn't see Popeye anywhere. In the kitchen she filled the kettle with water and put it on the stove to boil. She was thinking about Lee Jordon, and her thoughts of him were sweet and tingly, still coated with the pixie dust of dreams.

Nika regretted not returning to the steakhouse the evening before. She'd only fainted for a few seconds. The nearest cop had caught her in his arms, saving her from potentially bouncing her head off the sidewalk. He'd offered to take her to the police station, but she'd insisted she was fine. She wasn't. Her hands were trembling, and her anxiety and paranoia were sky-high. She was half-convinced the black SUV had only taken a whirl around the block and would return as soon as the cops left. So she hailed the first taxi she saw.

She told the driver Popeye's address in Tice Valley—a forested, rural neighborhood in Walnut Creek—because she had no other place to go. Whatever friends she'd had from her first two years in Stanford she'd lost while in prison, and she had no siblings. She considered texting Lee, giving him some excuse for her abrupt departure. But what could she say? She'd been semi-kidnapped on the way to the bathroom? She doubted he would believe that. And if he did, then she'd have to fill him in on Ari and her felony convictions and her prison sentence...and that was something she didn't want to do.

The kettle whistled. Nika made an instant coffee and took it outside to get some fresh air.

Popeye was lounging in a chair on the stone patio, smoking a cigarette.

"Didn't know you were out here," she said, sitting down across from him. "Still working hard on the habit, I see?"

"Two days straight." He coughed, covering his mouth with a fist.

"You really are a smoker now," she said. "Smoker's cough and everything."

He put the cigarette out in a ceramic ashtray. "Did you sleep well?"

"Like a baby. Nightmares and all."

"Nightmares?"

She sipped her coffee, nodded. "The wannabe kidnapper was stalking my date and me."

Popeye eyed her dress. "Got another date this morning?"

"I'm going to pick up some clothes at Broadway Plaza a little later. But I'm not going to go shopping wearing your pajamas."

"Do you want me to drive you?"

"It's only a couple of miles from here. I don't mind the exercise."

"In stiletto heels?"

"I'll borrow a pair of your running shoes."

"Do you need money?"

"Thank you," she said tartly, "but I'm not destitute."

"You're no longer paying restitution?"

"If you must know, I paid what I was ordered to in a lump sum before I was incarcerated."

"Gate money?" he asked.

"I didn't receive a penny when I was released. I got a job."

"Oh?" he said, raising an eyebrow.

"It's in IT," she said evasively.

Nika looked out at the backyard. A vast green lawn lined with garden beds filled with early-summer flowers led to a heavily wooded forest. A playset leaning slightly askew and weathered with age stood next to a blue elderberry tree smothered in creamy flowers and powdery blue-black berries (which she used to pick and eat during imaginary tea parties). Popeye had bought the playset for her shortly after her parents died and she moved in with him and her grandmother.

She said, "I'm surprised you never knocked that ugly thing down. It's an eyesore."

Popeye turned to look at it. "It's been there so long that it doesn't bother me."

"Nana's sewing machine and big mirror bothered you enough to toss them out."

"I didn't toss them out, Nika. I donated them. And they were inside stuff. Outside stuff is a different matter. Besides... I always thought the playset might come in useful if I had grandchildren."

"Did you want grandchildren?"

"Doesn't every grandparent?"

"I'm only twenty-seven," she said.

"Your mother was twenty-one when she had you. Here, you better take this." He reached into his pocket and produced two keys attached to a bright blue fob. "One is for the front door," he explained. "The other is for the back door. Also, I've written down the password for the alarm. It's on the kitchen table. But it's just your grandma's birthday."

"Thanks, Papi. But like I said, I'm only staying for a few days, and you're always home…"

"I'm leaving today."

Nika stared at him. "Leaving? Where are you going?"

"Overseas," he told her.

She blinked as if she hadn't heard him right. Anger rose inside her. "If you don't want me staying with you," she snapped, "just say so. I'll leave. You don't have to fly to Europe to get away from me!" She stood abruptly, nearly knocking the chair over.

"Scooter—wait. I'm not going to Europe. And it's not to get away from you."

"You've had this trip planned?" she challenged.

"Well, no," he said. "I decided to go last night."

"The night I showed up, huh?"

"You don't understand…"

"So explain, Papi! Where are you going?"

"Vietnam," he said. "I have some unfinished business there I need to take care of."

"You mean…from when you a soldier?"

He nodded.

Nika was incredulous. "That war was a lifetime ago! And you decide to take care of this 'unfinished business' the day after I come to stay with you? I'm not stupid, you know."

"You're reading too much into this. Last night I made up my mind to get this done, and now that it's been decided, I can't just sit around procrastinating and wasting time."

"Wasting time…" she said, nodding, her jaw clenched. "Right. Okay. Well, it was nice seeing you, Papi, for all of one evening. Have a good time in Vietnam."

Nika went back inside the house, waiting for her grandfather to call to her, to tell her to come back out, he'd changed his mind, he wasn't going anywhere.

She heard nothing except the thud of the door closing behind her.

\#

Ernest knocked on the door to Nika's old bedroom. She hadn't been in the guest bedroom, and he couldn't imagine where else in the house she might have gone.

"Nika…?" he said, entering the room.

"Not here," came her sulky reply from the closet.

"Strange," he said to nobody. "I thought I heard somebody in here."

Silence.

He went to the closet and opened the door.

Nika sat on the chair from her desk, her feet propped up on a shelf stuffed with her old toys.

She was smoking a cigarette.

"Christ, Scooter! What are you doing?"

"What?" she said, looking up innocuously at him.

"You don't smoke."

"It sure looks like I do."

"Since when?"

"College, off and on. But in prison it was something to do during rec time." She took another drag before putting out the cigarette in a Coca-Cola can. "Why did you send me to The Athenian School?"

The question surprised him. "It's one of the best private high schools in California."

"Why a *boarding* school?" she demanded. "I never really questioned that before. Why you would send me to a boarding school. You just wanted me to be prepared for college, that was all."

"That *was* all."

She shook her head and said, "That's B.S. You wanted me out of the house."

"Don't be ridiculous, Scooter."

"*Nika.*"

"Where are you getting this nonsense from?"

"Nana died when I was in grade eight. You didn't want to raise me on your own."

Ernest frowned. "That's not true," he said, although it was partly true…or maybe even mostly true. It wasn't that he didn't want to raise Nika on his own. It was more that he didn't think he could—at least, he didn't think he could do a decent job of it. Neeti had always been the one to read Nika bedtime stories, make her lunch each morning before school, take her to the mall on weekends, drive her to Girl Scouts and dance classes and ice-skating lessons. Ernest had never done any of that stuff, and he didn't believe the time to start was when Nika was twelve, on the cusp of becoming a teenager. Besides, it wasn't as though he'd shipped her off to an orphanage. Attending the Athenian School had been in the best interest of her future. He added, "You liked it there."

"That's not the point," she said. "You didn't want me around then, and you don't want me around now."

He sighed. "Look, maybe one day we can sit down with a shrink and talk through all this fun stuff, but right now's not the time." He held up his hands. "Hear me out. I came up here to ask you something. How would you like to come to Vietnam with me?"

Nika blinked. "Seriously?"

Ernest shrugged. "You can't go back to where you're living right now. So like I said. You can stay here while I'm gone, that's no problem. Or you could come with me to Vietnam. Nobody in the world is going to find you over there, and when we get back, I'll look into getting you a safe apartment somewhere—"

She jumped to her feet and threw her arms around him. Ernest patted her on the back affectionately, warmed by her reaction but not unsurprised; she, like her mother, had always been a bit of a paper tiger. "I take that as a yes?" he said into her chamomile-scented hair.

"Yes!" She stepped apart, her brown eyes sparkling. "Thanks, Papi! Vietnam! I can't wait! When are we leaving?"

"There's a flight to Ho Chi Minh City this evening."

"Let's go book our tickets before they sell out—"

"I've already booked them, Scooter." He cleared his throat. "Nika. So why don't we head over to Main Street to buy you some decent clothes to fly in?"

"You knew I'd say yes?"

"You did, didn't you?"

"Guess you know me too well," she said, planting a kiss on his grizzled cheek. "And even though I'm not a kid anymore...I think I like it better when you call me Scooter."

PART 2
HO CHI MINH CITY

CHAPTER 7
NUMBAH ONE

They touched down at Tan Son Nhat International Airport at five in the morning two calendar days after takeoff (they'd leapfrogged a day chasing the sun east), and Nika felt like crap.

As soon as the jet reached cruising altitude, the business-class flight attendant, wearing a yellow Star Trek-esque uniform, poured her a welcome glass of champagne. She had a second glass with dinner. She should have stopped there; she didn't have a high tolerance for alcohol. But later, while watching a movie on the in-flight entertainment, she had two blueberry mimosas. During a second movie she had two or maybe (probably) three glasses of red wine.

She didn't remember falling asleep but woke up when breakfast was being served. She didn't think she could keep anything down and settled for coffee while Popeye treated himself to a breakfast martini, French toast with poached peaches and mascarpone, a smoothie shot, and a fresh fruit salad. Then he asked the flight attendant for an Earl Grey tea while he browsed a two-day-old copy of *The San Francisco Chronicle*.

The long-haul flight might have been a boring slog for him, but for Nika it was the beginning of an adventure. She had never been overseas before, and despite her hangover, the anticipation of what Vietnam might be like had her imagination churning. Mostly she was just happy to be *doing* something. Watching ice melt in slow motion was preferable to the monotonous daily routine of prison.

God, prison, she thought. She tried not to think about the years of her life that she'd wasted there (just as she'd tried not to think about the outside world when she was locked up), but that was proving to be easier said than done. The memories were too recent and raw. One day she might be able to gloss over them without regret and bitterness, but that day was not today.

When the judge handed down her sentence, she had initially felt relief. The weeks of anxiety and uncertainty leading up to the trial were over. She knew her fate: five years. She could do that; it wouldn't be so bad. Of course, the understanding of what it would be like to be confined to a cage for five years hadn't hit her yet. It was only when she told her cellmate a couple of weeks into her sentence, "I don't think I can do this" and the woman replied, "You don't have a choice in nothing no more, honey, and that's just how it is in here" that Nika realized exactly how long five years behind bars was going to be.

In retrospect prison—at least her medium-security one—wasn't the hell you saw portrayed in the movies. The worst punishment Nika received was a forty-eight-hour stint in solitary confinement after she'd tried to free a bat that had gotten caught in the razor wire of the exercise yard fence. Nevertheless, prison was mind-numbingly soulless. You might see some of the new girls smiling or giggling when they first arrived, but it wouldn't be long before they had the dead eyes and slack expressions like everybody else.

Each day Nika woke at six. After changing into her khaki uniform (no jewelry was permitted except for a plain wedding band that didn't exceed $100 in value) and doing her make-up (it helped her to feel a little more human), she was marched in single-file to the cafeteria, where she had exactly thirty minutes to eat breakfast. Then it was off to her job. She did everything from collecting trash and mopping floors to serving food and folding laundry. For that she was paid less than a dollar a day. The money was held electronically and could only be spent at the in-prison commissary on basics like toothpaste and soap and snacks.

After lunch (also exactly thirty minutes) Nika returned to her job where she worked until three o'clock. At five o'clock, after two hours of "free time"—an oxymoron in prison—she ate dinner and then attended rehabilitation courses. She took cooking, hospitality, pottery, and computer studies. Cooking was everyone's favorite course and considered to be a privilege by the guards—one they revoked from her after they caught her smoking in a non-designated area.

At eight o'clock she was herded into her cell. Nika found the few hours before the lights went out at eleven to be the worst of the day. There was little to do to distract her from the reality of her predicament. Thankfully her cellmate, Robyn, had been relatively normal. She was a nurse serving an eleven-year manslaughter sentence for murdering her husband. She didn't plan his murder in advance. On the day it happened she'd had a bad day at work where two patients had died, and when she came home and saw him shirtless and sweaty, beer in hand, pushing around the lawnmower, something in her snapped. She floored the accelerator of her car, jumped the curb, and ran him over, lawnmower, beer bottle, and all.

The funny thing was, Robyn was a shy and mousy woman, and if Nika hadn't heard the tale straight from her, she would never have believed it. In any event Nika liked Robyn, and during those somber evenings before bed, they would often give each other shoulder massages or facials to pass the time. Sometimes they would play cards. They would rarely talk about their past lives; that was too painful.

Some inmates looked forward to visiting hours on the

weekends, but for most nobody came to see them—and that went for Nika, too. At first she waited expectantly every Saturday and Sunday morning for Popeye to surprise her and show up. She understood he was upset with her. He made that abundantly clear on the one occasion they spoke before her trial. He also made it abundantly clear that whatever sentence she received she would deserve, and he would not be visiting her in prison. Even so, she didn't really believe it.

Trudging through the bland airport corridors, Nika felt a strange mix of emotions. There was a surge of resentment toward Popeye for pushing her out of his life so easily, but also relief because he had let her back in. She didn't know where she would be right now if he'd turned her away from his house a few days ago.

They cleared immigration and then customs and followed the signs indicating the taxi stand. When they stepped outside into the crisp morning, the sky was overcast and everything was wet. However, the warm, exotic air reminded Nika that she was halfway across the world. She breathed it in deeply.

"Looks like it rained recently," she said, stopping next to her grandfather on the sidewalk.

"It's the start of monsoon season," he told her. "It's going to be raining a lot while we're here. Now where are the damn taxis?"

Just then a green taxicab swerved to the curb directly in front of them. A small, smiling man got out and asked, "You need taxi?"

"No, thank you," said Popeye. "We're looking for—"

"What are you talking about, Papi?" To the driver Nika said, "We're going to The Reverie Saigon. Do you know it?"

"Yes, yes, of course. Very nice. Numbah one hotel." He came over, took the purple suitcase she'd bought at Nordstrom, and dumped it into the vehicle's trunk.

"Where's the taxi stand?" asked Popeye when he came back to

take his suitcase.

"Not open," said the man. "Too early."

Popeye huffed. "Right."

"What's wrong?" Nika said, opening the back door for him.

Shaking his head, he got in the car, and she followed. A few moments later they were speeding away from the airport.

"Hey, sport," said Popeye, leaning forward. "Turn on the meter, okay?"

"Meter no work," the man replied.

Popeye huffed again. "How much to the city then?"

"One million."

"Stop the car. We're getting out."

"Okay, for you, 800,000 dong."

"Stop the car."

"Okay, okay, 700,000. Best price."

"500,000," said Popeye, sitting back with a grunt. "I told you we should have found the taxi stand."

Nika was frowning at him. "How much is 500,000 dong?"

"Almost thirty dollars, give or take."

"How long is it to the hotel?"

He shrugged. "Twenty minutes."

"What's the problem then? Thirty dollars seems reasonable to me. That's about what it would cost back home."

"We're not back home, Scooter," he said. "We're in Vietnam. The average daily wage here is maybe ten bucks."

She laughed. "You just paid…however much for business-class plane tickets, Papi? What's thirty dollars to you?"

"It's the principle. I don't like getting ripped off."

"No rip-off," the driver called back to them happily. "Numbah one price for you. Numbah one price in Saigon."

Smiling to herself, Nika turned her attention to the bustling, colorful city rolling past her window.

CHAPTER 8
AN UNUSUAL REQUEST

The twelve-mile drive from the airport to the hotel was a slog. Ernest had forgotten how bad traffic was in Saigon. Even in the early hours, the wide boulevards were clogged with motorbikes that outnumbered other vehicles fifty to one. The drivers obeyed the stoplights, but they didn't seem to follow any other rules of the road; they certainly didn't have any concept of lanes. The incessant honking was almost a language in itself.

There was no air conditioning in the taxi, and both the temperature and humidity had to be close to one hundred. Ernest hadn't known what to expect from Saigon after more than fifty years, but the former French colony known as the Pearl of the Orient was not exactly the Saigon he remembered. Most of the city blocks still consisted of uniform three-story buildings, presenting a neat yet repetitive aesthetic with red roof tiles, wooden louvered windows, and elegant balustrades or Indochinese iron balcony bars. And while all the old hand-painted signs had been replaced with digital printing and vinyl graphics and LED lighting, the bones of the structures hadn't changed.

What was different, what was hard to get his head around, was just how much the city had been developed over the decades. Skyscrapers, trendy shopping malls, hip bars, high-end restaurants, and well-kept green spaces were everywhere. Saigon's architecture, much like its culture, had always been a hodgepodge of international elements, and that remained the case now but on steroids.

Strangely, Ernest felt oddly neutral about the city. He felt no nostalgia. It was just another big, ever-growing metropolis to him.

"You want to sightsee?" the driver said to them a moment after swerving sharply to avoid a three-wheeled motorbike. "Where you want to go? Quan take you tomorrow." He offered a white business card over his shoulder. Nika accepted it. Ernest glimpsed Quan's handwritten name above a scribbled phone number. "Independence Palace? Binh Tay Market? Very good food. Very good. You take many pictures."

"We're fine," Ernest said curtly.

"Where you go?"

"Too far for you."

"Nowhere too far. Quan go anywhere. Take you anywhere you want."

"No, thank you."

"We'll see what happens, Quan," said Nika, pocketing the card. "Thank you for the offer."

District 1, the city's main cultural and financial area, was chock full of faded French colonial buildings, consulates, busy cafés, designer boutiques, and sleek glass-and-steel towers. The Reverie Saigon occupied the top floors of the Times Square Building, a forty-story high-rise building that would have been right at home in New York City or Chicago. Quan parked in front of the valet stand, retrieved their suitcases from the trunk, and handed them to a bellhop with a waiting trolley. Ernest gave him three 200,000 notes, the only denomination he'd requested when exchanging money at the airport.

"Thank you, thank you," said Quan, bowing.

"Hold on, sport," Ernest said impatiently. "We agreed on 500,000. You owe me change."

"Quan has no change."

"Bullshit!"

"Papi…" Nika rested a hand on his arm. "It's no big deal."

"You go sightsee tomorrow, you call me," said the driver, ducking quickly back behind the wheel of the car and driving off.

Nika smiled. "He was a happy fellow."

Ernest scowled. "We got scammed."

"Consider the extra you paid a tip."

"It wasn't a tip. It was highway robbery."

"Wow!" she said, turning to the building's large glass entrance, which was flanked by stone elephants. "Impressive."

The bellhop had already rolled their luggage inside, and a young man wearing a gold peaked cap and a white jacket with epaulets held open the door for them. They rode an elevator up to the marbled hotel lobby which featured a seven-meter vaulted ceiling, vibrant wall mosaics, a giant emerald-green monument clock, and gilded and bejeweled purple furniture which could be best described as a cross between Baroque, Rococo, and Alice in Wonderland.

After checking in Nika went to her room and Ernest to his, where he unpacked his suitcase, showered, and shaved. Dressed in fresh clothes, he found a tourist office two blocks from the hotel on the corner of a busy thoroughfare. The glass-fronted building was nestled between a rundown motorbike rental shop (which had hired a woman in a Snow White costume to entice customers inside) and a Vietnamese restaurant offering cooking lessons. Ernest entered and queued in an empty line. A few minutes later a Caucasian couple at one of the booths stood, thanked the employee for her help, made a joke about the weather, and left. The employee waved Ernest over.

"Good afternoon, sir," she said in fluent English. "Are you looking for a tour today?"

"Not today, no," Ernest said. "Tomorrow. And I require a private car."

"A private car?" The woman frowned. "I'm sorry, sir. We don't offer private tours." She indicated a rack stuffed with glossy tour brochures. "But we do have many exciting and affordable options. If you could tell me where you had in mind—?"

"The Cu Chi District, and if you only offer group tours, then I'll buy all the seats on the tour."

"Um, I'm sorry, sir, but we don't, um, really do that…"

"You have a tour of the Cu Chi District, don't you?"

"Yes, it's a popular destination to see the Cu Chi tunnels."

"How many seats are available?"

"Six is the maximum number for that tour. Customers are driven in a luxury van that offers air conditioning."

"Well, I'd like all six tickets then for that tour leaving tomorrow morning."

"Six tickets just for you?"

"What does it matter if they're just for me or not?" Ernest said, growing annoyed. "I'm paying for them."

"Yes, but I'm not sure if we…" She seemed flustered. "Excuse me a moment. Let me get my manager."

Ernest sat back with a sigh. Customer service was just as he remembered it: professionally polite but not exceptionally educated. A few minutes later a thin man dressed in a well-fitted suit approached the booth with a smile. He sat in the chair while the woman stood behind him with her eyes lowered and her hands clasped in front of her.

He said, "Hello, Mr.…?"

"Campbell," Ernest said.

"Mr. Campbell. I am Mr. Van Lam, and I'm more than happy to accommodate your request today. You would like to rent an entire tour van for yourself to visit the Cu Chi tunnels, is that correct?"

"No. I don't need an entire van. A private car would suit me fine. And I have no interest in the Cu Chi tunnels. I would like to visit an area northeast of the tunnels. I want a driver who is familiar with the Binh Duong Province—specifically, the Ho Bo Woods next to the Iron Triangle."

Mr. Van Lam frowned. "The Ho Bo Woods? We don't offer any tours to the Ho Bo Woods."

"Which is why I require a private vehicle. And I also have no interest in a tour or any sightseeing for that matter. I'm looking for a village. I don't know the name of it, but I'll recognize it when I see it."

"Ah, Mr. Campbell. Such a request is highly unusual…"

"I understand it's an unusual request, which is why I told this lovely young lady that I would rent an entire van for the trouble. I should finish my business the same day."

Mr. Van Lam's eyebrows went up. "*Should?* And if for whatever reason you are not able to? What is it you would have my driver do?"

"Return to the village in the morning. I'll compensate him for a hotel room in Cu Chi, and I'll pay the price again of the tour for him to bring me back here."

"This is truly an unusual request," said the man, frowning. "However, let me see what I can arrange."

#

Back at the Times Square Building, Ernest went to an eatery on the ground floor called The Long. He sat at a marble-topped bar that stretched fifty meters. A bartender dressed in a spiffy black and grey uniform arrived promptly.

"Wonder why this place is called The Long?" Ernest said.

"Because the bar is very long, sir," he replied proudly, missing the sarcasm. He waved his hand expansively. "It links Dong Khoi, Saigon's most fashionable street, with Nguyen Hue Boulevard. Do you require a menu? We have the finest pizza kitchen in the city. Or would you like to try one of our premier cocktails? They are *my* specialty—"

"Just a Vietnamese 333."

"Of course," he said a little too politely. He went to get the beer and set it in front of Ernest alongside a frosty glass. "If you require anything else, I'm at your service," he added and then went down the bar to serve a giddy young couple that had just sat down.

Ernest sipped the beer from the bottle. It was what he used to drink during the war, what all the G.I.s had called Tiger Piss back then. It tasted exactly as he remembered.

At a nearby table two drunk American vets were chatting about how great it was to be back in Vietnam. By the time Ernest ordered a second bottle of beer, they were reminiscing about their participation in the 1968 Tet Offensive. Ernest could still recall with vivid detail waking in the middle of the night of the Vietnamese Lunar New Year and realizing something big was happening. The generals and senior commanders might have had an idea of how big that something was, but the grunts like him were told simply to saddle up and hat out.

As he soon learned, the Viet Cong and North Vietnamese Army had launched surprise attacks on Saigon and other places across the South. The scale of the offensive shocked the brass in Washington who'd believed the war had been going well. Due to superior firepower and mobility, the Americans and ARVN had been winning nearly every encounter with the VC and NVA troops ever since their first major victory in the Ia Drang Valley in '65. While some NVA generals wanted to conduct a guerrilla operation to wear down the US's resolve, others preferred to stage a large assault that, they believed, would rally the South Vietnamese to the Communist cause and spark a general uprising against the Saigon government: hence the Tet Offensive. However, American intelligence suspected there would be attacks during the holiday season, so they weren't caught fully off guard, and the bulk of the fighting was all but over in a matter of days.

US Forces planned to counterpunch with 200,000 or so troops to exploit the enemy's debacle, and had they done this, the war might have ended very differently. But someone in the Johnson White House leaked the plan to the press. When the story broke, the American public, already wary of the growing scale of the war and its casualties, concluded that the government was lying to them about the overwhelming battlefield victory and that the extra troops were in fact needed to recover from a disastrous defeat. It was a psychological turning point in the nation that foreshadowed the beginning of the end of the war.

Less than a month later, President Johnson announced that he wouldn't seek reelection. Three years after that, in 1972, the last of US forces left the country. And three more years after that, in April 1975, Saigon fell to the North.

That was the same year that Ernest met Neeti. He was twenty-eight, living on the top floor of a mixed-use building in downtown San Francisco, and working at his family's printing company. Over the last few years he'd tried out a half dozen different positions, including an assistant to the VPs in marketing, sales, and accounting. Nobody took him seriously; he was just the boss's son getting an inside look at the operation so one day he could run it. That was what Ernest's father would have wanted, although it wasn't what Ernest wanted. He didn't know what he was going to do with his future then, but it wasn't wearing a suit and tie every day.

In any event he was young, healthy, and enjoying life; he had plenty of time to figure things out. Unlike a lot of other vets, he'd been able to put the war behind him, although he still had nightmares sometimes. A conversation with a sergeant who had no limbs; a room filled with jumbled bones that he had to rearrange into skeletons so the remains could be sent to the families; dark, unending tunnels in which he always woke up just before a boobytrap was triggered, or in which he heard Cowboy calling to him, begging him for help. But for the most part he was doing okay. No PTSD, or what would later become known as PTSD when it was recognized as a disorder.

On the fourth of July of that year, Ernest took a girl named Josie to watch fireworks in Golden Gate Park. At one point he went to a refreshment stand to buy them Pepsis and a bag of licorice. Neeti was in the line in front of him wearing a big straw hat, a colorful bohemian dress, and a whole lot of beads. Ernest's first impression was that she was busy and messy but beautiful, and he was immediately smitten. He asked her if she was enjoying the fireworks and led the small talk from there. She was polite but made it clear she wasn't interested in him. When she left the refreshment stand with two soft drinks, he figured she was spoken for.

Later that afternoon, after the fireworks had finished, Josie told Ernest that she had to get home because her parents were visiting from Michigan. He offered to walk with her, but she said she was already late and it would be quicker if she went on her own. While Ernest wandered the park alone, looking for the exit he had originally entered through, he spotted Neeti eating ice cream with a girlfriend beneath a tree. He struck up another conversation. The friend was more receptive than Neeti had been and invited him to sit with them. Eventually the girlfriend asked, "So, Ernie... are you interested in me or Neeti? Because you can't have us both." Ernest didn't remember what his reply had been, but he made it clear he was interested in Neeti and the girlfriend eventually left. Over the next hour Ernest won Neeti over and eventually walked her back to her apartment in North Beach. He invited her to dinner the following Friday night, she agreed…but he never called her. He didn't know why. He was just young and dumb and…didn't call her.

Seven years later, on New Year's Eve in 1982, Ernest was dining with some friends at a seafood restaurant located on Pier 7 along The Embarcadero. After they ate they moved to the patio to watch the fireworks over the Bay. The small space was so crowded that you could barely turn around without bumping into somebody—and that was exactly how he met Neeti for the second time. He turned around from where he had been standing at a railing, looking out over the water, and nearly knocked a glass of champagne from the hands of a beautiful woman.

"I'm terribly sorry," he said. "I didn't see—"

"Ernest?"

His eyes met hers, and he recognized her as if the seven years had only been seven days. "Neeti? Dear God, *Neeti*. You remembered my name?"

"And you remembered mine."

"How long has it been?"

"Too long. Where does the time go?"

"You look great. I mean it. You've barely aged."

She smiled. "You're very charming, Ernest. I remember that about you."

"Let me buy you a drink."

"I can't. I'm—I'm with friends. I just came over here to get a look at the view."

"Just one. I owe you that much. Champagne?"

"Well…all right then…thank you." When he returned from the

bar with two flutes of champagne, she said, "Given your track record, I was a little worried you might not come back…"

"I don't know what to say, Neeti. I was twenty-eight. I was stupid—"

"I'm teasing, Ernest. We were both young."

He raised his glass and said, "To this serendipitous reunion."

She raised hers. "To that."

They spent the rest of the evening together. He learned that Neeti was recently divorced, had a five-year-old daughter named Palak, and was a high-school math teacher. After the fireworks finished, he drove her back to her place, a well-kept Victorian near Chinatown.

"Thank you for a lovely evening, Ernie."

"Are you free for dinner sometime?"

"Where have I heard that before?"

But she agreed. Ernest took her to the Liholiho Yacht Club, and over two bottles of wine they shared their life stories. It was as though the two of them were the only people in the restaurant… and Ernest never had eyes for another woman again.

Five months later they were strolling through Union Square when Neeti stopped in front of Tiffany & Co. She pointed to a vintage emerald ring on display in the window and said, "If you ever do propose to me, Ernie, I don't need a diamond. I'd like something interesting like that."

The next day Ernest returned to the shop, bought the ring, and proposed to Neeti. They married a month later at a small ceremony attended by Neeti's parents, her sister, and her bridesmaid, a friend she'd known since college. Ernest's parents had both passed away within a month of each other three years earlier, he had no siblings, and so the only person on his side was his best man, a venture capitalist who'd backed his computer software company.

After the honeymoon in Italy, Neeti and Palak moved in with him in the San Francisco mansion which he had inherited from his parents. The years went by quickly. Palak left for San Francisco State University in 1995, met her future husband in her sophomore year (a pleasant if introverted man named John Hill), and fell pregnant with Kanika a few months later. The pregnancy wasn't planned, but having an abortion never crossed Palak's mind, nor did dropping out of school. In the end she managed to raise Nika while earning a Bachelor of Fine Arts degree. Her passion was photojournalism, as was John's, and the following summer they were both accepted to an internship with the National Geographic Society.

Yet that was the high point in their nascent careers. In the years that followed they struggled to find any sort of freelance work. It was the old Catch-22: established publishers wanted photojournalists with experience, but the only way to gain experience was to work for an established publisher. Eventually Palak and John decided to create their own nature expedition to obtain the experience they needed, so they borrowed $5,000 from Ernest and organized a three-week trip to Alaska's Denali National Park. They were due to return to Juneau on October 1st. When a few days went by with no word from them, Ernest notified the park rangers, who began aerial and ground searches. Ernest flew to Juneau and joined them.

The beat-up station wagon that Palak and John had purchased for $500 was discovered at the Savage East parking lot, and so the search focused on Savage River, Mr. Margaret, and Healy Ridge. Two days later the ground team that Ernest had been a part of discovered their remains near the north end of the Savage River Loop Trail. It seemed they had diverted from the riverside trail to do some scrambling on higher terrain when they fell and suffered fatal injuries.

Ernest and Neeti had been heartbroken, but they remained strong for Nika, who they took custody of, and who quickly became the centerpiece of their lives. Even though she was only four years old, she already resembled Palak, and over the next few years more and more of her mother began to shine through so that it was almost as though Ernest and Neeti were raising Palak all over again. Nika asked often about her mother and father, things like "What do they do in heaven every day?" and "Can they hear me when I say my prayers?" and "Are they friends with Jesus?"

A few weeks after Nika's tenth birthday, Neeti began seeing a new primary care physician after her longtime doctor retired. During his initial exam the GP thought her stomach looked a little swollen and ordered a CT scan.

After undergoing a barrage of other tests, Neeti learned she had Stage 3 ovarian cancer. Two tumors—one the size of a grapefruit, and the other the size of an orange—had grown on both sides of her ovaries. After several rounds of chemotherapy, she underwent a twelve-hour surgery to remove the tumors, along with her uterus, fallopian tubes, and ovaries. She went into remission but relapsed the next year...and her prognosis was not good. Because once Stage 3 cancer returns, you're automatically graduated to Stage 4.

Ernest and Neeti were told she had maybe three more years, but it turned out to be much shorter than that. She died four months later in a private room at John Muir Health-Walnut Creek Medical Center. Ernest was sitting by her side, holding her hand, when she took her final breath. Her funeral was as their wedding had been: small and intimate.

That summer Ernest made the decision to send Nika to The Athenian School in the fall. They still saw each other during the Christmas holidays and summer breaks, and he always took her somewhere special for her birthday.

Nevertheless, during those four years she was away, she grew up fast, and they grew apart. And then before he knew it she was heading off to Stanford University. He was incredibly proud of her...until she quit school to work for that jackass Ari Schwartz. He told her she was making a mistake, but she didn't listen to him, and they spoke less and less with each other. And then he learned—from her lawyer of all people—that federal prosecutors were charging her in a 19-count indictment.

He couldn't believe the magnitude of the fraud she had been accused of. Ari Schwartz was clearly the mastermind, but she had gone along with him willingly, and that was almost as bad in his mind. When they met on the weekend before her trial began, he had practically disowned her, telling her he wanted nothing more to do with her. He knew his words had been overly harsh, but he had been so disappointed in her; he and Neeti had not raised her to be a criminal.

And that was that. He didn't see her for five long years. Not until she showed up on his doorstep a few days ago, looking more than ever like her late mother...

Ernest was still musing over these memories when his phone rang. As he dug it from his pocket, he realized the two vets had paid their bill and left.

It was a local number. "Ernest Campbell speaking," he said.

"Mr. Campbell, my name is Pham Thang," said a man in fluent English. "The manager at Saigon Adventure Tours mentioned that you require a driver familiar with Binh Duong province."

"Yes, that's right."

"Then I believe I may be of assistance to you. However, there are a few details I'd like to discuss in person. I am near the Times Square Building right now if there is somewhere nearby where we could meet?"

"I'm in a place called The Long Bar. It's—"

"I'll be there shortly." He hung up.

Ernest went to the bathroom, ordered a third Tiger Piss at the bar, and then sat at the table that the vets had vacated. Soon a man dressed in tan slacks and a white Polo shirt entered the eatery. He had gray hair and a gaunt, severe face. But when he introduced himself to Ernest with a small bow, a kind smile softened his features.

"Thank you for seeing me, Mr. Thang," Ernest said when they were seated. "But we could have organized everything over the phone…"

"We could have, Mr. Campbell. But given the nature of your request, I assumed that you are a veteran of the Vietnam War. Would that be correct?"

"Why would my request make you think that?"

"I have met many American veterans over the years who have made requests similar to yours. Not to find a village in the Ho Bo Woods, of course. But they were in Vietnam searching for something of importance to them."

Ernest frowned. "Such as?"

"Different things, the same things." Mr. Thang shrugged. "Answers, mostly. The war was a difficult time for everyone involved. We all did things we regret—"

"We?"

"Were you with the 25th Infantry Division or the 173rd Airborne Brigade? Or was it the 82nd Airborne Division?"

Ernest said, "The 25th—2nd Battalion, 27th Infantry Regiment."

"1st Brigade?"

"Third."

Mr. Thang nodded. "I was a soldier in the National Liberation Front. I was born in Binh Duong province, and I was assigned there from 1967 to 1971. Perhaps you would prefer a different driver?"

Ernest hesitated. He'd never sat down at a table with a man he'd once been trying to kill. However, the war was a long time ago. He held no animosity against those he fought. He said, "No, Mr. Thang, I would not. Do you want a drink? It's on me."

"No, thank you."

Ernest sipped his beer and studied the fellow. He was soft-spoken and composed and seemed like a no-nonsense sort; he would have made a good soldier. "You were saying how we all did things we regret...?"

"We had little choice, didn't we? And I believe most of us want to understand why we did what we did. We want to be able to look into a mirror and not only see the man staring back now, but the man we had once been. We want to understand who he was so we can find a little more peace with who he is now. Am I making sense, Mr. Campbell?"

Perfect sense, Ernest thought. *Only I'm not here to come to terms with the shit I did. I've already done that. At least I've tried.*

He said, "Are you familiar with a village in the Ho Bo Woods that was razed to the ground by American soldiers?"

"Many villages were destroyed in the Ho Bo Woods during the war. As you well know, it was the headquarters of the Viet Cong Military Region 4 and a major thorn in the side of the Americans—until, that is, it was flattened by your B-52 bombers in 1970."

"This village was razed in May of 1969. There was a very large banyan tree in the center of it, although I don't know if it would have survived the fire."

Mr. Thang said nothing for a few moments, and then he nodded. "I know the village that you speak of. It is called Tân Hòa. It was rebuilt in '72 or '73, and the banyan tree is still there."

Ernest sat straighter. "How do you know this?"

"I have relatives in a nearby village who I visit occasionally. I have driven past Tân Hòa several times. So it seems I can be of assistance to you, after all, Mr. Campbell."

"Excellent!"

"However," he added with a cautious note in his voice, "I must ask you why it is you would like to go to Tân Hòa. It is a very small and impoverished village. It would not receive many, if any, outsiders. I do not wish to…disrespect…the people who live there."

Ernest understood what he meant. Bringing an American G.I. back to a village that he had once had a hand in destroying was likely not going to earn Mr. Thang any brownie points with the locals.

"There are tunnels in the jungle to the north of the village," he said. "I fought in them. A dear friend of mine died in them. I promised him I would not leave him there…" His jaw tightened. "I have cancer, Mr. Thang." It was the first time he had said it out loud, and the admission sounded brazen and unreal. "I don't have much time left, and I'm here to fulfil the promise I made to him."

"I see," Mr. Thang said thoughtfully. He assessed Ernest for a prolonged moment without blinking. And then he added, "When would you like to depart?"

"Tomorrow," Ernest said. "Early."

CHAPTER 9
HAPPY JACK'S

Nika had never stayed in such an opulent hotel room before, and she didn't quite know how to describe the décor. The color palette was an eye-popping gold, red, and chocolate; decorative mirroring and floral hand-painted motifs adorned the walls; the hardwood floor looked as though it was waxed at least once a week; a crystal chandelier dangled above an ultra-modern bed, flanked by a sleek leather chaise; and the bathroom with all its marble and decorative tiling could have been lifted straight from the Taj Mahal.

She kicked off her shoes and flopped onto the bed, landing face-first without bothering to get under the covers.

She was asleep before she knew it…and awoke groggily to someone knocking on the door. It seemed to take an immense effort to pull herself out of sleep, but she called, "Coming!" She took another few moments to clear her head before she went to the door. Popeye stood in the hallway wearing shorts, a linen shirt, boat shoes, and a white Panama hat with a black bow.

"How can I help you, Mr. Hemingway?" she said.

"Wrong Ernest, Scooter. Is that what you're wearing?"

She looked down at her jeans and T-shirt. "What?"

"You just spent seventeen hours on a plane in those clothes."

"What time is it?"

He checked the big silver wristwatch that her grandmother had given him on one of their anniversaries. "Five fifty-nine. Exactly one minute before the time we agreed to meet."

"I slept all day?"

"Welcome to the world of jetlag."

"Ugh, give me ten. I need a quick shower to wake up."

#

Ernest was sitting in a throne-like chair with plum-colored leather cushions and ornate gold trim (it looked ridiculous but was damned comfortable) when he saw Nika come out of the elevator. He stood to greet her. "Nearly on time."

She stopped next to him, wearing a breezy white summer dress and sandals. "I just set a world record," she said. "Where are we eating?"

"I thought we'd walk until we find somewhere."

Outside they crossed the busy road to a tree-lined pedestrian promenade. It was bustling with locals, tourists, street performers, and young people.

"Want a balloon, Scooter?" Ernest said as they passed a woman holding so many metallic helium balloons that he wouldn't have been surprised if she simply lifted off the ground and floated away.

"I like that guy," she said, nodding at a bare-chested man standing on an overturned milk crate. He was painted head to toe in silver with a pair of angel wings on his back. He didn't move a muscle and was doing a great job impersonating a statute.

Nika dropped a few small notes into his tip box; he didn't react.

"Be careful with your money," he told her. "It's easy to confuse a 500,000 note with a 50,000 one."

"Gee, thanks, Papi," she said. "I wasn't quite sure how money works. Higher is better, right?"

"Left leads to the Saigon River. Right to the city hall and opera house. Both are impressive French colonial buildings if you're interested in that sort of thing."

"Of course I am. 'If you don't know history, then you don't know anything. You're a leaf that doesn't know it's part of a tree.'"

He looked sidelong at her. "Who said that?"

"Michael Crichton," she said. "I read all his books while I was in prison. You'd be surprised how good the library was there."

After walking a short distance, Ernest said, "How about we try something in there?" He pointed to a mid-century apartment building overlooking the promenade. At some point all the residential units had been converted to vibrant restaurants, cafes, and boutiques.

She scanned the brightly lit signs and said, "I know we're in Vietnam, and I should be adventurous and try something authentic. But to be honest right now all I really feel like is a cheeseburger."

"Let's have a look anyway."

The entrance to the building was in the back next to a sprawling bookstore. A pink sign informed them that there was a fee of 3,000 VND (per person) to use the elevator. They took the stairs—not to save the twenty cents or whatever it was but because the elevator didn't look as though it had been serviced this century.

The staircase was painted orange, poorly lit, and decrepit…the kind of place that should have smelled of urine but thankfully didn't.

They eventually made their way all the way to the roof to

discover an American restaurant named Happy Jack's Tavern. It was crowded and rowdy with loud music playing. A waitress showed them to a recently vacated balcony table with a view of the promenade below. Next to them billiard balls clacked loudly as four men stood around a red-felt table. When the waitress returned with their drinks—a diet Coke and a beer—Nika ordered a cheeseburger and fries. Nothing caught Ernest's eye, and so he settled for chicken wings with blue cheese dressing.

"Fun atmosphere," said Nika, glancing about. Raunchy fairy lights and Chinese lanterns decorated the ceiling, and pictures of Michael Jackson and other iconic singers hung on the wood-paneled walls. Motley Crue's "Girls, Girls, Girls" began blasting out from a nearby speaker.

"Too many ex-pats for my liking," Ernest said. A lot of them, he noticed, were middle-aged men with Vietnamese dates in their twenties.

"Probably means the food is good. So what's the plan tomorrow, Papi? You told the taxi driver that we're going somewhere far from here. Was that to brush off his offer to take us around the city? Or is this mysterious business of yours not in Saigon?"

"It's not in Saigon," he told her. "I should only be gone tomorrow. Two days at the most—"

"Papi!"

He frowned at her. "What?"

"*What?* Do I really have to explain? You tried to ditch me back in San Francisco. If I hadn't made such a fuss, you would have. Now I come with you halfway across the world, and you're at it again!"

Ernest grimaced. "I'm not 'at' anything, Scooter. Where I'm going is remote. It's no place for you. Have fun in Saigon when I'm gone, and when I get back, we'll do whatever you want together."

"No offense, Papi, but I'm a third of your age. Anything physical that you can do, I can do just as well. So this place is remote? So what? It sounds like an adventure to me."

Ernest summoned the waitress, borrowed a pen, and flipped over his brown paper placemat. He drew an elongated S shape. "This is Vietnam," he told Nika, angling the placemat toward her. "We're down here." He made a dot near the bottom of the S. "I need to go over here." He made another dot to the left of Saigon. "That's about two hundred kilometers away. Once I get there I need to get to an old North Vietnamese Army base in the jungle somewhere around here." He made an X to the north of the last dot.

"Why do you need to go to some old army base in the middle of the jungle?"

"During the war I was one of the guys who went into the tunnels, looking for documents and weapons and occasionally scaring the Viet Cong up to the surface. I have some unfinished business to take care of in the tunnels beneath the NVA base."

"You came all the way back to Vietnam to *crawl around some tunnels*?"

"We're here, aren't we?" he said. "Now please don't argue with me, Scooter. Where I'm going is no place for you. It's as simple as that."

#

Buck Rafelson sipped his whiskey and ginger ale.

Around him the rooftop bar buzzed with a lazy kind of energy. Americans, Australians, Brits, and other foreigners were drinking from mugs of beer in the sweltering evening heat. Some were watching cricket or tennis on the wall-mounted TVs, others were engaged in rambunctious banter, and others still (a good many, in fact) were eyeing every young Vietnamese woman who trotted through the bar's entrance.

And a steady stream of them, svelte and smiling, were doing just that. They knew Happy Jack's was an expat hotspot, and they were on the prowl for a rich foreigner. "Rich," of course, was subjective. All foreigners were rich to these girls, many of whom grew up in the tin-roofed huts crammed along the canals of Binh Thanh, or some of the other slummy districts, where barefooted kids ran amok and there was an illegal cockfight or two down every twisting alleyway.

Originally from Boonville, Missouri, Buck lived month-to-month on a $1007 pension, and he was rich enough to show one of the girls a good time on any given night. The only problem was, tonight none of them seemed interested in him.

It's still early, he told himself, tipping whiskey down his throat. *You'll find one. You usually do...even if it's the ugly one that nobody else wants.*

Buck went to the bathroom. Battered record sleeves covered the walls. The one in front of his face while he stood at the foul-smelling urinal was The Beatles' "A Hard Day's Night." A fat guy Buck recognized but had never spoken to stumbled into the bathroom while Buck stumbled out. They exchanged a nod and a grunt.

Back at his table Buck found his friend, Shelby Papadopoulos, sitting in Buck's temporarily vacated seat. Shelby was a short, stocky, deeply tanned Greek American who'd been living in Saigon—HCMC would always be Saigon to Buck—for close to twenty years. At sixty-one, he was a decade younger than Buck, but with his cherub face and thick brown hair he looked even younger.

Buck sat across from him and frowned. "Where's my drink?"

Shelby looked up from his mug of beer. He wore a Hawaiian shirt with the top three buttons undone to reveal a heavy gold chain. It matched the gold fillings in his mouth and the gold bracelet on his wrist. "Waitress took it."

"Hell she did! I wasn't done!"

"Looked done to me," Shelby said and glanced out at the city. The table was at the edge of the nine-story building with views of Lam Son Square, Saigon Opera House, and Notre Dame Cathedral. The drone of traffic battled with a Latino-style lounge band that had just started playing in the corner of the bar beneath haphazardly strung fairy lights. "Nice night, huh?"

Buck was too drunk to decide whether it was a nice night or not. He caught Mamma-san's attention and signaled another whiskey.

Shelby leaned forward conspiratorially and cocked his head to the left. "See the American broad over there?"

Buck squinted, which seemed to help keep his vision from swimming. A young woman was sitting a couple of tables over. She was dark-complected with raven-black hair and long-lashed eyes. Across from her was a smallish fellow with silver hair who, Buck guessed, was approximately his own age. But unlike Buck, he appeared to be a rich prick. It wasn't the preppy clothing or the leather boat shoes. It wasn't even the expensive-looking watch on his wrist or the fact he wasn't wearing any socks with the topsiders. He simply had that air of money about him, that self-assuredness that you could wear like a crown when you had nothing in life to worry about. Buck hated assholes like him.

To Shelby, he said, "Looks like she's taken."

"She ain't taken. That's her grandad. But I ain't interested in her like that. I overheard them talkin' when I was shootin' stick…"

He zipped up when Mamma-san arrived with Buck's Jim Beam over ice.

"You have new fren, Buck? Wow! Good for you," the stout, middle-aged woman said in pidgin English. "How many fren now? Two? But this one handsome fren."

"I like this place," Shelby said, watching Mamma-san walk away with a flat-footed swagger.

"I've invited you plenty times before."

"Like I don't got nothin' better to do than sit around with an old drunk."

Buck snorted. "You're no spring chicken yourself."

"At least I still get laid." He raised his beer.

Buck raised his glass and took a belt. The whiskey burned a trail down his throat and warmed his stomach.

"So that broad over there and her grandad were talkin'," Shelby continued. "The guy's a vet like you—only he don't dress up in his old uniform like an asshole."

Buck was wearing a black beret and a fatigue shirt; it was his standard getup most nights when he went out on the town to meet women. He took a second belt of whiskey and then crunched on an ice cube.

"He was a rat," Shelby said.

"Rat?"

"Tunnel rat. One of those motherfuckers who crawled around in them tunnels lookin' for the little man."

"So?"

"So he's goin' back down into some tunnels tomorrow, somewhere up in the Hobos."

The Ho Bo Woods was about fifty miles north of Saigon and just west of the Iron Triangle. During Operation Circle Pines in '66, the 5th Infantry Regiment discovered an extensive subterranean bunker and tunnel system there…and an entirely new kind of guerilla warfare that would come to haunt Uncle Sugar for the rest of the war.

"Good for him," Buck said, wondering what his friend was getting at. "Do I look like I give a flying fuck?"

"Don't you wanna know *why* he's goin' back in them tunnels fifty years after the war?"

"I expect you're about to tell me."

"He left somethin' important in them."

"And what the hell would that be?"

"Didn't say. But he's come back to Vietnam after all these years to get it, so it's gotta be somethin' important down there. It's gotta be somethin' real important."

Buck was frowning even as what might have been excitement (a foreign feeling for old Buck) churned in his gut. "You're talking about…"

"Gold, man!" Shelby hissed quietly.

"Gold?"

"Or cash. You're the one who told me the fuckin' stories!"

Buck sat back, floored. He looked over at the tunnel rat…and he no longer looked so much like a rich prick. In fact, Buck had no problem picturing him as a young man covered in dirt and sweat, a pistol in one hand and a flashlight in the other as he got ready to crawl into a hole.

Something important down there, he thought.

Something real important.

Beaucoup dinky dau was an expression Buck had picked up during the war. It was a bastardization of French and Vietnamese, and it meant "very crazy." Every vet had a beaucoup dinky dau story to share if you cared to listen, and Buck had heard some very, very crazy shit over the years.

Nevertheless, the stories that got his sluggish mind racing now were of the G.I.s on search-and-destroy missions in the Cu Chi district. He was aware of at least a half dozen different instances of patrols finding canvas sacks stuffed with US greenbacks or wooden crates filled with Chinese gold. Typically the grunts would radio in the discoveries to their First Sergeant. However, Buck had heard tales of shady point squads that loaded their rucksacks with the loot and, once back in the division's rear area, sent it home to the States without raising any eyebrows.

Which begged the question: Had the rich prick been one of those lucky bastards who'd come across a Viet Cong make-shift bank and kept the loot for himself? It would explain the air of money about him. Asshole had been living off the ill-gotten gains his entire life. And if that were the case, was he, like Shelby was suggesting, back in Vietnam now to collect the cash or gold, or whatever it was he hadn't been able to smuggle out of the country during the war?

"Lordy, Lord, Lord," Buck muttered to himself as he rubbed the stubble on his jaw thoughtfully. Then to Shelby: "Where'd you say this section of tunnels you heard them talking about was?"

"Somewhere in the Hobos, some village."

Made sense, Buck thought. That was how all the tunnels started. A family would dig one beneath their hut, and it would connect with others that their friends and neighbors were digging, and then they would all keep on digging together, connecting their village with other villages until all of a sudden you had thousands of tunnels stretching for hundreds of miles, all the way from Saigon to the Cambodian border.

He said, "You want to follow him to the village?"

Shelby nodded. "See what he brings up. What the fuck else you doin' tomorrow?"

"And if it's a small fortune in cash…he's just gonna hand it over to us?"

"You still got that pistol, don't ya?"

He was talking about the .380 Colt that Buck had purchased illegally in Cambodia a few years ago. "I'm not shooting anyone."

"You don't gotta shoot no one. You just gotta have the pistol to wave around. You think an old man and his granddaughter are gonna argue with that? So whaddya say, amigo? Worst case, he finds nothin', and it's just a little daytrip for us." He wagged a finger, and his gold bracelet slid from his wrist to his hairy, muscular forearm. "But best case, he brings up a bag or two of cash that was never his to begin with, and we take it off his hands, thank you very much…"

Buck wondered how much cash that might be. A hundred grand? Two hundred? More? Christ, was he finally going to catch a break in his pisser of a life? It would be about fucking time. Two tours of duty—two goddamn years of his life spent in hell—and what did he get for that? Enough shrapnel lodged permanently in his ass to set off metal detectors in airports, for starters. A lifelong limp. Third degree burns on his left arm and shoulder. An ungrateful public when he returned home. People on the left calling him a baby killer; people on the right telling him he was a pussy that didn't fight hard enough. Armchair assholes who had no idea what it had been like living in the fetid jungles, being eaten alive by mosquitos, jumping at every shadow, carrying your dead buddy to a medevac point in a body bag.

So hell yes, this was his just desserts, and it was long overdue. Screw the rich prick and his granddaughter. The greedy bastards had already lived a life of leisure. Now it was Buck's turn. He deserved the loot. He'd *earned* it, one body bag, one purple heart, and one God-forsaken day at a time.

Buck tipped his highball to his lips. Only ice cubes remained, which were melting quickly in the evening heat. "Lemme think it over," he told Shelby and waved to catch Mamma-san's attention again. "In the meantime, next round's on me."

\#

Nika said, "Do you know those two men, Papi?" She was

looking past him.

Ernest turned in his seat. The men she was presumably referring to were at a nearby table. One of them wore a black beret. The other looked smug and smarmy. Black Beret tipped Ernest a nod. Ernest turned back around and said, "Ignore them."

"Why's the army guy smiling at us?"

"He's not smiling at *us*. He's smiling at *you* because you're a young woman and he's an old pervert."

"Oh, shoot," she said. "He's coming over."

"Howdy, folks," said Black Beret, setting a glass of whiskey on their table. "How goes the evening?"

"My granddaughter and I are having a private dinner," Ernest told him, emphasizing both *granddaughter* and *private*.

He didn't take the hint. "You a vet?"

Ernest glanced up at the man, not bothering to hide his annoyance. Beneath the tilted beret, he had a doughy, cocky Steven Seagal face. There was a generic 75th Infantry Ranger scroll on the right shoulder of his army fatigue shirt but no division or field force patch below it to identify the unit he served in. He said, "Good guess."

The man shrugged. "I can just tell, you know?"

"Where did you serve?"

He frowned. "Where?"

"Which corps area were you in?"

"Oh. Different places," he said, shrugging. "I did a few tours. I was with the Second Batt."

"That right?" Ernest said, feeling his blood boil.

"Yup. And wanna know something?" He rested his forearms on their table, leaning in close as if the CIA had bugged the restaurant. "It's Top Secret. Never been declassified. Probably never will be." He winked at Nika.

"We're listening," she said, looking bemused.

"I killed Ho Chi Minh." He rapped his knuckles on the table in sync with each syllable of the North Vietnamese leader's name.

Whatever tall tale Ernest had expected to hear, it wasn't that. "Who?" he asked to make sure he'd heard the moron right. A Latino band was playing lively music nearby.

"The commie leader, man. *Ho Chi Minh*."

Nika appeared impressed. "And you killed him?"

"That's what I said, honey. My team was on a LURP—that's a Long-Range Reconnaissance Patrol. Basically black ops. We came across a heavily fortified jungle base with an entire company of North Vietnamese soldiers. And we soon learned why: they were guarding Ho. So we radioed it in and were given the green light to take him out. It was a suicide mission, but we did it anyway. We went in during the night, and I put a bullet in his head."

"And everyone escaped?" she said.

He shook his head. "Just me. There were five of us. The others wiped."

Ernest had had enough of this nonsense and said, "Last I heard, Ho Chi Minh died of a heart attack."

"No, man," said the drunk, looking left and right to make sure nobody was trying to listen in. "That's what the brass *wanted* everyone to believe."

"You're full of shit," he said, his voice steel.

"Papi!" said Nika.

"Scooter, quiet! He's full of shit!"

"But you don't have to be *rude*."

"That's right, old man," snapped the drunk. "I'm just—I was just saying hello to a fellow vet."

Ernest shot to his feet, his hands balled into fists at his sides. The drunk was at least a half foot taller than him, but he shied backward a step. "You're right. I *am* an old man," he said. "Because I actually served in the war, you lying vermin."

"Hey, man, I served. I served, man."

"Not Special Forces, you didn't."

"Yeah, m'man. Rangers, 2nd Bat—"

"There wasn't a 2nd Ranger Battalion! There wasn't a First or Third either. Ranger battalions didn't exist back then, only individual units and companies. Now get the fuck out of my sight before I clean the floor with you."

The drunk huffed, looking sheepishly at the nearby diners watching the confrontation. "I don't need this shit! I'm outta here." He stormed out of the restaurant.

Shaking his head, Ernest sat back down. Nika was staring at him with wide eyes. "I deployed with Rangers in the kind of behind-the-lines combat he was talking about," he told her. "They were the best of the best. For that drunk to pretend he was one of them, to wear a combat patch that he didn't earn, goes against everything a soldier stands for."

"I get that. It's just that I've never seen you so upset."

The waitress arrived with their food, setting the chicken wings in front of Nika and the cheeseburger and fries in front of Ernest. When she left, they swapped plates.

"*Chúc ngon miệng*," Ernest said, wanting to get off the topic of the war and all the shit that anybody who hadn't fought in it could never fully understand. "That's their version of bon appetite over here."

"*Chook ngawn meeng*," Nika parroted, taking a bite of her cheeseburger. "And just so you know, Papi," she added, wiping some juice from her chin, "I *am* coming with you tomorrow. It's as simple as that."

CHAPTER 10
THE FRENCH GUY

Nika had been lying in bed, wide awake, for at least an hour. It was nine-thirty, which meant it was like six thirty in the morning in San Francisco.

"I should be waking up now, not going to sleep," she said to herself in the dark.

And she wasn't going to get to sleep, she knew. She'd just keep lying there, thinking about Ari Schwartz and what she was going to do when she returned to the US and how shitty her life was at the moment.

Sighing, she threw the covers aside and sat up. She turned on the lights and then the TV. The channel was set to CNN. She left it on for company while she dug through her suitcase for her cigarettes and lighter. She assumed the room was non-smoking and decided to go down to the promenade.

The elevator, like the rest of the hotel, was adorned with alabaster and marble. She initially pressed L for Lobby but then changed her mind and selected 6 for the floor with the swimming pool.

Purple lights illuminated a vast outdoor space offering city views. She approached one of the Jacuzzis, removed her sandals, and submerged her feet in the hot water. Lighting a cigarette, she tilted her head back to gaze up at the neon-lit tower soaring into the night sky above her.

She was putting the smoke out in a nearly empty water bottle she'd brought with her when a young, barefooted guy with scruffy blond hair pushed through the glass doors.

He waved at her; she waved back tentatively. He peeled off his shirt to reveal a lean upper body, tossed it on a lounge chair, and dove into the swimming pool. He swam underwater for a dozen meters before surfacing next to the Jacuzzi.

"*Bonjour,*" he said, smiling at her. His wet hair was flattened back from his forehead, and a goatee gave his round face a slightly more angular appearance. His icy blue eyes were intense, yet his smile was disarming and playful.

"Hi," she said.

"Ah, you are American?"

"I'm not French."

"I am Claude," he said.

"Hi," she said again.

He frowned. "You don't have a name?"

"I don't usually give it out to strangers."

"But I am not a stranger anymore because you know my name." He opened his arms in an expansive gesture. "I am Claude!"

"You might be Claude, but you're definitely still a stranger."

He laughed. "Maybe you are right." He pushed off from the swimming pool wall with his feet and swam away with slow, graceful backstrokes. Nika lit another cigarette. There wasn't much to look at other than the buildings on the other side of the tall glass wall that bordered the outdoor area, and she stole a few glances at the French guy, who seemed content to splash around in lazy circles.

When she finished the smoke, she got to her feet.

"Hey!" he called. "Where are you going?"

She shrugged. "Back to my room."

"Why?" He swam to her again.

"To watch TV."

"Come in the water."

"Do I look like I have a bathing suit on?"

"Maybe you do under your dress."

"I don't," she said. "I didn't even pack one."

He raised his eyebrows. "You came to Vietnam without a bathing suit? There are so many beautiful beaches here!"

"This trip was a last-minute decision. I didn't think about it."

"Are you traveling by yourself?"

"Why would I be traveling by myself?"

"Some people like to travel by themselves."

Nika had the feeling he was trying to figure out whether she was single or not. "Not me," she said simply.

"Are you wearing underwear?"

She blinked. "Excuse me?"

"It is just like a bathing suit, no?"

She folded her arms across her chest. "I'm not swimming in my underwear."

"Why not?"

"It's not appropriate."

"Something is only not appropriate when someone does not approve," he said sagely. "And I approve." He turned his back to her. "I won't look."

Nika stood indecisively for a moment. Then she decided, to hell with modesty. It was hot and muggy, and the water looked refreshing. She slipped her dress over her head and jumped straight in.

She yelped. The pool wasn't heated, but the chilly shock lasted only a moment.

The French guy—Claude, she thought—turned back around. "Nice, yes?"

"It's nice," Nika said, treading water. "So how old are you?"

"How old are you?"

"Older than you."

"You don't look that old. What are you doing tomorrow?"

"Why?"

He shrugged. "We can do something together."

"Sorry," Nika said. "I have plans."

"What kind of plans?"

"I'm going to a jungle village with my grandfather."

"Fantastic!" he said. "My friend did that in Thailand. She stayed with a hill tribe for a week and smoked opium."

"I'm not going there to smoke opium with my grandfather. He has some kind of business to take care of, and I'm just tagging along for something to do."

"Business in a jungle village? What kind of business?"

"I don't know. He won't tell me. But something from when he was a soldier in the war here."

"Ah..." he said, nodding.

"What does 'ah' mean?"

"In wars, occupying soldiers often come into contact with locals. Sometimes there are, you know...intimate relations and such."

Nika was shocked and insulted. "You're saying my grandfather *raped* a woman fifty years ago?"

"No, no, no," he said quickly. "I'm sure it was consensual. A lot of villagers worked at the American bases as cashiers and waitresses and that sort of thing."

Nika considered the idea that Popeye might have had a consensual relationship with a Vietnamese woman. He didn't know Nana then, after all. He would have been single, far away from home, probably lonely. She said, "My grandfather hasn't been back to Vietnam since the war. Why would he decide to come now to visit a woman he had known for only a short time over a half-century ago?"

"Maybe he's not here to see the woman. If she had a child..."

Nika laughed; this was absurd.

"He could have left the country without knowing. The kid might have only recently tracked him down."

She shook her head. "No way. You're nuts." And then she remembered something. "He said he's going to the village to find some tunnels. If there's a secret love child, I don't think he or she would be living underground in tunnels."

"Well, you didn't tell me that." Claude shrugged. "I guess you'll find out for yourself tomorrow, huh?"

"I guess so," she said, suddenly feeling bad for imposing herself on Popeye. Whatever he needed to do, it was his private business. She should have stayed out of it.

"You don't have to go," said Claude, seeing that he'd gotten her down. "You can stay here with me. We will do something fun together."

Nika had an idea and said, "Do you want to come?"

He looked surprised. "To the jungle village?"

"I don't know what's going to happen tomorrow, but you've got me thinking now that it might be something awkward. And you know what they say. The more the merrier. It might not be as awkward with you there. We could give my grandfather some space…"

Claude grinned. "Sure, I'll come! What time do we leave?"

"We're meeting at 7:00 in the lobby," she said. "I'll get you on my way down. What's your room number?"

"1712," he told her. "Think of the War of 1812, but 100 years earlier."

A cleaner entered the swimming pool area with a wheeled bucket and a mop in hand. "Here is closed now!" he said loudly to them. "Ten o'clock. Everybody go!"

"Guess we're 'everybody,'" said Claude as they swam to the ladder. "Ladies first," he added when they reached it.

"I don't think so," she said, heat rising to her cheeks. "Get going, Mr. Chivalrous. And no looking until I'm dressed."

CHAPTER 11
THUNDER ROAD

Ernest woke at 3:35 a.m. and didn't bother trying to get back to sleep. He showered, shaved, dressed, and then watched a current affairs show on ABC Australia, followed by yesterday's news on the BBC.

Every so often his eyes would wander to the framed photograph on the dresser below the television. He and Neeti stood in front of the Rome Cavalieri hotel, his arm hooked around her shoulder, both smiling. The color was faded, no surprise since it was taken in 1983 during their honeymoon in Italy.

Ernest remembered that day well. Shortly before the photo was taken, while they were standing in a line to enter the Basilica San Clemente, a kid snagged his wallet from the back pocket of his trousers. Young and fit, Ernest gave chase. The kid was fast and knew the neighborhood, ducking through back alley after back alley. He kept glancing over his shoulder and yelling at Ernest in Italian, likely surprised Ernest wasn't giving up.

It turned into a scene out of a Jason Bourne movie as they skirted fruit and vegetable carts, dodged laundry hanging on washing lines, and narrowly escaped collisions with pedestrians and vehicles. The locals they passed cried out and made either rude or encouraging gestures. The only word Ernest understood was "Americano!" How they knew he was an American, he wasn't sure; he supposed the only people targeted by pickpockets were tourists. In any event nobody tried to stop the kid, but he made a mistake when he cut through a mom-and-pop restaurant. Instead of emerging from the back door into another alleyway, he found himself trapped in a small yard surrounded by six-foot stone walls. Ernest caught him while he was attempting to scale the back one. He plucked his wallet from the kid's grubby hand (the leather was slick with sweat), and said, "Nice try, punk."

Ernest wasn't going to screw around with the cops; Neeti was waiting back at the church. So he returned through the restaurant. He held up his wallet and explained in English that the kid had stolen it from him. He got only blank faces until someone said something in Italian, and then several customers broke into applause.

The man who had spoken in Italian followed Ernest outside and introduced himself in English as a reporter for *Il Messaggero*, one of Italy's national newspapers. He told Ernest pickpocketing was a major problem in Rome, and he'd like to interview Ernest for a story about his "heroic actions." Ernest, amused, agreed to meet with him later that afternoon at the Rome Cavalieri. After the reporter got his interview and a photograph of Ernest, Ernest asked him to take a picture of Neeti and himself. The reporter delivered it to the hotel the following day, and it had been on Ernest's dresser ever since. When he packed his suitcase for the trip to Vietnam, he never thought twice about taking it with him.

At six o'clock Ernest packed a rucksack with supplies he had purchased the day before and went down to the hotel's restaurant for breakfast. He ordered a strong Vietnamese coffee, a bowl of beef Pho, and rice topped with fried onions and quail eggs. He read *The Saigon Times* until seven when he went to the lobby to meet Nika. Unsurprisingly, she wasn't on time. He was thinking about calling her phone to make sure she was at least awake when she emerged from the elevator alongside a young blond man.

She was smiling as she approached. It was a smile he was familiar with: she'd used it when she was home from The Athenian School and wanted something from him, usually money, new clothes, or to borrow his car.

"Hi, Papi!" she said brightly. "This is Claude. He's from France."

"Hello, Mr. Hemingway."

Ernest scowled at him. "It's Ernest. Who the hell are you?"

"I met him at the swimming pool last night," explained Nika. "And, well, get this. I invited him to come to the village today…if that's all right with you?"

Ernest's initial response was to say no. But he hesitated. Nika, of course, was not going down into the tunnels with him, and he would be gone for hours, possibly into the evening, so having someone else around aside from Mr. Thang to keep her company in the village wasn't such a terrible idea.

He said, "What's your name again, sport?"

"Claude," he said, smiling. "Claude Deschamps."

Ernest eyed him up and down. He wore a pair of Reebok sneakers, khaki shorts, and a white tank top with 98% CHIMPANZEE scrawled across the front in black letters. "Do you think your attire is appropriate for where we're going?"

He looked down at himself. "Do they have a dress code?"

Ernest sighed. The kid wasn't his responsibility. If he was okay getting eaten alive by mosquitos and black flies, that was on him. At least Nika had taken his advice. She wore blue jeans and a long-sleeved shirt.

"If you want to join us," he said, "you're free to do so."

Nika and Claude grinned at each other. Then Nika noticed the rucksack at his feet. A tent was attached to the bottom of it with compression straps.

"We're sleeping over in the village?" she said, surprised.

"No. At least, I doubt it. I bought the tent in the unlikely event that I can't make it back to the village before dark."

Nika frowned. "What about us?"

"Guess you two get to sleep under the stars."

"Won't they have a guest hut or something for us?"

"Sure they will, Scooter. Complete with air conditioning and a Jacuzzi, no doubt." He slung the rucksack over his shoulder. "Let's get this clown show moving. The driver should be outside already."

#

Buck Cowley had been sitting on his tan Honda motorbike across from the towering Times Square Building since the crack of dawn. Shelby's blue Yamaha was parked in front of him; his friend had gone to a 7-Eleven to buy them a couple of Gatorades. It wasn't yet 7:00 a.m. but it was already hot as hell, and it was only going to get hotter.

Buck and Shelby had followed the smart-mouthed tunnel rat and his granddaughter to the Times Square Building from Happy Jack's the night before. No doubt they were staying at the Reverie Saigon, which occupied the upper twenty floors or so.

Rich prick indeed, Buck thought with a spike of jealousy. What did a room there cost? Four, five hundred US a night? That was what Buck paid in rent all *month* for his two-bedroom house in District 4. In the past the district had been run by a mobster named Nam Cam who reigned as the Godfather of Saigon. It was one of the poorest in the city, filled with brothels and gambling dens and locked doors and barred windows. Hell, if you parked your motorbike in the wrong spot, you could end up with a knife between your ribs. However, after Nam Cam was arrested and executed by a firing squad in the early aughts, the area developed into an up-and-coming neighborhood.

Buck's house was old and needed a lot of work that neither he nor the landlord was willing to do, and the street it was on smelled like sewage, especially during the monsoon season. But it was built from fired bricks and solid ironwood, and if he kept the curtains drawn it stayed relatively cool during the daytime. There was even a room for worshipping ancestors (which he used as a giant walk-in closet) and a little garden out back where he would sit and smoke and watch industrious ants go about their business, which was often a hell of a lot busier (and more interesting) than his.

So Buck liked the place well enough. Of course, that wasn't to say he wouldn't mind living it up in a five-star hotel like Mr. Rich Prick and his granddaughter.

And maybe you will be, buddy old pal. Maybe very soon if everything goes to plan today...

Buck was looking forward to confronting the tunnel rat when he returned to the surface with the loot. He was still steaming about the way the asshole confronted him about his claim to be an Army Ranger. The truth was, he'd reached the rank of Spec 4 with the Big Red One and had known some of the guys in the Ranger units, but he'd never gone on any missions with them. They were cocky motherfuckers who thought they were better than everyone else except maybe the Special Forces. But he'd always liked their smart black berets. Which was why he'd picked one up, along with a matching shirt, a few years ago from a vendor selling old war memorabilia in Ben Thanh Market.

Buck looked up at the bright morning sun and then back at the hotel. Where the hell was the rich prick? In Saigon you started your days early before the heat made it too hot to do much of anything but sleep—

Right on cue the tunnel rat and his granddaughter exited the hotel, along with some guy around the same age as the girl. An older Vietnamese fellow got out of a silver Nissan sedan that had been parked near the front doors. They appeared to make introductions before getting into the car.

Buck glanced over his shoulder, but Shelby was nowhere in sight.

Fuck it, he thought. *Just means more loot for me.*

The Nissan merged into the busy morning traffic.

Buck started up his motorbike, zipped away from the curb, and followed.

#

They spent the first thirty minutes of the drive crawling through Saigon's stop-and-go traffic. Claude sat in the front seat because he was the biggest. Nika was to Ernest's left with her nose glued to her window, fascinated by the crowds and energy and ramshackle buildings all stacked one on top of another as if built by a terrible Jenga player. She kept piping up with observations like "That temple is so *old*!" or "Those guys are sitting on *top* of the truck!" or "That guy has a *pig* in his trike!"

When the concrete and smog of Saigon finally receded behind them, the vista became one of farmland and vegetation as far as the eye could see. Military checkpoints manned by American troops were no more, and Ernest had a hard time getting over just how peaceful and—normal—it all was.

Cu Chi Base Camp, where the 25th Infantry Division had been stationed, was just a short distance to the northwest of them. When it was completed in 1966, it was home to some 50,000 men and women. Four convoys of about sixty vehicles, known as the Cu Chi Express, traveled from Saigon or Long Binh Post to resupply the base each day. That was done via the highway they were on now, only back then it had often been littered with mines. If an ammunition or fuel truck ran over one, you had a blazing fireball blocking the route, making the convoy a sitting duck for Viet Cong small-arms fire and mortar rockets until a tractor could drag it out of the way. Bulldozers with Rome plows had cleared all the vegetation along the highway to improve visibility and limit the effectiveness of the ambushes, and gunships flew overhead to provide artillery cover. Even so, it was probably the most dangerous stretch of road in the world at the time.

Ernest didn't have many good memories of the war, but the ones he did have were from Cu Chi Base. It had been home, a place of normalcy in what had otherwise been a fucked-up and alien country. It had all the facilities of a permanent base such as clubs for the officers, NCOs, and enlisted men; sports fields; miniature golf courses; swimming pools; a radio station; a chapel, you name it.

Ernest's hooch had been filled with books and what few other personal possessions he'd owned. A box beneath his bed contained letters and photos from his high school sweetheart, a girl named Wanda McCloud, who stopped writing abruptly during his final tour of duty (he later learned she married a man who'd avoided the draft because of a bad heart). In the evenings there were steak barbeques, cold beer, Vietnamese dancing girls, pop groups from Saigon, an occasional visiting American celebrity, and Red Cross recreation volunteers named Doughnut Dollies who wore light blue seersucker outfits, floppy field hats, tennis shoes, and big smiles.

Despite all these comforts, Ernest was never completely at ease on base because the enemy wasn't only in the jungles and marshes of the boonies; it was inside the wire as well, a fifth column. During Operation Crimp documents retrieved from a tunnel complex revealed that all twelve barbers on base were Viet Cong spies. The locals who worked at the base were screened when they came from their villages and hamlets every morning, and they were counted when they left at night. Yet boobytraps rocked the base once or twice every week. One bomb hidden in the mess hall caused a dozen casualties in '69. It went off near the table where Ernest's squad usually sat; two of his buddies died in the blast.

Ernest coughed into his hand.

Nika looked at him. "You should probably get that checked out, Papi."

"Thanks," he said.

"I mean it. You've been coughing a lot."

"I'm seventy-one, in case you've forgotten."

"I'm just saying, it doesn't sound so good."

"I'll get it checked out when we get home," he said dismissively. He felt her studying him, and it went on long enough he finally turned to her. "What?"

"It was just a joke."

"What was?"

"The Ernest Hemingway stuff."

"I don't care about that."

"Yes, well...you seem like you're in a bad mood."

"I'm not in a bad mood."

"You've been quiet for most of the car ride."

"Have I?"

"Yes, you have. Anyway, you don't even look like him today. More like...Indiana Jones."

"But no whip," said Claude from the front.

"Thank you, Nika," Ernest said. "I rather like Indiana Jones, so I'll take that as a compliment."

"Is it all like you remember?" she asked him after a brief lull.

"Is what like I remember?"

"Vietnam!"

"It's not the country I left in '69."

"Of course it isn't. The entire world has changed since then. We had just landed a man on the moon in 1969. Now there are rovers on Mars and billionaires flying people into space just for the fun of it—"

"I get your point, Scooter," he said, cutting her off. "But I don't think you get mine. We used to call this highway Thunder Road."

"Thunder Road?" said Claude, glancing back over his shoulder with a cheeky grin. "Are you sure you're not confusing your war memories with *Mad Max*, Ernie?"

"It's not Ernie to you, sport. It's Ernest. And if I have to tell you that again, I'll stop this car and you can walk back to Saigon."

"*Désolé! Désolé!*" He held up his hands in a gesture of apology. "*Je suis désolé.*"

"Why Thunder Road?" asked Nika.

"There were a lot of military skirmishes along it."

"Along the *highway*?"

"The war wasn't only fought in the jungles like you see in the movies. Nowhere in the country was safe."

Claude said, "What did you do in the war, Monsieur Ernest?"

"Is he having a dig at me?" Ernest asked Nika.

"He's being polite, Papi."

"Why can't he simply call me Ernest?"

Claude said, "I am right here. I can hear you perfectly fine. If you would like me to call you Ernest, and only Ernest, that is no problem. So were you a sergeant, Ernest? A lieutenant? A cap-e-taine?"

"I reached the rank of corporal," Ernest told him curtly. "I had no interest in a leadership role. I liked doing what I was doing."

"He crawled around in the tunnels, remember" said Nika helpfully. "I can't believe you did that, Papi."

"Somebody had to clear them out."

"Why didn't they just use dogs?" asked Claude.

It was a semi-intelligent question. The US had been employing service dogs in military operations since WW1, and Vietnam was no exception. German Shepherds were the most common breed, used for everything from scouting, sentry duty, and mine/trip-wire detection. They could even detect Viet Cong submerged in rivers, breathing through hollow reeds while they waited to ambush American watercraft. Labrador Retrievers were also used, primarily as trackers (they were much quieter than beagles and bloodhounds) to find enemy troops after a battle or missing soldiers and downed pilots.

Nevertheless, when it came to the tunnel networks, the K-9 units were often maimed or slaughtered by booby traps, leading their handlers to refuse to send the dogs down. Hence the creation of a tunnel rat school for human volunteers. In an area of heavy vegetation on the western side of Cu Chi Base, the Americans paid the local Vietnamese farmers to maintain about five thousand feet of Viet Cong tunnels. This was where prospective tunnel rats would train to get an idea of the conditions they would be facing.

When Ernest heard about the tunnel rat school, he volunteered for no other reason than it was something to do. He didn't know that the grunts who succeeded were the ones with a little bit—or a lot—of craziness in them. And he certainly didn't know then that he had that craziness in him. But as it turned out Ernest was one of the few soldiers that didn't crawl back out of the tunnels soon after they entered. During the five-month training period, he excelled in the claustrophobic spaces filled with false walls, multiple levels, and mock booby traps. Out of the fifty grunts who hadn't been weeded out early, he was one of only five to graduate as a bona fide tunnel rat.

To Claude he said simply, "Dogs couldn't disarm booby traps, sport."

"And you could?" asked Nika.

"I wouldn't be here now if I couldn't, Scooter."

"I really can't believe you did that stuff, Papi. What if you got *stuck* or something?"

"That wouldn't have been ideal."

"Must have really sucked," said Claude.

"Everything in the war sucked, sport."

"Tell us more about the tunnels," said Nika. "What did you find in them? How far did they go? Did you ever run into the Viet Cong? Did you *kill* any—"

"Maybe another day, Scooter," he said dismissively. Mr. Thang had not spoken since Ernest introduced him to Nika and Claude at the hotel. He sat straight-backed with his hands planted neatly at the ten and two positions on the steering wheel. He stared impassively ahead as if detached from the conversation. But of course he was listening. "I've done enough reminiscing for now."

"Do not concern yourself with me, Mr. Campbell," said Mr. Thang as if reading Ernest's thoughts. "I speak often with Americans about the war. I respect everyone's perspective on it."

"Did you fight in it, too?" Claude asked him.

Mr. Thang nodded. "I was in the 272nd Main Force Regiment."

"Which side was that on?"

"I fought with the North Vietnamese Army against the South's government in Saigon and its American allies."

"So you and Popeye fought against each other?" said Nika, sounding surprised.

"Popeye?" he said.

"That's my grandfather's nickname."

"Popeye!" said Claude. "Like the sailor?"

Mr. Thang said, "I know that I fought against the 1st Infantry Division, the 25th Infantry Division, the 4th Division, and the 173rd Airborne Brigade. But whether I engaged in combat directly with Mr. Campbell, that I cannot answer."

"Were you in any of those divisions, Papi?"

"I was in an infantry regiment that was part of the 25th, yes."

"So you *did* fight against each other!"

"That's enough, Scooter," Ernest said sternly. "Please ignore her, Mr. Thang."

"Your granddaughter is merely curious, Mr. Campbell," he said, "which is an admirable trait indeed. I am happy to answer any questions she might have."

"Well...I don't really have any questions," she told him. "I just find it neat that you and my grandfather might have been trying to shoot each other—"

Ernest scoffed. "Neat?"

"You know what I mean, Papi. You guys might have been trying to kill each other during the war, and now you're hanging out in the same car together as happy as Larry."

"Happy as who?"

"It's what they say in Australia. I heard it on an episode of *Home & Away*."

"We're not exactly 'hanging out,' Scooter. Mr. Thang is simply—"

"What I'm getting at, Mr. Thang," Nika went on, "is that shouldn't you...I don't know...kind of not really like Americans?

We invaded your country."

"The war was a very long time ago," he told her. "The Americans caused my people much pain and suffering, and I would say we caused them much pain and suffering also. But it wasn't personal for me then, nor is it now. I was simply fighting for our liberation and independence. It was what all my comrades were fighting for, and it was why we fought so hard. The question for many of us, what we never understood, and what I still don't quite understand, was why the Americans fought so hard. What was it, Mr. Campbell, that you were fighting for that was so important to you?"

Ernest frowned, caught off guard by the question. After the first few years of the war, he didn't think anybody on his side knew what they were fighting for.

"I guess we fought so we could go home one day," he said. "We all just wanted to go home."

Except for you, chief, he thought. *Everybody except for you. Because you don't stick around for three tours of duty if you're raring to go home, do you? You don't volunteer for the most dangerous job in the war time and time again if you're raring to go home. You don't look forward to engaging Charlie in the blackness of the tunnels if you're a sane person who wants to return to the World and work a nine-to-five job. You were a crazy motherfucker who was addicted to spilling blood. You found that out when you were a kid, and you pretend you're not anymore, but you were and you are exactly that.*

Want to go home, my ass.

Ernest looked out his window and said nothing more.

PART 3
BINH DUONG PROVINCE

CHAPTER 12
THE VILLAGE

In contrast to the authentic grittiness of Saigon, Nika thought the town of Cu Chi felt kind of...cheap. American restaurants and billboards lined the streets. Souvenir shops spilled onto the sidewalks selling everything from pith helmets and "I ♥ Ho Chi Minh" T-shirts to Kiwi shoe polish and bowls filled with fake dog tags. Camouflaged baseball caps hung like piñatas from rickety kiosks, and she even saw a sign advertising a shooting range where you could fire an AK-47 or a rocket-propelled grenade.

Most of the tourists, Mr. Thang explained, would be on day trips to the Mekong Delta and Cu Chi tunnels. When Nika asked Popeye if they were the same tunnels he had crawled through, he said they were. She left it at that. He seemed upset that what he'd experienced during the war was now being monetized as a tourist trap. She didn't know much about the tunnels and their importance during the Vietnam War. Truth be told, she didn't really know much about the war in general. It had occurred decades before she was born, and she hadn't been taught about it at The Athenian School. What she did know came from movies like *Forrest Gump* and that one by Stanley Kubrick (which she'd never finished because she'd been too upset by what happened to the poor chubby soldier in boot camp). In any event the war seemed like a pretty hellish time for everyone involved.

Nika liked Mr. Thang. He was quiet but seemed very polite and respectful. The fact that he and Popeye had once been mortal enemies and were now traveling together in the same car, acting perfectly nice to one another, reinforced her belief in how pointless wars are. Soldiers on one side fighting soldiers on another side, no different from one another really, killing each other for the stupid reason that they are told to by ambitious politicians. And then when it's all over they go back to their lives to make sense of what they did, as enemies become allies and killers become neighbors and neighbors become friends.

Popeye, Nika noted, was once again in one of his silent, grumpy moods, so she chatted with Claude for the next while. Mostly she asked him about France. What was it like to live in Paris? (Crowded.) Was it really as beautiful as everybody said? (Yes.) Had he ever been up the Eiffel Tower? (No.) Did they eat American food? (Krispy Creme donuts were a big hit despite all the authentic boulangeries.) Did they understand much English? (They pretended not to.) And so on. When she ran out of questions, she let him be, and her thoughts drifted to other matters.

She didn't want to think about San Francisco, but she knew she needed to figure out what she was going to do with herself when she got back home. Her life at the moment was in a depressing limbo. The high of being released from prison didn't last long when you had no boyfriend, let alone husband, waiting for you. No job. No car. No money. And no apartment —at least no safe apartment because a narcissistic sociopath knew where she lived and wanted to film her being chopped up into little pieces. Yes, she was only twenty-seven. She had time to start her life over from scratch. Nevertheless, that wasn't an especially enviable task, nor would it be easy, since she was now a convicted felon with a criminal record.

Nika felt as though an ominous mountain stood in her path. She knew she had to find a way over the summit to the other side, yet she had no idea how exactly she was going to accomplish that. It was exhausting even to think about. Thankfully she had Popeye in her corner, whether he was happy to be there or not. He would let her live with him until she got on her feet, she knew. He even said he would find her a safe apartment. That was a generous offer, and she would take it if he insisted…but the truth was, she would prefer to stay in the big old house where she had grown up. It wasn't the same there without her grandmother puttering around in the kitchen or the garden or knitting in her study, which had unceremoniously been turned into the guest bedroom.

However, Popeye was still around. Despite that cough of his, he appeared to be in good health, but he wasn't a young man anymore. And it didn't really matter what kind of shape you were in at his age. All it took was one stroke, one heart attack, one bad fall in the shower…and that would be that. Nika wanted to spend as much time with him as she could before any of those things—knock on wood—happened. She hated that she'd wasted the last five years in prison, partly because it had been during the prime of her life, but mostly because it had been during the twilight of her grandfather's. What made her feel even more lousy was that he had been alone all that time. No wonder he'd been acting like such a grouch ever since she'd showed up unannounced on his doorstep.

Nika decided that when they returned to San Francisco, she would add life back into the house. Each morning she would draw back the heavy blinds and open the windows. She would dust off her grandmother's old recipes and fill the kitchen with the smells of casseroles and roast vegetables and apple pie. Of course, she would have to be careful not to get in Popeye's way; he was a private person who liked his personal space. Yet she didn't think that would be a problem. The house was a mansion, after all. Two people could live there without ever bumping into each other if they so pleased.

Popeye had mentioned that he didn't even use the second floor, let alone the third. Maybe Nika could turn one of the rooms into an art studio. She could easily spend hours each day painting with oils or acrylics on canvas. That had been a passion of hers at The Athenian School. She had often remained in the art room for an hour or two after school had finished each day to continue working on one painting or another. She hadn't had time—or space in her little dorm—to paint at Stanford, but she'd gotten into it again during her final months at AS Solutions. The daily fraud and lying had made her a lightning rod for anxiety and stress, and she painted in the evenings to try to relax and forget about what she had become entangled in.

She had talent, too. Everyone said so, from her art teacher to her classmates to Popeye himself. Even Ari Schwartz, while on a rare visit to the apartment he'd rented for her, commented on an oil painting of a frangipani that she'd recently completed, saying something along the lines of, "Not bad. Shame you can't make money from doing that shit."

But what if I could *make money?* Nika wondered with a faint echo of excitement somewhere deep inside her. She would have to practice and find an original style and build a portfolio... but perhaps one day she could sell her work. She was under no illusion that that would be easy, but it wouldn't be impossible either. Other artists made a living from their work. She imagined her paintings under spotlights in a gallery in Union Square as important people sipping champagne flitted about, critics and collectors and maybe an Arts and Entertainment reporter from the *Chronicle* or *Examiner. That* was the life she wanted. As a successful artist, she wouldn't need Tinder to meet someone (not that Lee Jordan had been a bad catch). In fact, she could get back in touch with Lee one day. She wouldn't be a penniless felon anymore. She wouldn't be defined and embarrassed by her past mistakes. She would be confident, strong, a somebody...a somebody worthy of dating a brain surgeon.

As these fanciful thoughts danced inside her drowsy head, Nika felt weights tugging at her eyelids. She fought the urge to close them, not wanting to succumb to jetlag again. After they'd landed, Popeye had advised her to try to stay awake until the evening; that way she would have a chance of sleeping through the night. But the bed in her hotel room had looked so tempting. What she told herself would only be a short nap turned into a daylong comatose slumber. Consequently she spent most of the night lying wide awake in bed. Around three o'clock she turned on the TV and flipped through the channels for half an hour before having a look at what was on pay-per-view. She was surprised to find the hotel offered softcore pornography, and she considered renting one of them.

She'd never watched porn before, but she'd read *Fifty Shades of Gray* in prison, and she'd appreciated the steamy stuff more than she would have thought. However, she could only imagine Popeye's reaction if he discovered *Orgy of the Living Dead* on his credit card statement, and so she settled for a Robin Williams flick. She never got back to sleep, and when she knocked on Claude's door at a few minutes past seven o'clock he said, "Thought you'd decided to ditch me."

"My grandfather's not going to be happy that I'm late. And he's probably not going to be happy that I invited you either."

"What's his name?"

"Ernest. But call him Mr. Hemingway—it's a joke between us. It might break the ice."

*Yeah, right...*she thought now as she felt her head nodding forward. She snapped it upright and opened her eyes.

"Did you sleep much last night?" Popeye asked her.

"Not really," she said.

"I told you—"

"I know what you told me, Papi." She rubbed her tired eyes. "That's why I'm trying to stay awake now."

"Did you eat breakfast?"

"There wasn't time."

"The hotel buffet opened at six."

"I didn't know that."

"We can stop somewhere to grab a bite if you make it quick."

She shook her head. "I'm fine. I'm not really hungry."

Claude said, "I wouldn't mind stopping somewhere…"

"You can wait until the village, sport," Popeye told him. "Order room service to your air-conditioned hut."

Ten minutes later Mr. Thang took an offramp from the highway. After nearly half an hour traveling through remote backcountry, they ended up on a narrow, dirt road with fields on either side of it. Nika glimpsed a collection of ramshackle huts in the distance.

"Is this the village, Papi?" she asked her grandfather, unimpressed.

He was peering past her out her window. His eyes were intense, his jaw clenched.

"Yes," he said.

#

They parked along the margin of the road. When Nika got out of the air-conditioned car, she felt as though she had stepped from a refrigerator into an oven.

"Oh my God," she said. "It's so *hot*."

"Maybe not for too long," said Claude, looking up at a bank of low-lying storm clouds scrubbing out the bright blue sky to the north of them.

"I think I'd prefer rain to this heat. Papi, you didn't happen to pack an umbrella, did you?"

"There's a waterproof poncho in the rucksack," he said distractedly. He mentioned something to Mr. Thang and pointed to a monstrous banyan tree in the center of the village. Hundreds of woody aerial roots dripped from its branches, some of the mature ones half as thick as the original trunk.

"Looks like the villagers don't get out much," said Claude, going over to examine a Honda Civic they'd stopped behind. It was the only other vehicle parked on the road and was covered with dirt and dust and bird droppings. He peeked into a grimy window, then kicked a front tire.

Nika joined him, breathing in the rich, pastoral smell of raw earth, fresh vegetation, and chicken manure. "What are you doing?"

"I wonder if it still runs."

"Why did you kick the tire?"

He shrugged. "I'm checking it out. That's what you do when you check a car out."

"Kick a tire?"

He nodded.

"That's the stupidest thing I've ever heard."

"It's what you do," he insisted.

"Papi?" she said. He was still talking to Mr. Thang but looked over at her. "Do you kick car tires?"

"What?"

"When you check out a car, do you kick the tires?"

"Why the hell would I do that?"

"See," she said to Claude. "Nobody kicks tires."

"It's just..." He scratched his head. "How do I say? It's how you express skepticism. I don't think the tire's going to fall off. But it's just what you do, trust me."

He kicked the tire again to double down on his point. This time a small green snake darted from beneath the vehicle.

Claude yelped, leaping backward. "Look!" he said, wagging a finger at it as it slithered away into the tall grass.

"So what?" Nika said. "It was tiny."

"It was a snake!"

"Are you scared of snakes?"

"It doesn't have legs, and it's not a fish. That's not cool."

"What color was it?" asked Popeye, coming over.

"Green," Nika said.

"And yellow," said Claude. "On the sides."

"Probably a pit viper," said Popeye. "They're fairly common."

"Are they poisonous?" Nika asked.

"Charlie used to rig them to boobytraps in the tunnels. If you tripped one, the snake would drop onto your head and bite you. We nicknamed them Two Steppers because you'd only make it a couple of steps before you keeled over and died."

"*Mon Dieu!*" Claude had gone white. "It could have killed me?"

"Doubt it. Soldiers indulged in exaggeration back in the day."

"Why did you call Vietnamese soldiers 'Charlie'?" Nika asked him.

"Has a better ring to it than Claude, doesn't it? Now, Mr. Thang and I are going to talk to the villager under the tree over there. You two wait here."

"What are we supposed to do?"

"Beats me. You're the one who wanted to tag along."

"I thought we were going to…I don't know…a proper village with streets and shops and things. This is just like twenty huts in a field."

"Good thing you have the chimp to keep you company."

"Ninety-eight percent chimp," said Claude, tugging at the hem of his T-shirt to emphasize the graphic. "And you are, too, Ernest."

"Whatever you say, sport."

Popeye returned to Mr. Thang, and they started toward the banyan tree together.

"I think we should put on some sunscreen." Nika went to the Nissan, opened the trunk, and rifled through Popeye's rucksack until she found a bottle of SPF 60 sunscreen. "Guess we won't be getting a tan," she said as she squirted a blob onto her palm and passed the bottle to Claude. She smoothed her hands together and rubbed the cool cream over her face and the back of her neck.

"Need any help?" asked Claude.

"Uh, no."

Dressed only in the chimp T-shirt and shorts, he had a lot more bare skin to cover than she did, and when he passed back the bottle it was half empty. "Glad you left some for my grandfather," she remarked.

"Why does he need sunscreen? He's going to be underground all day."

She tossed the bottle back in the trunk and closed the lid. "Let's catch up with him."

"He told us to wait here."

"I'm not going to stand around in the sun," she said. "And I want to hear why he flew halfway around the world to crawl through some dark, forgotten tunnels."

#

The village was an anachronism from the war, Ernest thought. It was much smaller now, perhaps a quarter of its original size, but the wood-and-thatch huts were as they had been in 1969, rebuilt at some point but constructed just the same, and he had no problem remembering the scorching flames and asphyxiating black smoke and cries of dying water buffalo on the morning that he had torched them with the flame of his Zippo lighter.

Ernest had been dozing in his hooch when Sergeant Little stuck his head into the room and yelled, "First Platoon's in deep in the Hobos! Saddle up, mos tick!" A few minutes later Bravo Company was airborne on ten gunships zipping in tight formation over the jungle. A hot landing zone was always a possibility, so during the descent the door gunners lit up the tree line surrounding the small clearing with automatic machine-gun fire, decimating the vegetation.

On the ground Ernest's platoon leader, a clean-cut second lieutenant named John Stevens who everyone simply called L.T. or Loot, explained that a large NVA unit had ambushed 1st Platoon a little earlier and caused some casualties. Bravo Company's mission was to find and destroy the NVA's base camp.

After two days of humping through heavy jungle, Ernest's platoon came across a village dominated by a huge banyan tree. When the village headman insisted to the unit's South Vietnamese translator that the VC hadn't been by in months, L.T. ordered the villagers herded into common spaces and homestead yards. A security sweep of the shacks uncovered gas masks, AK-47s, ammunition, and VC propaganda leaflets with the face of Ho Chi Minh.

Slicks were radioed in and the villagers were flown out. The women, children, and elderly would be relocated somewhere else while the men between fifteen and forty-five would be sent to the provincial headquarters of the national police for questioning. The ones believed to be Viet Cong would be sent on to the Combined Military Interrogation Center. The rest usually went to Chieu Hoi centers, where they would spend a couple of months being "reeducated" before being drafted into the ARVN or recruited to serve alongside U.S. forces as Kit Carson Scouts.

A second and more thorough search of the village uncovered a tunnel entrance beneath a chest of drawers in one of the huts. Sergeant Little ordered the tunnel rat squad down to bring up anything of value that they might come across. As usual Ernest went point.

Progress was slow and methodical as he scanned the tunnel for boobytraps with his flashlight before moving forward. He kept the light high and away from his head. He'd started doing this two years earlier after the Limited Warfare Laboratory in Maryland—a real-life version of the Q Division in the James Bond books and films responsible for creating new field technologies—shipped a Tunnel Exploration Kit to the 1st and 25th divisions. One bright idea was to substitute a tunnel rat's flashlight with a headlamp attached to a fatigue cap. It was meant to keep your hands free and sounded good in theory, but the lamp put a big X-marks-the-spot right in the middle of your noggin. Ernest learned this firsthand when a VC fired at him before retreating. Aboveground he discovered a bullet hole in the front and back of his helmet. Cowboy had joked that he should mail the helmet home to keep as a souvenir, and that was what he did.

The tunnel led to several other tunnels and eight or nine small rooms. Some were empty. Others were dormitories with simple sleeping arrangements. One was a field hospital filled with American medical equipment likely purchased on Saigon's black market. The entrance to the furthermost room had been boarded up. They hacked through the wood planks with their bayonets and discovered stacks of boxes stuffed with documents they couldn't read. They lugged these back to the surface (in the past such papers often turned out to be a goldmine of intelligence data including staging plans, transport routes, and arm cache locations), and then Ernest and Cowboy returned underground to blow the tunnels.

They set eight bricks of C-4 explosives in strategic locations before realizing they had only brought a foot of fuse wire with them. Crouched in the dark, Ernest said, "That's not enough fuse." Cowboy replied with a big grin, "No, it ain't, Soup, so you best start hauling ass." He lit a cigarette, took a drag, and then touched the ember to the fuse.

Ernest had never scrambled through a tunnel so quickly, skinning his elbows and knees and losing his flashlight. He shot out of the shaft like a bat out of hell with Cowboy right behind him, cackling madly.

A moment later the one hundred pounds of plastic explosives detonated. The ground behind them erupted with a thunderous *crack-boom!* "You motherfuck—" Ernest started to say before being cut off by dirt and stone raining down on top of them. When the smoke and dust cleared, they saw that the entire lid of the tunnel system had lifted like a scalp from a skull, revealing the tunnels they had searched. Most of the platoon came over to have a gawk.

Grinning like a kid, Sergeant Little slapped them both on the backs and congratulated them on a job well done. L.T. wasn't as enthusiastic, telling them they'd just alerted every enemy soldier within a ten-mile radius to their presence.

"Yeah, but look on the bright side, sir," said Sergeant Little. "Now we can burn this commie shithole to the ground and not have to worry about the smoke giving us away."

When Ernest and Mr. Thang reached the shade beneath the banyan tree, which was even bigger than Ernest remembered, the white-haired villager they had seen from the road looked up at them. He was seated on a roughly hewn wooden bench partly overgrown with roots. Dressed simply in a white tunic and black pants, he was carving a block of wood with a rusty stiletto knife.

The knife was similar to the Randall Model 2 Ernest used to carry during the war, and he guessed it had once belonged to an American soldier.

Mr. Thang spoke to him in Vietnamese. His bushy eyebrows, the same snow-white as his hair, knitted together. His eyes went to Ernest and narrowed. He said something back.

"He wants to know why we're here."

"Tell him that I was one of the American soldiers that set fire to this village during the war. Tell him I apologize for that."

Mr. Thang translated. The man looked at Ernest again. This time he didn't look away when he replied. Ernest didn't need Mr. Thang to tell him it was the same question he'd asked previously.

Ernest said, "There was an NVA base camp about two klicks north of here. Does he know of it?"

A brief exchange.

"He wants to know why you want to know."

"Tell him what I told you, Mr. Thang, about my friend, and my desire to return his remains to the US."

He heard a gasp behind him and glanced over his shoulder. Nika and Claude stood a few yards away, close enough to overhear him. Nika's hand was pressed over her lips. He scowled disapprovingly at her before returning his attention to Mr. Thang. After he translated, the villager spoke quietly and indifferently and resumed carving his block of wood.

Mr. Thang said, "Yes, he knows of the base, but he says the jungle reclaimed the road that led to it a long time ago."

Ernest was disappointed but not surprised. He checked his wristwatch, turned around, and said to Nika, "It's 9:30 now. With no road to follow, I won't get to the base until noon or so. But if all goes well, I should still be back before dark. If not, I've arranged for Mr. Thang to drive you and Claude to a hotel in Cu Chi. He'll come back here to pick me up in the morning."

"A hotel?" said Nika, surprised. "What happened to sleeping under the stars?"

"It's not as romantic as it sounds. You'd be eaten alive—and maybe not by the bugs."

She frowned. "Are you sure you want to do this on your own, Papi? What if you get lost?"

"The base is next to the river. It won't be hard to find."

Claude said, "If it's next to the river, why don't you just take that boat over there?" He pointed to the river. "That will be faster than walking through the jungle, yes?"

Ernest squinted. It took him a moment to spot a traditional fishing boat pulled up onto the bank of the river. It was mostly obscured by vegetation but looked to be in working order.

"I'll be damned," he said, grinning. "You're not as useless as you look, sport. Mr. Thang, can you ask our friend if I could rent the boat over there for the afternoon?"

Mr. **Thang** translated.

"*Không*," said the old villager, shaking his head.

Ernest slipped his wallet from his back pocket and produced two 500,000-dong notes. "Here," he said, holding out his hand. "I'll be back in four hours. Five at most."

The man eyed the money but didn't take it.

Ernest plucked out another 500,000 note, then thought to hell with it and held out everything he had on him: 5,000,000 dong, equivalent to $200 USD.

"Okay?" he said, wondering why the old villager was so conflicted; the money could feed the entire village for a month.

Finally common sense took hold. The man snatched the money, waved dismissively in the direction of the boat, and went back to carving what appeared to be some sort of bird.

#

Back at Mr. Thang's car, Ernest retrieved his rucksack from the trunk and was strapping it on when Nika said, "So, with no dangerous jungle to hike through, we can come with you now, right?"

He chuckled. "I don't think so, Scooter."

"Come on, Papi! A jungle cruise is way more exciting than hanging around here all day."

"Forget it."

"What's the big deal?"

Ernest frowned. It wasn't a big deal anymore, he supposed.

"And don't forget," Claude chimed in, "that the boat was my idea."

"Great!" said Nika, seizing on his hesitation. "This is going to be fun!"

He sighed. Then to Mr. Thang he asked, "Would you like to come, too?"

"No, thank you, Mr. Campbell. I'm happy to wait here for your return."

#

Buck straddled his idle motorbike on the road where the jungle met the field. He had watched through a pair of ten-dollar Made-in-Thailand binoculars as the Nissan pulled over to the side of the road in a cloud of dust, and the four occupants got out. Buck had assumed this was where the tunnel system was. But then the rich jackass and the two kids got in a fishing boat and went north along the river.

That had alarmed Buck...but only for a moment. Wherever they were going, he thought, they were also coming back from. He could simply wait where he was until they returned with the loot. It would be risky to hold them up with an entire village as witnesses, despite how backwater the villagers might be, but there was little that could be done about that.

And then he saw the canoe.

It was on the bank of the river not far from where the fishing boat had been, inverted on its top, resembling a log. He could get to it easily enough without anybody in the village seeing him. The fishing boat had a good head start, but he would catch up with it wherever the tunnel rat and kids tied it up and disembarked.

And that would be the ideal place to confront them.

No witnesses.

Even more, once the loot was his, Buck could leave with both boats, forcing the suckers to hike back to the village on foot. And by that time Buck would be well on his way to Hanoi, incognito in a country of one hundred million people.

Lowering the binoculars from his eyes, he started toward the river with an excited spring in his step.

CHAPTER 13
INTO THE HEART OF DARKNESS

The moss-covered trees along the banks of the murky river leaned eerily over the water. Their branches met in the middle, casting deep shadows over everything below. Vines and creepers dangled in knots from the dense foliage, while the gnarled roots of mangroves sank into the brown water like hundreds of bony fingers. Occasionally a mysterious sound would echo through the dark, humid jungle, which smelled unpleasantly of wetness and decay. But for the most part the boat ride down the narrow channel was preternaturally quiet.

This created an uncomfortable sense of foreboding, and on more than one occasion Nika thought: *We shouldn't be here.* Each time she chided herself for being a frightened, superstitious city girl. They were fine. When was the last time she'd heard of a tiger or crocodile eating a person? Besides, they were in a boat. Nothing could get them there.

Except for a giant anaconda. You saw that movie with Jennifer Lopez and Ice Cube. Their boat was a lot bigger than this one, and the anaconda turned it into matchsticks. She swallowed a lump in her throat as she imagined a giant snake coiling around her body, squeezing tighter and tighter until her ribs splintered and she could no longer breathe and its fanged mouth slid over the top of her skull...

"Are there anacondas in Vietnam?" she asked her grandfather.

"No," said Popeye. He stood behind her at the boat's stern, using a large paddle mounted to a pole to propel them forward.

"Are you sure?"

"I never saw one."

"That doesn't mean there aren't."

"There aren't," he said matter-of-factly.

"I thought you weren't scared of snakes," said Claude. He sat next to her on the seat in the middle of the boat.

"I'm not," she said. "Not little ones. But I don't like things that are bigger than me."

"I'm bigger than you, and you like me."

"That's up for debate. Hey, Papi," she said, turning around. "Want to hear why Claude thought you were returning to that village?"

"Not particularly," he said, looking past her at the water as he worked the oar.

"He thought— Ow." Claude had elbowed her in the side.

He shook his head.

She continued anyway: "He thought you shacked up with a villager and had a secret love child. You know, during the war. And you came back to adopt her."

"I never said *adopt* her," said Claude, turning red.

"You want to know what I think, Scooter? I think you shouldn't spend any more time with him when we get back to Saigon. His stupidity may be contagious." Popeye eyed him. "What are you doing in Vietnam anyway, champ?"

"I teach English."

"You never told me that!" Nika said.

He shrugged. "You never asked."

Popeye said, "You teach English?"

"That's right," said Claude.

"You're French."

"Yes, but my English is very good."

"Don't you need to be a native English speaker to teach English as a second language?"

"In most of the big schools. But I work for a very small school. They don't care that I'm French. Besides, I don't really 'teach' English. Not grammar or anything. I just talk."

"What do you mean?" Nika asked him.

"They're called conversation classes. There are usually only two or three students in a class, and I just chat with them."

"And you get paid for that?"

"The best way to learn English is by speaking it, not studying syntax. Anyway, most of my students don't come to the classes to learn English. They are bored housewives who want something to do when their husbands are at work."

"That sounds so sketchy," Nika said. "Are you sure 'teaching' is all you do with these desperate housewives?"

"What do you mean?"

Popeye said, "She means, do you have any side hustles, sport? Outside of the classroom."

Claude frowned—then looked sheepish. "Oh." He shook his head. "Of course not. I'm a professional."

"A professional conversationalist, right…"

"Maybe I can do this?" Nika said.

"Teach English?" said Claude.

She nodded. "I need a job. Is it hard to get hired?"

"No, it is very easy for an American. Do you have a university degree?"

"Um…no."

Popeye grunted disapprovingly.

She ignored him and said, "I went to Stanford, but I dropped out before I finished my degree."

"The big schools want you to have a university degree. But you could get work at a small school like mine. I could even ask the owner if you want. The male students would love you."

She eyed him suspiciously. "I'm not doing anything outside of teaching."

"Of course! That is all we do. Teach English. I don't know why you think it is some sort of brothel or something."

"What do you think, Papi?" she said, turning around again. "Maybe I'll stay in Vietnam and teach English?"

"Sounds like a promising career path," he said sardonically.

"At least I'll be safe here."

"Safe?" said Claude.

"My ex-boyfriend is trying to kill me."

"For real?"

She nodded but didn't say anything more; she didn't want to think about Ari Schwartz.

Claude took the hint and didn't press her. "Well, if you want me to talk to the owner of my school, just let me know—" With a shrill shout, he leaped to his feet. He tripped over the seat and fell hard onto his back. "Get it off! Get it off!"

Nika stared as a huge centipede scampered across his lap. Its segmented, reddish-brown body was the length of her foot and as thick across as a flattened wiener. Pointed, yellow-orange legs wiggled like synchronized maggots, propelling it forward with surprising speed.

It dropped onto the wooden floorboards of the boat but got only a short distance before the thick rubber heel of Popeye's boot crushed its head. Its disgusting body curled and thrashed and then went still. Popeye picked it up with his bare hand and held it before him proudly. "Big sucker."

"Gross!" Nika said. A cold shiver seemed trapped beneath her skin, which had broken out in gooseflesh. She shuddered and looked away.

Muttering in French, Claude pushed himself into a sitting position. He looked like he might puke.

Popeye tossed the dead centipede into the river and said, "Lucky it didn't bite you, sport. That would have hurt like hell." He was grinning.

#

A short time later they approached a wooden dock jutting from the riverbank like a severed limb. Some of the pilings had collapsed on one side so it was half submerged in the brown water. Ernest maneuvered the fishing boat up along the good side and tied the painter line to an exposed stringer. He climbed out first where the planks were still level, then helped Nika. Claude came last.

He led the way through the incredibly dense and towering triple-canopy jungle—nature had erased the original path—until they came to a bunker. It had been constructed with hand-hewn logs, large stones, and hard-packed earth. Now it was little more than an odd-looking lump on the ground hidden beneath deadfall, shrubs, and elephant grass. Only a grave-black entrance hole that hadn't been overgrown with vegetation gave away its identity. There were dozens more like it, Ernest recalled, strung along the base's outer perimeter.

Nika stooped down to peer inside the entrance. "I can't see anything inside. It's too dark."

Claude crouched next to her. "Should I crawl inside?"

"Sure, champ," Ernest said. "Maybe you'll find another of your centipede friends. Even better, a nest of scorpions." He went around the bunker and pushed deeper into the lush, emerald-green jungle. Soon he began to see what had been the NVA base camp. Most of the structures were skeletons of posts and support beams. Some still had partial walls or roofs, although they were all sagging or collapsed.

Claude and Nike moved ahead of Ernest, enthusiastic and sprightly.

"It's like the jungle ate this village up," said Nika with awe in her voice.

"It wasn't a village," Ernest told her. "It was a fortress that was home to a couple hundred Viet Cong. When my unit discovered it, there were trucks and motorcycles and enough stores and equipment to man a small army."

"There were roads?"

"Just the one from the village. It was covered with a manmade canopy of vegetation so we couldn't spot it from the air."

"Was there a battle here?" asked Claude. "If this was an important base, the Viet Cong must have put up a fight to keep it."

"It was deserted when we arrived. The VC had left on patrol looking for us—"

"A bug!" exclaimed Nika.

Claude stopped dead in his tracks. *"On me?"*

"No, *there!*" She pointed past him to a bamboo structure that had stood the test of time remarkably well. Parked inside it was a Volkswagen Beetle.

"Well, well, well," Ernest said as they made their way toward the vehicle. "That was here in '69. Hell of a lot better condition then, mind you."

It was hard to tell what color the car had been (although

Ernest remembered it being beige) as the weather had stripped the paint down to the rusted metal frame. Moss and leaves and branches covered what little remained of the cloth roof, and some ferns had even taken root there. The tires were all missing, so the car sat on miserable-looking rims. The round headlamps dangled from their sockets by wires. The chrome bumper hung askew like a dumbly smiling mouth. Cobwebs dusted the dashboard and steering wheel, and foam rubber stuffing and metal springs poked through tears in the seats. Ernest wouldn't have been surprised if the interior had served as home to several generations of rats.

Claude peered through a glassless window and wrinkled his nose. "Smells like urine."

"Aren't you going to kick the tires?" Nika asked him.

"There are no tires."

"Kick the rims then."

"I don't think so."

"Claude kicks the tires on cars," she told Ernest. "It's how he can tell if it's a good car or not."

"I never said that," he protested. "It was just something my father used to do it. It was part of his car inspection ritual, okay?"

Nika rolled her eyes. "I'm just teasing you."

After passing dozens more structures that had fallen apart to reveal the bunkers beneath, they came to a ten-by-twenty-foot pit dug into the orange clay ground. Well-worn steps, oddly free of vegetation, led to the bottom. The small, square entrance to the tunnel system was uncovered and as black as night in the bright daylight.

"That's it?" said Nika, standing at the lip of the pit.

"That's it," Ernest said, taking a drink of water from his canteen.

"Weren't the tunnels supposed to be secret? It's like they were advertising where this one was. There are even steps leading right to it."

"Those steps led to a cooking fire. The hole was hidden beneath a woven mat and a large cauldron. It was only luck that we discovered it." He forced his eyes from the hole and the memories he knew were waiting for him down there. "Why don't you two go have a look around?" he said, realizing he wanted a few minutes alone. "I'm going to take a short rest."

"Let's go, Claude. Maybe I'll find a souvenir to take home."

"No you won't, Scooter," Ernest told her sternly. "Don't touch anything. There might still be boobytraps around."

"Are you serious?"

"I'm deadly serious. Don't go inside the bunkers and don't touch anything."

\#

"I feel bad for him," Nika said, ducking beneath a vine as they moved through the remnants of the jungle base.

"Your grandfather?" asked Claude, one step behind her. "Why?"

"Because he doesn't want to do this."

"Go down that hole?"

She nodded.

"He kind of seems to be looking forward to it if you ask me."

"No. He's scared. Or at least he's reluctant. And I don't blame him. He was younger than us when he was in the war. That was a long time ago. He's seventy-one now..."

"It's his choice. He doesn't have to go down."

"You heard him. His friend is buried down there. I think it's noble what he's doing."

"I think it's creepy," said Claude, moving up beside her. "His friend is a skeleton now. What's your grandfather going to do? Carry his bones to the surface in his arms? And then what? Are you going to be sitting next to a pile of bones on the drive back to Saigon?"

"Stop it," she told him. "There was some sort of bag rolled up in the rucksack. And he'll put them in the trunk."

"That's still creepy."

She glanced sidelong at Claude. "Why don't you like him?"

He frowned. "I like him. He just doesn't like me."

"He likes you."

"Why does he keep calling me 'sport'?"

"He calls everyone that."

"It sounds belittling."

"It's not. That's just how he is. He's always been a little distant. Nicknames are how he keeps people at arm's length."

"He doesn't call you 'sport.'"

"I'm his granddaughter, dummy. And he calls me 'Scooter,' in case you haven't noticed. When I was a kid, he never called me anything else. Never 'honey' or 'sweetie' or 'darling' or any of those normal things."

"Yes, you guys have a strange relationship."

"What? Why?" she said, insulted. "I didn't say that. I just said—"

"He calls you 'Scooter' and you call him 'Popeye.' That is kind of weird."

"What do you call your grandfather?"

He shrugged. "*Grand-père. Grand-papa*—"

"Hey, look at that." Nika went over to a rusted watering can with a spout. It lay on its side next to the trunk of a tree, partially buried in the earth. "Maybe that would be a good souvenir."

"What would you do with it?"

"Grow flowers in it?" She bent down to free it from the dirt.

"Stop!" said Claude.

She froze, looking up at him in surprise.

"Don't touch it. Remember what your grandfather said. It could be boobytrapped."

"Who would ever boobytrap a watering can?" She reached for it.

He grabbed her arm and tugged her to her feet.

"Hey!" she said, whirling angrily toward him—and finding her face very close to his.

Claude kissed her on the lips.

It was brief, more like a peck.

Nika blinked at him, her eyes wide. "What was that?"

He shrugged. "A kiss."

"Why did you kiss me?"

He studied the ground. "It seemed like a good moment."

"A good moment? You were attacking me."

He looked up at her. "I was saving your life."

"Well...next time make sure you ask first."

He grinned. "Can I—"

Nika kissed him quickly on the lips and then broke away. "That's all you get," she told him, blushing; the last person she'd kissed had been Ari Schwartz, and that had been more out of duty than affection. "You're too young for me."

"Too young? I'm...twenty-five."

"No way you're twenty-five!"

"I'm twenty-five," he insisted.

"Let me see your ID."

"What are you, a bouncer?"

"Let me see it."

"I don't carry ID in a jungle."

"You're not twenty-five."

"Yes, I am. So can we kiss again?"

"No way, junior," Nika said and continued walking in the direction they had been going. She kept her back to Claude so he couldn't see her smiling.

CHAPTER 14
THE AMBUSH

Ernest sat on the edge of the pit, surveying the remains of the NVA base camp as his mind spiraled back to the day of the ambush.

"Wherever they are," said Sergeant Little to the platoon huddled around him, "they left in one hell of a hurry."

Holding his M-16 across his chest, L.T. said, "They heard the fireworks show back at the village and went looking for us."

"They'll likely be back by dark. We need to set up a protective perimeter."

L.T. nodded and took the radio handset from the Radio Telephone Operator. A few minutes later he handed it back to the RTO and said, "Command is sending the rest of the company. Nearest LZ is back at the village, so they won't be here for another two or three hours."

"Three hours, shit," said Sergeant Little. "What do we do until then?"

"Captain wants us to avoid unnecessary contact but be ready to pop some caps if Charlie comes back early."

"Gonna be a real fuckin' Chinese fire drill if that happens."

Ernest said, "May I make a suggestion, sir? A base this size, I'll bet a year's worth of MPCs that it's sitting on top of a shitload of tunnels. We should look for an entrance."

"Soup's right," said Sergeant Little. "We don't want any unexpected guests."

L.T. ordered a thorough search of the area in three-man groups. After about half an hour he called for Ernest and the other rats to come to his location. He stood at the bottom of an outdoor kitchen where a large white bird was roasting on a spit. He pointed at a hole next to a cast-iron cauldron. "Private Jennings found it beneath the cooking pot."

"What's for lunch?" said Lynn. "Smells good."

"Crane stew. Fuckin' head and all."

"Goddamn," said Cowboy. He was slurping up ham from a can with his boot knife. "And I was getting ready to catch a few Zs."

"Cooler down there than up here," said Lynn, dropping his pack to the ground with a sigh.

"Let's rock 'n roll," said Pig, swinging the M60 machine gun off his broad shoulders, which glistened like oil beneath a sheen of sweat.

"I'll go point," Ernest said, shedding his gear.

"Slow down, pal," said Cowboy. "You went point in the village. I'll go point."

"Toss you for it."

They flipped the lid of Cowboy's C-Ration can. Ernest won and went to the hole, kneeling next to it and looking down.

Sergeant Little said, "Be careful, men. There's a good chance this one is hot."

Ernest said, "Wouldn't want it any other way, Sarge."

Wouldn't want it any other way, Sarge...

Ernest dwelled on the memory for several more moments before pushing it decisively aside.

#

He was impatient to go underground when Nika and Claude returned. He had removed his khaki shirt so he wore only his jungle boots, trousers, and a white tank top. In his left hand he held a black rechargeable flashlight. It was a lot smaller, lighter, and brighter than the clunky L-shaped one he'd carried in the war; it also lacked a red lens, which most tunnel rats had adopted so they wouldn't be mistaken by their own troops for Viet Cong when they exited a hole. A Bowie knife was in a sheath on his belt, and knee pads were strapped snugly to his knees. He was no longer a young man, and he was going to be doing a lot of crawling.

Nika eyed him skeptically. "I was wrong, Papi. You're not Ernest Hemingway, and you're not Indiana Jones. You're like a cross between Crocodile Dundee and a plumber. What's the knife for?"

"Snakes," he said simply. "And rats. They grow as big as house cats over here." He picked up the Nike duffel bag that had been rolled up in his rucksack and went down the worn steps of the pit. Nika and Claude started after him, but he said, "Wait up there for a moment." He crouched next to the hole and set the bag down. He flicked on the flashlight and aimed it into the inky darkness, looking for a trip-release wire. He stuck his arm down and felt carefully with his flattened hand along the roof where he couldn't see. All clear. "Okay, you two. Come here and give me a hand."

When they joined him, Nika said, "Were you looking for a boobytrap?"

"Yep."

"Jeez, Papi, I really don't think this is such a good idea…"

"I appreciate your concern, Scooter. But it's a little late to turn back now, don't you think? Sport, hold my ankles while I go down. I'll tell you when to let go."

Shoving the Nike bag ahead of him, he shimmied headfirst into the darkness.

#

The hole went straight down for three feet and then angled away at a gentle gradient. When Ernest's hands touched the sloped floor, he said, "Okay!"

Claude released his ankles, and he slid down the final few feet to where the floor leveled out. He hand-walked forward until he was on all fours. It was already almost completely black.

Hello darkness, my old friend.

"Are you okay, Papi?" Nika called down.

"Fine!"

Ernest clicked on the flashlight and aimed it around the narrow tunnel. It was three feet high and two wide, leaving little room on either side of his shoulders. He remained unmoving for several long seconds, taking it all in: the texture of the hand-dug earth, the musty smell of somewhere Time forgot, the perfect silence. *You're back, chief. Jesus Christ, you're back.* A bead of sweat trickled down his forehead. And then: *Get moving. The sooner you get this over with, the better.*

Ernest started forward on his hands and knees. He didn't make much noise, but the confined space amplified and reverberated even the small scuffing that his kneepads and boots made on the hard-packed clay. Anything much louder would create an echo, which had always made it difficult to pinpoint Charlie's exact position. Ernest and some of the other rats had coined the term "Black Echo" to describe the sensory deprivation and disorientation they experienced while navigating the tunnels, and it was as apt now as it was then. One wrong turn could leave him hopelessly lost.

He didn't think there were boobytraps in the tunnel; there weren't any in '69. Nevertheless, he wasn't taking any chances and probed every suspicious root and cranny that he came across.

He had gone perhaps thirty feet when he heard something ahead of him, a rustling of dirt. His war instincts triggered, and he snapped off his flashlight. He listened, blind in the darkness. He heard the noise again and recognized it immediately.

A trapdoor lifting.

Somebody was in the tunnel with him.

Ernest's heart shifted into high gear. A small voice inside his head yelled at him to get out of there. Instead he lowered the flashlight to the ground and silently removed the Bowie knife from the sheath on his belt.

More noise as the trapdoor lid was set to the side. It wasn't any louder than a dead leaf blowing along a deserted October street, but in the black tunnel it was *loud*…and the silence that followed was even louder.

The person was right in front of him, within an arm's reach. He could smell overwhelming body odor. More than that, he could sense the person's exact presence almost as if he had evolved some sort of primitive bat sonar—and given all the time he had spent in the tunnels, who the hell knew, he very well might have.

Ernest struck like a snake, grabbing the person by the hair and tugging the head back. With his other hand he slid the knife's blade across the exposed throat. Hot blood slapped him in the face and coated his hand. He released the hair and the body fell back down through the trapdoor.

He listened for others in the tunnel below but heard nothing.

"Clear?" whispered Cowboy from behind him.

Ernest clicked the flashlight back on and aimed the beam down the hole. A girl, no older than eighteen, lay sprawled on her back, blood staining a checkered scarf around her neck.

"Clear," he said.

"Why do you get to have all the fun?" Sergeant Mercado called up to him from the number-three spot.

"It was a girl."

"So what? She ain't down here playing hide and seek. She'll kill you just as quick as her daddy would if you gave her the chance."

"Tunnel continues straight," Ernest said. "Or we can go down a level. Your call, Sarge—"

Suddenly a muffled *thud!* shook the entire tunnel, throwing Ernest onto his chest. Dust and dirt fell on top of him. Almost immediately there was a second, heavier WHUMP. More dirt and dust. Ernest coughed and gasped for a clean breath of air.

"Arty!" shouted Mercado. He was also coughing.

Cowboy said, "Back! Go—"

Four more artillery shells landed aboveground—*whump, whump, whump, whump*—although they sounded farther away than the first two. The staccato cadence of automatic gunfire followed.

Ernest twisted around in the tunnel, feeling his way with his hands because the dust was in his eyes, abrasive like sandpaper, blinding him. He crawled back the way they had come, still coughing.

And ran into Cowboy's backside.

He blinked his watery eyes and could see again.

"What is it?" he demanded, aiming his flashlight past Cowboy. Sergeant Mercado's rear blocked most of the tunnel, but he could make out light from the entrance shaft ten feet ahead. "What's the holdup, Sarge?"

"Fighting's over," he said.

Ernest realized the machine gun fire had ceased.

"Then let's di di up there," said Cowboy.

"We don't know who won," said Mercado.

"Fuck," Ernest muttered. Then, "Lynn! Where's Pig?"

Lynn crawled forward until he was lit up from the daylight coming through the opening. "Pig?" he whispered, looking up. "You there, man? Pig!"

There was no response, and they all knew what that meant.

"He's waxed, man," hissed Cowboy.

"Might've ducked into a bunker during the shelling," Ernest said.

"Fuck that. He's dead. They're all dead. *The entire fuckin' platoon.*"

"Backup's coming," said Mercado. "They're already on their way. We just need to hold position—"

"'Nade!" shouted Lynn.

That word was a tunnel rat's greatest fear, and Ernest backpedaled frantically. Two seconds later—which felt infinitely longer in the slow-motion scramble—the grenade detonated. A blast of heat knocked him flat on his back. He couldn't hear anything; it was as if somebody had turned the volume down to zero. He couldn't see anything either. The smoke was as bad as the dust had been earlier.

He sat up and reached blindly in front of him and found Cowboy's shoulders. "Sarge? Lynn?" he said—or thought he did; he couldn't hear his voice.

Cowboy crawled forward. Ernest followed. Almost immediately he felt something wet and sticky beneath his hands and smelled the metallic stench of spilled blood. The gray veil of smoke was clearing, and he couldn't immediately comprehend what he was seeing in the beam of his flashlight.

Cowboy held Mercado in his lap. The sergeant's eyes were closed. He looked at peace, like he was sleeping, only he no longer had a lower body. Close to where his legs should have been was a torso…and then Ernest realized that was what was left of Staff Sergeant Ricky Lynn from Minnesota.

"Oh, Jesus," Ernest said, and now he could hear himself. The volume was back up, accompanied by a maddening ringing in his ears.

Cowboy was sobbing.

"You hurt?" Ernest asked him.

He didn't seem to hear the question. His legs were bleeding from shrapnel, but they were intact. Ernest squeezed past him, crawled through the blood and guts of his friends, and came to a wall of dirt where the tunnel opening should have been. It had collapsed in the explosion, and that was probably for the better. He crawled back to Cowboy, who was still sobbing.

"Cowboy?" Ernest shook his shoulders. "Cowboy!" He pointed toward the cave-in. "That bought us some time, but we gotta *go*."

"Go…?" His eyes focused. "*Go?* Go where, Soup!"

Ernest wiped his sweaty face with the back of his wrist. He was parched and hyper-alert, and that was making it difficult to think clearly. "Back entrance. There's always a back entrance."

"You don't think Charlie knows that? The fuckers are probably already pouring down it right now. They have us cold." He paused. Then: "He don't got no legs, Soup. Sarge don't got no fuckin' legs—"

"He's dead! *Dead.* You dig it, Cowboy? And we're going to be dead too if we don't haul ass."

Ernest pushed past him without waiting to see if he was coming. When he reached the trapdoor with the dead girl, he looked back. Cowboy was right behind him, looking scared but determined.

Ernest leaned into the hole and quickly fired three shots into the blackness. Then he dropped down, careful to avoid trampling the female guerilla's body. He continued along the new tunnel until he came to another trapdoor. He removed the lid, fired his last three rounds, and dropped down again. He crawled for twenty yards before coming to a wall.

Dead end, he thought with a jab of panic…and then noticed a trapdoor in the ceiling.

He was reloading his pistol when Cowboy caught up to him and tried pushing past.

Ernest didn't move. "I got this one."

"You've already had your two," he said. "This one's mine."

There weren't many rules underground, but there were three that Ernest's tunnel rat squad abided by. The first was that you never fired more than three shots at a time; if you fired six Charlie would know you were out of ammo. The second was that the point man always stayed at least five meters ahead of the others in case he tripped a boobytrap. And the third: the point man rotated off the lead after going through two trapdoors.

Ernest hesitated, then eased aside to let Cowboy pass him. He cocked his pistol, then aimed it, along with his flashlight, at the twelve-by-twelve-inch trapdoor. Cowboy placed his hands on the underside of the lid a foot above his head, drew a deep breath, and pushed it up. He set it down crosswise on its beveled frame and pulled himself up to the new level.

He kicked wildly, his boot dinging Ernest's helmet. His legs went slack.

"Cowboy!" Ernest yanked his lower body, trying to pull him back down. He was stuck. Ernest could guess what happened, and he slipped his head between Cowboy's legs and stood. When a bit of space opened between Cowboy's chest and the lip of the tunnel, he stuck his pistol through and fired two shots. Then he stood at his full height and did his best to rest Cowboy on his side in the higher tunnel. He climbed through the now unblocked opening and crouched next to his friend.

A short bamboo spear skewered Cowboy's chest like a martini pick through an olive. He was looking at a foot or so of wood that protruded to the left of his heart. His hands gripped it weakly as if to pull it free.

"Don't," Ernest said, cupping his friend's bloody hands with one of his. "You'll bleed out if you remove it."

"Imma shiskabob..." he said with a very pale grin.

"You're going to be okay, man," Ernest told him, fighting tears because he knew it was a lie. "You're going to be fine—"

Cowboy seized his wrist with surprising strength and said in a fading rasp, "Don't leave me down here, Soup. Promise me you won't leave me down here. I don't wanna be buried in no Charlie-made anthill."

"I won't, Cowboy. I promise you, I won't. You're going home."

#

Ernest opened his eyes. He was curled forward on his knees and drenched with sweat. The trapdoor that had set off the flashback was right in front of him. He looked at his wristwatch. Half an hour had passed since he'd entered the tunnel.

"Get your shit together, chief," he muttered to himself and dropped down the hole.

CHAPTER 15

THE ATTACK

When thunder rumbled somewhere in the distance, promising rain, Nika and Claude spent twenty minutes pitching Popeye's tent in a patch of jungle relatively clear of undergrowth. Then they went through the rucksack to see what food he'd brought. It was an unimpressive selection of trail mix, crackers, hard cheese, granola bars, instant noodles, and four bananas.

"Do you think I could have a granola bar?" asked Claude. "I haven't eaten today."

"Go for it," Nika said. She picked up a pack of ramen and tossed it back down. "How does he think we're supposed to cook this stuff? He didn't pack a stove."

"Guess he didn't want to carry it."

Nika's cigarettes and lighter were in her handbag, which she'd left in Mr. Thang's car. However, she discovered a box of waterproof matches in a zippered pouch on the top flap of the rucksack. "Do you know how to build a fire?"

"Of course," said Claude as he fiddled in frustration with the wrapper of the granola bar.

"Are you sure? You can't even open that."

"There!" he said proudly, tearing the plastic. He offered the granola bar to her.

"No, thanks. I might have a banana." She looked around at the quiet, still jungle. It was as though God had run out of every color except for green and brown. The gray sky and dark clouds made everything even more drab. "I hope Popeye's not gone for too long. It's kind of creepy here without him."

"You don't think I can protect you?"

"Protect me? Right. You're scared of snakes and centipedes."

"You would have freaked out too if that centipede had been on you."

"It was pretty disgusting," she admitted. "But Popeye wasn't scared."

"Guess he ate his spinach for breakfast."

More thunder echoed across the sky, closer. A raindrop struck Nika's face. Then a second, third, more. "Aw, great. It's started already." She dragged the rucksack toward her, rifled through the few items inside it, and withdrew a small polyester bag with a drawstring. From it she produced a brown poncho. She stood and held it against her body. "It's huge."

"You're just small," said Claude.

Nika pulled the poncho over her head. It billowed around her like a moo moo dress, only with oversized sleeves and a hood that obscured her face.

She heard Claude laughing and pushed the hood back.

"You look like a Jawa," he said.

"A what?"

"From Star Wars."

"At least I'll be dry."

Claude took a Ziploc baggie from the pocket of his shorts. It was filled with colorful gummy bears. "Want some?" he asked.

"No, thanks. I don't have a sweet tooth."

"These are special. They're green gummies."

"Are you color blind—?"

"No, *green* gummies," he said. "Like...THC gummies."

Her eyes widened. "Ganja bears!"

"Yes, those. Would you like some?"

"Yes, please!" She took the bag and added, "This is going to be so fun—"

"Not so fast, honey."

Nika whirled around at the sound of the stranger's voice. Claude shot to his feet.

A man was leaning against the trunk of a tree less than a dozen feet from them. His arms were folded across his chest, and he was smiling arrogantly as though they should be impressed that he'd sneaked up on them.

Nika's first thought was that he must be from the village, but that was ridiculous. He was Caucasian, spoke English, and was dressed like a soldier—

"You!" she exclaimed, recognizing the man as the fake Army Ranger from the restaurant the night before. He wore the same black fatigue shirt and cockishly raked beret.

"Who?" asked Claude.

"I met him at a restaurant last night," Nika explained. I was having dinner with Popeye. He came over to our table."

"And you invited him *here*?"

"No way! I never mentioned anything about today." During the exchange with Claude, she never took her eyes off the man. The only explanation for his presence was that he followed them from Saigon, which made him a world-class creep and stalker.

"Popeye the Sailor Man, huh?" said the man. "Is that what you call the squirt? Cute."

"You followed us here?" she said. It was as much a statement as a question.

"Where is he?"

"Who?" she said, playing dumb. She didn't know why, but it seemed the right thing to do.

The man smiled thinly. It was lipless and mirthless, what a snake might look like if it could smile. "Your granddaddy, honey. Did he go down into the tunnels already?"

She blinked. How could he possibly know about the tunnels?

"Why are you here?" demanded Claude, taking a step forward. "Why did you follow us?"

His aggressive posturing encouraged Nika, and she realized they didn't have anything to fear from the fake Ranger, stalker or not. There were two of them, and he was old.

"He claims he killed Ho Chi Minh," she said tauntingly.

"What!"

"That's right, kid," said the man. "What do you think about that?"

"I think you're crazy," said Claude. "Is that why you followed us all the way out here? Are you crazy?"

Nika said, "He's a fake Army Ranger. He bought that shirt and hat at a tourist kiosk."

"The hell I did!"

"And Popeye almost beat him up last night for lying about being in the Vietnam War."

"I *was* in the war, you little shit!" His face had flushed scarlet. "Now shut up and sit down! Both of you!"

Claude said, "Do you have any rope in your bag, Nika? I think we should tie him up until your grandfather gets back."

She said, "We can use tent rope—"

"*I said sit the fuck down!*" He lifted his shirt to reveal a pistol stuffed between the waistband of his pants and his taut belly.

Nika and Claude exchanged apprehensive glances.

"Sit. The Fuck. *Down.*"

They slowly sat down.

He dropped the hem of his shirt, but his face remained red. "You shithead kids these days... Where's the tunnel?"

"What tunnel?" Nika asked, still playing dumb. Had this nutjob come all the way out here because Popeye had embarrassed him at the restaurant? Was he on some bizarre revenge mission? Did he want to collapse the tunnel entrance to entomb her grandfather underground?

Claude was right. The guy was crazy.

Crazy and armed, she thought uneasily.

"Don't dick me around, honey. My friend overheard you and your granddad talking last night. I know he came out here to find a tunnel from the war. I know why he went down it, and I want what he brings up. So where the fuck is it?"

Nika stared at him. "You want what he brings *up*?"

The man frowned. "That's right. The loot."

"Loot?"

"The cash."

Nika looked at Claude, who was shaking his head. He mouthed the word, "Crazy."

The man tore the gun from his waistband and aimed the short barrel at them. "I'm losing my patience here, kids. *Where's the fucking tunnel?*"

Nika raised her hands and tried to sound reasonable. "I don't know why you think there is money in the tunnel, mister. My grandfather was a tunnel rat during the war. They—"

"I know what the hell they did, okay?"

"His friend was killed in a tunnel, and I guess his body was never recovered. Because that's why my grandfather came to Vietnam. That's why he's *here*. He went down into the tunnel to bring up his friend's remains."

The fake Ranger looked like he'd stepped on a rake. His expression was so incredulous it might have been amusing had he not been aiming a gun at them.

"It's true," Nika insisted. "The tunnel's right over there." She pointed to the ditch, figuring her cooperation might convince him that she was being sincere.

The man stalked past them to the edge of the ditch and stood there for almost a full minute with his back to them. Then he took a silver flask from the pocket of his pants and knocked back a belt. He began to pace, muttering a litany of curses.

When the rain increased to a steady patter, Nika and Claude stood up.

"Sit the fuck down," he snapped.

"I'm cold," said Claude, rubbing his bare forearms. "Can we move under a tree?"

The fake Ranger hesitated, then waved the pistol indifferently.

Nika and Claude went to a large, stately tree with numerous bromeliads growing on the twisted branches. They stood with their backs pressed to the trunk, out of the rain, watching the crazy guy pace and talk to himself.

Nika was still holding the baggie of weed gummies in her hand. She stuck it in her jeans pocket beneath the poncho and whispered, "I think he's seen too many pirate movies with buried treasure."

Claude whispered back, "He might've escaped from a psychiatric hospital."

"Maybe he'll just leave."

"Or fall over drunk and hit his head."

"Or maybe he'll shoot us."

"Don't say that. What should we do?"

Nika shrugged beneath the too-big poncho. "Wait until Popeye comes back."

Claude frowned. "That won't be for a while."

"Then I guess we should try to get comfortable."

\#

As if a celestial tap had been turned on directly above them, the rain became a torrential downpour, tearing through the canopy and churning the earth around them into mud. Puddles formed and swelled and joined with others. Thunder boomed loud enough that Nika felt the shockwave reverberate through her bones. Forked lightning shredded the dark sky. From somewhere in the canopy birds squawked and cawed. The poncho clung wetly and uncomfortably to her body, but at least it was keeping her mostly dry. Claude looked as though he had just jumped into a swimming pool.

So much for getting comfortable, she thought.

She said, "Do you want my poncho? It will fit you better than me."

He shook his head. "I'm already wet. I can't get any wetter."

"He keeps glowering at us." She was referring to the fake Ranger. He had taken shelter beneath a nearby tree and sat facing them with his knees pulled up against his chest.

"Don't look at him," said Claude. "You don't know what might set him off."

"Should I ask him if we can go inside the tent?"

"I'd rather stay out here. At least I can keep an eye on him that way."

"I'm sorry, Claude," Nika said. "This is my fault. If I hadn't invited you to come here, you would have been warm and dry back at the hotel."

"And bored out of my mind. At least now I'm having an adventure."

"Pretty crappy adventure if you ask me."

"But the company is okay."

"Just okay?" She smiled at him, but he seemed too wet and miserable to smile back. "Hey, what are you doing staying at The Reverie anyway? Don't you have a house somewhere?"

"My parents are visiting from France and staying at the hotel. They wanted me to be close to them, so they got me a room for the week."

"What do they do?"

"They're bakers. They own a bakery."

"Do they make those long loaves of bread?"

"Baguettes, yes. Do you know that we have a baguette competition every year?"

"I'm not surprised," she said. "Why don't you work in the bakery?"

"Because I am teaching English in Vietnam."

"I mean, why not go back to France? You could probably take over the bakery one day."

"That is what my father would like." He shrugged. "But I don't want to be looking at bread for the rest of my life."

"What do you want to do then?"

"I like teaching," he said.

"You're not going to live here and teach English forever."

"No, but I haven't thought about what I will do next. Maybe I will go to America."

"People already speak English there."

"Not to teach. I might like to be a talk show host."

"Just like that, huh?"

"There are many in America. I see them on TV all the time."

"You can't just walk into NBC with a resume and say you want to be a talk show host. Are you messing with me?"

Claude smiled and rubbed rain from his eyes; it was falling so hard now they had to raise their voices to hear each other. "What do you do?" he asked. "You never told me."

Nika groaned. "You know those phone stores in every mall? You go in to buy a charging cable or SIM card or something and you walk out with a new phone that you didn't need. Well, I'm one of those annoying salespeople."

"Huh," he said. "I thought you'd have a more interesting job than that."

"Thanks, Claude."

"I meant it as a compliment. You are a smart, interesting person, so I thought you might have a smart, interesting job."

"I used to have a smart, interesting job. I worked at a tech start-up. The ex-boyfriend I mentioned was the founder. But then we committed fraud…like massive fraud. I went to prison for five years. And now that I have a criminal record, it's tough to get another smart, interesting job."

Claude eyed her. "Now you're messing with me."

She shook her head. "I was released a few weeks ago."

"That's so cool!"

"Yeah, really cool, Claude. I'm twenty-seven and a convicted felon. I have no college degree. No job prospects. No savings. I own nothing but a few drawers of clothes. And my ex is trying to kill me. My life sucks. So let's not talk about me." They fell silent for a little and watched the rain fall. Eventually she said, "I need to go pee."

"Me too," he said.

"I'm going first. He's only going to let one of us go at a time." She got up and hurried through the rain to the fake Ranger's tree, her head ducked against the storm.

He scowled at her. "What do you think you're doing, shortcake?"

"Don't call me that, please," Nika said. "And I need to go to the bathroom."

"Then go." He gestured to the ground.

"I'm not going where you can watch. I'd like some privacy."

"Pick a tree then," he said. "But if you don't come back, your boyfriend gets a bullet in the head, got that, *shortcake*?"

Nika went almost thirty yards into the jungle before stopping to urinate. The fake Ranger had followed them all the way from Saigon, after all. What was to prevent him from following her through the bush to get a perverted peek?

While buttoning her jeans back up, she noticed a spot of bright green not too far away. It was clearly not a plant.

Curious, she picked her way through the wet foliage and discovered a badly beat-up tent. Not far from it were two more tents, one blue and one black, both flattened to the ground. Blinking rain from her eyes, she turned in a circle, looking for others. There seemed to be only the three of them.

Campers out here? she thought.

She supposed they could have been wildlife photographers or academics who had come to explore the remains of the jungle base camp.

But why leave their stuff behind?

She went to the still-standing green tent. The zippered door flap hung open. She looked inside. A large rucksack sat in a corner, surrounded by some of the contents it had carried: a bottle of water, a battered paperback novel, and a single sock. In another corner were a pair of neatly folded khaki pants, a matching shirt, and muddy boots. In the center of the ground sheet lay a sleeping bag, smeared with mud as though someone had trampled on it.

Nika dropped the flap and looked around the abandoned camp again. There was a firepit roughly in the middle of the three tents. Little remained but ashes surrounded by a ring of stones.

Did they get lost? Forget where their camp was? Or did one of them have an accident or medical emergency and there was no time to pack up? But what happened to the flattened tents? They look like they'd been savaged.

Nika went to the blue one and saw several long, vertical slits split the nylon fabric. It was almost as though someone had been trying to get out in one heck of a hurry...

Or someone had been trying to get in.

"Shit," Nika muttered, and a chill colder than the rain shot down her spine. She turned to get out of there—and spotted a black Doc Marten boot a short distance from the tent.

Only it wasn't just a boot; there was also a black-clad leg and an arm in a zebra-patterned shirt.

All at once she realized what she was looking at, what was right in front of her.

A body.

It was mostly covered with deadfall. But the shape was unmistakable. And there was something more, something she wasn't quite seeing—

She gasped in understanding and horror.

#

"Slow down!" said the fake Ranger. "What the hell are you talking about? Whose body?"

"I don't know!" Nika cried, raising her voice above the torrential downpour. She was out of breath from her sprint back from the abandoned camp. "I don't even know if it was a man or woman. There wasn't a head!"

Claude joined them. "What's going on?"

"There's a camp that way." She jabbed a finger in the direction of it. "Two of the tents were destroyed like someone took a knife to them. And there was a body. It didn't have a head!"

He frowned. "A *body*? Are you sure—"

"Yes, Claude! I know what I saw! Go look for yourself!"

"Where was it exactly—?"

"Slow down there, kid. You're not going anywhere."

"You can come with me."

The fake Ranger's hand had been resting on the grip of his pistol, and now he withdrew the weapon from his waistband and took a step back from them. "What is this? Some sort of trick? You kids set up an ambush for me?"

"No!" Nika said. "And I'm not going back there. We need to..." She was about to say they needed to leave, but she realized they couldn't do that. They couldn't leave Popeye. "We need to wait until my grandfather gets back, and then we need to get out of here—"

A strange call echoed through the jungle. It was somewhat muted by the drone of the rain but still audible and sharp, almost like a bark.

Nika's heart leapfrogged up her throat. "What was *that*?"

Claude said, "I don't think it was a bird."

A second call answered the first, then a third, all from different directions.

Nika's nerves, already frayed from her ghastly discovery at the camp, were now as taut as catgut. "I have a really bad feeling—"

"*Shut up*," hissed the fake Ranger. Rain streamed from his beret and streaked his face. He had raised the pistol so that he held it at the ready next to his head, and Nika was suddenly very glad he had the weapon. He appeared to be listening intently.

She listened, too, but heard only the storm...which would mask the approach of anything sneaking up on them.

And then she saw it.

Thirty feet away, leaning out from behind a tree.

There! she cried, only the word never left her mouth. Her throat had constricted to the size of a straw.

"There!" she said finally. She pointed with a very slow hand.

But it was gone.

"What?" said Claude. "Where?"

"Someone," she said, her voice a croak. Her chest was so tight that breathing, let alone speaking, had become difficult. "Over—over there. Behind a tree. It was watching us."

"A person?" asked the fake Ranger.

"I think..."

"You *think*? *Was it a fucking person or not?*"

"It was standing upright. But it was too far away. I couldn't see its face."

The fake Ranger looked from her to Claude and back to her. His beady eyes were intense and scrutinizing...and afraid.

"Fuck this," he grunted. "I'm outta here."

He started toward the river.

Claude grabbed his arm. "You can't leave us—"

"Let me go, you shit!"

He took off into the jungle, making a clumsy racket, and then was gone from sight.

\#

As Buck pushed wildly through the vegetation, nearly blinded by the pelting rain and the branches and palm fronds flapping in his face, his mind kept coming back to the same thought: *The Montagnards*. They were an ancient tribal people who had occupied South Vietnam for centuries. The Vietnamese called them *moi*, which meant *savage*, and it was a fitting description.

During his first tour of duty, Buck's unit came across a Montagnard village while on a patrol in the central highlands. The wiry little bastards shared their huts with pigs, sacrificed chickens to their gods, and ran about barefoot. The men wore loin cloths; the women carried baskets on their heads with their tits out. A Green Beret once told Buck that if a 'gnard died giving birth, the baby, alive or dead, would be buried right alongside her in a hollowed-out log. Goddamn savages, all right. The green beanie also told him that the fuckers ate monkey brains and drank blood soup.

So maybe they've expanded their diet to include human *brains*, he thought as he lurched over a mossy log. It would explain the headless corpse that the girl had been going off about.

In any event Buck wasn't going to end up on any savage's menu. Not old Buck Rafelson from Boonville, Missouri, no sir. He might not be going home with a bagful of cash as he'd hoped, but he was going home, damn right he was, and under the circumstances he was grateful for even that. Let the savages feast on the two kids for all he cared, as long as they kept the fuckers busy while he got to the boat—

Buck tripped on a root and sailed forward through the air. He landed face-first next to a tree, and he counted himself lucky that he didn't strike his head against the trunk. Yet searing heat radiated up his left wrist. He could move it, although just barely, and he suspected that it was broken.

Getting awkwardly to his feet, swearing at his carelessness, he looked up and found himself face-to-face with a savage... although it was no Montagnard. Beneath a mop of tangled brown hair, its snarling, Playdough-like face was grotesque and disfigured, with a sloping forehead that tapered into a bulging ridge across the brow. Its rounded boxer's nose protruded prominently, while its recessed chin disappeared beneath a long beard.

Buck stumbled away from it. The misshapen creature stepped forward. Hooded, deep-set eyes sized him up, gleaming with malicious intent. He realized it wasn't human, and it wasn't ape either. Buck didn't know what the fuck it was, but he had no problem imagining it eating human brains for breakfast.

He raised the .380 Colt and fired a round at point-blank range. The report was like a clap of thunder. He hadn't realized that the creature was bare-chested until it began to bleed from below its left shoulder. It grunted in what might have been pain or surprise, and then its bonelike brow creased into a pissed-off frown.

With incredible swiftness, it swung a stone cudgel that it had been holding low at its side.

Buck heard his skull crunch inward but was dead before he felt any pain.

#

Claude seized Nika's hand and said, "We have to go!"

She said, "We can't leave my grandfather!"

"They're here! Whatever you saw! Whatever killed those campers! They're here! What else is the crazy guy shooting at? *We have to go.*"

Claude's already wide eyes turned into saucers. But he wasn't looking at her anymore; he was looking past her.

Nika spun about just as something hideous bowled into her.

Screaming, she fell onto her back. It dropped on top of her and gripped fistfuls of her hair. She thrashed and kicked. It lifted her head and slammed it down. A black wave of pain swept through her skull, but the rain had softened the ground and she held onto consciousness.

As the horrible beast continued to drive her head into the muddy earth over and over, she thought witlessly, *Why couldn't this be quick?*

CHAPTER 16
CLUES IN THE STORM & THE PUNJI TRAP

Heaving the Nike bag above him—bones didn't weigh that much, he discovered, even a complete human skeleton—Ernest pushed it out of the tunnel opening before climbing out himself...and found himself amid a raging thunderstorm. The thunderheads earlier had portended it, but he was still surprised by the storm's ferocity. The slanting rain chewed the ground like automatic gunfire, while palm fronds and entire trees swayed in the howling wind. He spotted his tent, which Nika and Claude had unwisely pitched beneath a copperpod tree. They likely believed the sprawling canopy would offer protection from the rain, but they didn't consider the threat of large falling branches (what his father used to refer to on family camping trips as "widow makers").

Ernest hurried through the rain to the tent. "Scooter?" he said. When she didn't reply, he unzipped the door and looked inside. It was empty. The rucksack, he noticed, was on the ground nearby, completely soaked.

Why had the nitwits left it in the rain? And where had they gone?

He decided they likely went back to the fishing boat when the storm broke. The thatch roof would have kept them dry, and they wouldn't be stuck in a flimsy tent.

Leaving the Nike bag behind, he started toward the river, trampling through mud that sucked at his boots and ankle-deep puddles. He was talking to himself, cursing the storm and the kids for running off. He had spent nearly four hours in the tunnels and was exhausted, and the last thing he wanted was to be searching for them in the wet and cold.

When Cowboy died in '69, Ernest had buried him in a temporary grave that he dug in the side of the tunnel and marked with a large C. It had been well into the rainy season then, and the soil, a mix of sand and earth, was almost like sugar and easy to excavate. Today the rainy season was just getting underway, the rain from the daily monsoons had yet to saturate the ground, and the soil had been as hard as concrete. Digging through it with the Bowie knife was painstakingly slow work. Moreover, placing a dear friend bone by bone into a bag was also psychologically draining—

Ernest stopped so abruptly he grabbed a tree branch to keep his balance.

Frowning, he rubbed rain from his eyes.

It was still there, a man's body, sprawled face down on the ground at his feet. He'd nearly stepped on it.

A man's body with no head.

Ernest had seen his fair share of corpses during the war, even some headless ones (Ricky Lynn's had been the last but the not first), and he suspected this was another of his medication-produced hallucinations.

Even so, he knelt next to the body and touched the left hand. It was cold. He felt beneath the black shirt and found the flesh slightly warmer.

His hallucinations of Cowboy were realistic but also a little like watching TV. Cowboy was there before his eyes, picture-perfect, speaking in his Texas drawl, but Ernest always knew at the same time, in the back of his mind, that he *wasn't* there, that he was a manifestation, nothing more.

He wasn't convinced that was the case now.

He wiped more rain from his eyes and noticed the 75th Infantry Ranger scroll on the right shoulder of the black shirt.

"What in the Sam Hill...?" he muttered, realizing this person was the drunk from the restaurant the night before. He glanced where the head should have been above the crudely butchered neck, and while there was nothing there now, he could recall perfectly well the cocky Steven Seagal face beneath the black beret.

What was he doing out here in the middle of the jungle?

And who cut off his fucking head?

And why?

Standing abruptly, Ernest experienced a wave of dizziness. He braced a hand against the wet bark of a tree and squeezed his eyes shut until the faintness passed.

Maybe I'm hallucinating, after all.

But he wasn't. He wasn't dreaming either. This was vivid and real.

Too real.

And then he thought with alarm, *Scooter*.

\#

Ernest reached the river less than a minute later. The storm had turned the previously tranquil waterway into a frothing torrent. The fishing boat bobbed up and down at the end of the taut rope like a kite caught in the eye of a tornado.

Nika and Claude were not in it.

"Scooter!" he called. Lightning, white and silent, lit the sky above the river. Thunder rumbled, crackled, and boomed. "Scooter, damn it! Where are you?" His voice was muted beneath the curtains of rain.

His thoughts raced, but he couldn't make heads or tails of what might have happened while he was underground. However, he was certain the drunk had something to do with Nika's and Claude's absence. Did he frighten them off into the bush? Were they hiding somewhere, scared but safe? He hoped that was the case, but he wasn't sure he could believe it. Someone had decapitated the drunk, and that someone was presumably still around.

"Scooter!"

Rain.

"Scooter!"

A haunting, resonant, *Hoo!*

Ernest stiffened.

A series of hoots followed, rising in pitch, piercing the storm as his own voice could not.

An owl, he realized.

"Scooter!" he shouted one last time before retracing his steps.

\#

Ernest searched around the drunk's headless body for footprints or some other clue that might shed light on what happened to him. He discovered a Colt Mustang partly submerged in the mud—basically a smaller version of his 1911. He retrieved the lightweight pistol and swung out the cylinder. Cartridges were loaded into two of the six chambers.

Did the drunk shoot whoever attacked him?

Ernest examined the nearby foliage and ground for blood but found none. Not that it proved anything. Had there been any, the rain would have likely washed it away.

But not the blood underground…

Ernest waited out a sudden coughing fit—the rain and chill were taking a toll on his weakened immune system—and then checked his knees and elbows. Both were muddy and wet, but he was sure the darker stains were blood.

While leaving the tunnels earlier, he had noticed blood on the ground between the first trap door and the entrance shaft. He didn't pay it any attention—in fact, he had done his best to push it completely from his thoughts—because he was sure that his mind was playing tricks again, and the trail of blood was nothing but an imaginary thread that, if probed, would unravel another flashback of the attack that had killed Mercado and Lynn.

But the blood was real, wasn't it?

And that meant…what? he wondered. Was the drunk's attacker, shot and bleeding, hiding in the tunnels? But hiding from whom? Or was the blood from Nika or Claude? When the shit hit the fan, did they flee underground to hide or perhaps to look for him?

Both scenarios seemed implausible…yet *somebody* had gone down there, somebody who had left behind a trail of blood.

\#

"Nika!" he called as he crouched next to the tunnel entrance, aiming the flashlight into it. He could see blood, all right. A trail of it stained the earth dark where the rain didn't reach. Whoever left it was seriously injured, and Ernest no longer entertained the idea that it was his granddaughter. Short of someone pointing a gun at her head, he couldn't fathom any circumstance in which she would crawl headfirst into a hole in the ground.

As a child she had climbed into one of those plastic tubes at a McDonald's PlayPlace and had some sort of panic attack that had left her bawling until he went in and led her out. And then there was the time he'd made her a maze out of cardboard boxes in his study. She'd taken one look inside the entrance and ran screeching from the room. He also knew she didn't like the dark. She'd insisted on having a nightlight in her bedroom up until she left for The Athenian School, and if she ever got up to make a midnight snack, she would turn on practically every light on her way to the kitchen.

And if Nika didn't go into the hole, Ernest didn't believe Claude did either. In the face of danger they would most likely stick together.

Which meant the blood belonged to the sick sonofabitch who took the drunk's head, and it didn't come from the head itself. A human head doesn't hold much blood, certainly not enough to account for the volume spilled in the tunnel. Ernest didn't have a clue why the killer would go underground, and right then he didn't care; he had the much more pressing matter of finding where his granddaughter had gone.

He stood and turned in a circle, surveying the small clearing. Lightning and thunder continued to duel it out upstairs, and the rain fell in sheets. Would Nika and Claude have taken shelter in one of the still-standing structures? he wondered. One with a mostly intact roof? He had warned them that they may be boobytrapped, but when was the last time Nika had listened to him? Not only that, boobytraps had likely been the last thing on their minds when the drunk and his killer showed up.

Ernest started through the derelict base camp, calling Nika's name and sticking his head in every third or fourth building. When he reached the outer perimeter of bunkers, he scanned the thick jungle ahead of him in frustration. Had they attempted to return to the village on foot? That was a reasonable scenario, and it put him in a difficult position. Keep searching around the base or make his way back to the village, too? He decided on the former option. If they had gone back to the village, then they were safe. Mr. Thang would take care of them. On the other hand, if they were still nearby, then they were in danger until he found them.

"Scooter!" he called into the storm.

"...Ernest...?"

The voice was thin, distant, but clearly it belonged to Nika's friend.

"Claude?" he shouted.

"Ernest? I'm here! Help me!"

Pinpointing the Frenchman's exact location was difficult in the storm, but Ernest guessed he was due south.

"Ernest?"

"Coming!" he said as he struggled through the old-growth thicket. Thorny brush tore at his skin and clothing, fallen trees and upturned roots impeded his way, and patches of elephant grass as tall as cornstalks nearly caused him to go in the wrong direction.

But then the beam of his flashlight illuminated the Frenchman. He was seated on the muddy ground with his back to the trunk of a large palm tree. In the bright LED light, he looked like a specter, withered and afraid.

"What the hell are you doing out here?" Ernest demanded. "Where's Nika?" He noticed a sharpened piece of bamboo protruding from the top of the kid's sneaker, which was stained red with blood. "Ah, shit."

Claude pointed to a hole in the ground a short distance from where he sat. "I never saw it."

The Viet Cong had deployed a lot of devious boobytraps during the war, but one of their favorites had been punji sticks. The most basic version of the trap involved sharpened bamboo stakes pointed upright at the bottom of a camouflaged pit.

Ernest didn't go near the hole that Claude had stepped in; the

VC had often dug a second punji pit next to the first to injure the unlucky American G.I. who went to rescue his buddy. Instead he beelined to the Frenchman and knelt next to him to examine his wound.

"I can't get it out of my foot," said Claude, his voice shaky. "And it hurts. It hurts so much."

"Where's Nika?" Ernest asked again.

"You won't believe me…"

"Jesus Christ, man! Tell me what the fuck happened when I was gone, and then I'll help you with your foot. *Where's my granddaughter?*"

"These things… They weren't human…" He bit his bottom lip to stop it from trembling. Tears mixed with the rain streaming down his face. "They attacked us."

Lightning lit the jungle like a strobe light. The following peal of thunder was so loud that Claude flinched and looked up apprehensively at the sky.

"What did?" Ernest asked sternly.

"Things! One of them knocked Nika to the ground. But there were others. We heard them. So I ran."

Ernest clenched his jaw. "You *left* her?"

"*They weren't human!*" he yelled. "They look like us, sort of, but they're not us. I don't know *what* they are. And they attacked this guy. You met him in a restaurant last night. He followed us out here. We heard him fire his gun."

"Why did he follow us?"

"He overheard you and Nika talking, or his friend did. He thought there was money in the tunnels. He was crazy."

Ernest frowned. *Money?* But the dots connected quickly; he knew the stories of American soldiers discovering underground Viet Cong banks. Clearly the drunk did, too, and when his friend overheard an old vet talking about returning to a tunnel in the Ho Bo Woods…

"Scumbag," he muttered, but he was happy to have one mystery solved. Then, "He's dead."

"See!" said Claude. "And I would be, too, if I didn't run."

"These things…"

"I only saw the one that attacked Nika. It was like an ape with a big forehead and no neck. But it wasn't an ape. I can't describe it. Can you help me with my foot? It really hurts."

"Where did it attack Nika?"

"Where? *Where?*" He threw up his arms. "I don't know! By the tent. Nika came back from going to the bathroom… She found a body. The person had been dead for a long time. Nika said the head was missing."

"*What?*" he said, thinking, *Two decapitations?*

"Their camp wasn't far from ours. Then we heard these howls or whatever you want to call them. The crazy guy ran away, he left us on our own, and then the thing attacked Nika, and then I ran, too."

"Nika wasn't there. She wasn't by the tents. Her…body…wasn't there."

"Then I guess they took her!"

"Human-like non-apes?"

Claude closed his eyes and sighed. "Can you do something about my foot? Please, *monsieur*? I think I am losing too much blood. I feel dizzy."

If Ernest was somewhere back in civilization, and someone had told him that humanoid creatures had abducted his granddaughter, he would have thought they had lost their marbles. But it was a different situation when you were in a remote jungle in the middle of a stormy night, and someone you knew, someone who up until that point had been a relatively intelligent and sensible young man, told you that was what happened. Besides, what Claude was saying explained why the drunk was here. Even the trail of blood underground now made more sense. Because while he had a very hard time believing any sane human being would venture into long-forgotten tunnels for the hell of it, it wasn't as hard to believe that something else, something less than human, something that decapitated its victims, might do that, might, in fact, even call the tunnels home.

Setting these thoughts temporarily aside, Ernest examined Claude's foot. It was not a pretty sight. The bamboo spike had pierced the sole of his sneaker. About three inches of it was now poking out through the laced-up tongue. Given all the blood, it had likely severed a vein or artery, and it needed to come out so he could stop the bleeding.

Ernest told Claude he would be right back. He forged his way back through the jungle to the tent where he grabbed the first-aid kit from his waterlogged rucksack (which he'd packed to treat a potential sprained ankle or bee sting, not a punji stick through a foot). When he returned, he said, "Always come prepared, right?"

Claude said, "I didn't think you were coming back."

"I told you I would, didn't I?"

"You don't like me."

"You're...all right. Do you want a stick to bite on?"

Claude's eyes widened. "What? Why?"

"This is going to hurt. But I'll be quick."

"What are you going to do?"

Ernest stepped on the Frenchman's ankle so he wouldn't jerk his foot away.

"Hey! What are you doing? No! Wait—"

Ernest gripped the larger section of the spike on the underside of Claude's foot with both hands and yanked it free.

Claude cried out.

Ernest tugged off the bloody sneaker and sock, splashed the ugly wound with sterile saline solution, slathered it with a layer of antibiotic ointment, and then wrapped it tightly with a bandage. He dumped several Aspirin from a small bottle onto the palm of his hand.

Claude stared at them dumbly for a moment before picking them up one by one and placing them in his mouth. He chewed slowly.

"Now sit tight and don't make too much noise," Ernest told him, standing back up. "I'll be back for you when I can."

"Where are you going? *You can't leave me.*"

"Sorry, sport. I need to find my granddaughter."

CHAPTER 17
A LONG-LOST COUSIN

Nika could feel her brains trying to ooze out from the back of her shattered skull like a yolk from a cracked egg. The only thing preventing this from happening—which would have been mortifying in front of the hundreds of people in the audience—was her graduation mortarboard.

She stood on an outdoor stage in a black gown alongside faculty members and other students she didn't recognize. She felt like an imposter because she wasn't supposed to be there. Yet no one seemed to know that she had dropped out of university before earning a degree, and she figured if she could blend in for long enough to shake hands with the school officials and receive her diploma, then everything would be all right. Popeye would love her again. She would find a good job. She would meet a nice man, get married, have children, and lead a normal, happy life.

The president of Stanford University, serving as the master of ceremonies, introduced the keynote speaker—and Nika was horrified to see Ari Schwartz strut onto the stage. He tipped a wink her way, and then went to the microphone to brag about his past successes and his current company. And then he began confessing to the fraud that he and Nika committed, including all the nitty gritty details. The audience became increasingly irate, and they directed their anger at her. She tried to tell them it wasn't entirely her fault, she had been doing Ari's bidding, but they didn't care. They shouted and jeered and threw things. A tomato struck her in the head, knocking off her mortarboard, and she felt her brains slip down her back and splatter on the floorboards of the stage.

She dropped to her knees and tried to scoop them up, to put them back where they belonged, but the pieces were gel-like and slippery, and she couldn't grab them. The audience roared with laughter. Popeye stood next to Ari, both shaking their heads and staring at her with pity.

Nika wanted to die, yet she kept trying to put her Jell-O-like brains back inside her head, all the while thinking, *Why couldn't this be quick?*

#

She shot awake, momentarily relieved. *A dream. Just a dream.* The room was dark and unfamiliar. Then she remembered she was staying at Popeye's… No, she was in Vietnam with Popeye… *No, no, no—she was in the jungle, in a storm, and—*

Nika gasped. That *thing*.

She probed the back of her head gingerly and winced. Her skull was intact, but there was a tender lump the size of a tennis ball beneath her hair.

Where was she?

The room was tomb black, yet she could hear the storm, muted and distant, almost as if she was…

Underground. Oh, God, no, please, no. Don't tell me I'm underground in one of those tunnels. Anywhere but there.

A light switched on and off very quickly.

It wasn't until the following boom of thunder that Nika realized the light had been lightning. She scrambled forward to where the lightning had momentarily illuminated a window in the ceiling. The ground there was wet and muddy. Rain fell on her. Nevertheless, she kept her face tilted upward until another burst of lightning lit what she now saw was some sort of vertical ventilation shaft.

The surface appeared to be nearly twenty feet above her, and even if she could somehow pull herself up into the shaft, it was far too narrow to ascend through.

Nika's predicament was so incomprehensible and frightening she nearly burst into tears. But she held herself together. There were too many questions that needed answering. What was the thing that had attacked her? Why had it brought her down here? Where was Claude?

"Claude?" she hissed, fighting a swell of panic inside her chest.

No reply.

"Claude!"

Nothing.

Was he unconscious? Or was he…

Dead? I think you know the answer to that, NC. And maybe that's for the best because when you're dead you don't feel anything anymore. You don't feel the cutting and snapping and tearing as they take your head from your body. You don't feel the inhumanity and indignity of the savagery. And you want to know something else, NC? I think you're jealous of Claude, and if you're not, you should be. Because he may be dead and can't feel anything anymore. But you're not, and why's that? Why did they keep you alive? I'll bet it's so your brain stays fresh and tasty until they get hungry again, and they will get hungry again, and likely soon…

Her phone, she thought frantically. Did she have it?

Nika patted her pocket and nearly melted with relief when she felt the rectangular shape of her cheap Nokia. She took it from the pocket beneath her poncho. The screen was cracked but the phone was on and working. Unsurprisingly, she had no reception. She activated the flashlight.

The "room" was no larger than her prison cell had been with crude clay walls and a low ceiling. A narrow, child-sized tunnel directly before her burrowed into inky darkness. She shuffled in a circle—and frowned. In the thick shadows against a far wall there appeared to be…

Oh no, come on, no…

Nika forced her stiff legs to move, and then she was at the wall, looking down at a pile of human remains. The poor person had been dead for a long time. They were just bones now, partly clothed.

And there was something strange about the skeleton…

Nika's hand went to her mouth to stifle a cry.

There's no skull. Her eyes scanned the ground. It hadn't rolled away anywhere, and that confirmed her earlier fear. *They really are brain eaters.*

Go! she thought. *Run!*

But run where? The tunnels might be a maze of twists and turns, ups and downs. She could become hopelessly lost. Worse, however, she suspected those things had made the tunnels their home. Why else would they have brought her down into them? She had heard at least three creatures earlier, but what if there were more? What if there was an entire colony of savage brain eaters? She would never reach the exit alive.

Nevertheless, she knew that she had to try because…

I'm next.

Nika wasn't sure if it was all the water she had drunk during the day, or if the fear of being devoured by monsters had turned her bladder to mush, but she suddenly needed to urinate again, and badly.

She wasn't going to go next to the skeleton, so she moved farther along the wall until she reached the corner. She couldn't get her pants down quickly enough. Her fingers fumbled with her stubborn belt. She freed the tongue from the buckle frame, slid her thumbs inside the waistband of both her jeans and cotton underwear, and shoved them down her thighs.

A moment later the excruciating pressure left her bladder. Nika heard herself whisper "Oh God..." although it was barely audible over the steady stream of her urine hitting the hard-packed ground. She squatted for at least half a minute before she finally stood, pulling her underwear up her legs—

Two very strong hands gripped her arms and threw her away from the wall. She yelped, stumbling sideways. With her pants around her ankles, she couldn't keep her balance and landed hard on her hip and elbow.

She didn't have time to consider the pain. She scanned the blackness, but before she spotted the beast hands grabbed her by the hair, yanking her to her feet.

Nika cried out, and although she couldn't see the thing, she could smell it: an overpowering stench that fell somewhere between rotting onions and turpentine.

Leave me alone! What do you want!

She discovered the answer to that question a moment later when it spun her around. She felt something rock-hard and hot smack her bare butt.

Oh no...no, no, no please no—

The tip of its erection pushed between her thighs.

Adrenaline surging, Nika tore free from its grip while swinging a fist in a wild arc, striking its cheek or temple. It snarled and released her. She yanked her underwear and jeans up her thighs but stumbled again in her panic. However, she managed to button up her pants a second before landing on her hands and knees. She probed the ground blindly for what she knew must be somewhere nearby—and then her right hand closed around a leg bone from the skeleton.

She swung it like a baseball bat with all her might. She didn't know where she struck the creature, but she heard it fall to the ground.

Panting, crying, Nika scooped up her phone—the camera's LED shone like a beacon from the corner where it had landed—and ran to the wall with the low door where the thing must have been waiting and watching for her to regain consciousness. She dropped to all fours and scrambled into the hole. A few feet later the grave-black tunnel forked. She went left.

From behind her a wicked, inhuman howl cut through the darkness.

\#

The tunnel kept going and going and going like in a bad dream. The creature had fallen silent after its ungodly wail, but Nika knew it was behind her, knew it was coming after her.

Knew it wanted to rape her.

No! her mind shrieked. She would die fighting tooth and nail before she let it do that.

How was this even possible? she wondered desperately. How could a race of prehistoric beasts exist without anybody knowing about them? Was she really the first person on this planet to encounter them?

You're not the first, NC. Don't be silly. That headless person you discovered must have encountered them before you did. Maybe a whole lot of people have encountered them, only they've never lived to tell their tale.

Was she going to die? Was it going to catch her, rape her, and then cut off her head, too?

This didn't happen in real life. This happened in movies and nightmares.

But it *did* happen because it *was* happening.

She was going to die.

And it's kinda funny, the irony, don't you think? You came to Vietnam to get away from a killer, and now you're being pursued by an even worse one. You know what they say: out of the frying pan and into the fire.

Nika wanted to scream, but she couldn't. Her lungs felt like deflated beach balls that had been set on fire. Each breath seared her throat. She could run five miles without much trouble, but suddenly she couldn't scramble a hundred yards on her hands and knees without feeling as though her chest was about to burst open. Was that her fear messing with her biology? Or was there less oxygen underground—?

Who cares! You're about to die! Shouldn't you be thinking about something more important? Like how not *to die? Because maybe, just maybe, you can outrun the thing behind you. Maybe you can make it back to the surface. Maybe it won't follow you. Maybe it's already stopped following you—*

Ahead a passageway opened to the left.

Nika glanced back over her shoulder.

Now a scream escaped her lips, a shrill *Waa!* that might have come from a small bird that suddenly forgot how to fly mid-flight.

The beast was right behind her, its rounded, muscular shoulders filling the entire tunnel.

Without thinking, Nika darted into the new passage, scraping her back on the low ceiling and smashing her elbows against the walls in her haste. She emerged in a room where a woman was staring at her in utter surprise.

"Help me!" Nika blurted, falling down next to her and watching the entrance of the room.

The creature appeared at the threshold, its baleful eyes

flicking between Nika and the woman. Reality slowed and everything became amplified: the pounding of her heart, the blood thumping through her head, the sour taste of fear in her mouth…and most of all, the hideous creature crawling into the room on its hands and knees and then rising to its full height.

It was as tall as a man. And as it stood there on two feet, erect, Nika thought it *was* a man. With its tangled brown mane, naked and harry upper body, and crudely fashioned tiger-skin leggings, it was a hideous parody of David Lee Roth in his early Van Halen days. Yet it was not lithe and slim but dense and compact, with a wide chest and pelvis, and stubby limbs that were ropey with muscles. And its face…oh, God. A sloping forehead with a bony brow pushed down and distorted everything below it. Sunken in deep sockets, the eyes were too far apart. Flattened and wrinkled, the nose was too broad. Sneering and jutting outward, the mouth was too wide, further exaggerated by the clipped chin. Everything about it was just *wrong*, but perhaps nothing more than how its large head seemed to rest directly on its shoulders in a freakish, protruding way as if it were trying to peer far into the distance.

Although Nika was sure that it was not human, the similarities of its features were enough to make its otherness even more repugnant and uncanny, and that triggered a fresh wave of terror.

"What is it?" she hissed, barely aware that she had asked the question.

"A long-lost cousin," said the woman beside her.

CHAPTER 18
END OF THE ROAD

The trail of blood continued from the entrance shaft to the trap door and then past it. That explained why Ernest had not encountered the injured person—or creature if he were to believe what Claude had told him. It had continued along this level while he had been in the ones below.

Dragging Scooter behind it by her hair? By her ankles? She would never have gone with it freely, and he wasn't willing to believe she was dead, so he had to assume she had been unconscious.

He wormed his way faster on his elbows through the tight, black tunnel, the .380 Colt in one hand, the flashlight in the other. Rage was driving him forward with reckless alacrity—rage and, perversely, enjoyment.

An adversary was ahead somewhere in the darkness. Not an invisible coward that hid inside his cells, but one he could fight face-to-face.

He had trained for this.

He had been the best there was at this.

He may not have relished returning to these tunnels to retrieve the remains of a once-close friend. That had been a chore and a ghoulish one. But this, this was different. This was a hunt, and damn right he *was* enjoying it…at least a part of him was, the crazy-motherfucker part he had left behind in country when he returned to the World.

The tunnel became larger, allowing him to continue forward in a duckwalk. He should have remained focused on what he would find at the end of it, but his mind kept drifting back to Nika. If the fucking thing had done something to her, if it had killed her...

Again, Ernest wouldn't let himself believe that. He loved his granddaughter dearly. She had given him a second chance at being a father figure, and at being a better one than he had been to her mother, Palak. He had been so busy building his company in the 80s that he never made much time for his stepdaughter. He would be in his office writing code before she went to school in the mornings and was still there when she got home. He rarely had dinner with Neeti and Palak at the dinner table as he preferred to eat at his desk.

For him, the weekends were no different than weekdays, and he kept his office door closed so as not to be disturbed. He had been a selfish prick who had put his pursuit of success over the well-being of his family. It was no wonder that Palak had never even said goodbye to him when she left for university. He recalled coming out of his office one Saturday evening for dinner and asking Neeti where Palak was, and Neeti telling him that Palak had moved out a week ago.

When Palak died a few years later in **Denali National Park, and Neeti had told Ernest that she wanted to take custody of Nika, he had been vehemently opposed.**

"We have to take her in, Ernie," insisted Neeti on a chilly spring morning the day after Ernest had returned from the search operation in Alaska.

"We can't, love," he said, smoking one of his Winstons. "She's not *ours*."

"She's our granddaughter. She's our blood."

"She's four years old. Four. Do you remember what it's like

having a child running around the house?"

"Do *you*?" she asked tartly.

"Look," he said, ignoring the dig at his parenting skills or lack thereof, "we've been through that. We're not young anymore. This is our time. How are we going to travel? You keep talking about going back to Europe. We can't do that if we take Nika in. We can't go anywhere if we take her in."

"We're not giving her up to strangers! God, I can't believe you're even considering that."

"Let John's parents take her then," he said, even though he knew that Palak's parents-in-laws weren't up to the task. John's father had suffered a stroke two years earlier and needed a full-time nurse, while John's mother was a low-earning salesclerk working full-time at a department store.

"If they could, I'm sure they would, but they can't, and you know that." Neeti leaned forward, her dark eyes bright with challenge. "Ernie, this is something you have to do whether you want to or not. In the war, you would have done anything for the boys in your squad, am I right?"

"Don't bring up the war," he snapped.

"You would have. I know you would have. I've heard how you talk about them. You would have done anything for them. You would have given your *life* for them. I'm not asking for that much; I'm just asking you to give some of your time to our granddaughter who has lost her parents. Maybe even give her some love if you can spare it. Isn't that something you can do, Ernie? And if you can't do it for Nika, can you do it for me?"

Ernest eventually relented, and the next day they filed the paperwork at the local social services agency to take custody of Nika. For the next week he kept himself locked away in his office, preoccupying himself with work. And then, one morning, there was a timid knock at his door.

"Busy!" he called out.

"Papi?" said Nika. "I made you something."

Grunting, he got up and opened the door. Nika stood on the threshold in a colorful fuzzy jumpsuit. She held a piece of lined paper in her hand.

"What's that?" he said, kneeling so they were at eye level.

She handed him the paper. On it, in purple crayon, she'd drawn a stickman holding something in his hand. Below the figure, written in all capitals with backward Es, was:

POPƎYƎ

And then he realized the stickman was the iconic sailor and what was in his hand must have been a tin of spinach. There was even a pipe sticking out from his mouth.

"What's this?" he said, eyeing her curiously.

"You!" she said.

"Me?"

"Papi!

"Papi?" And then he realized the phonetic similarity of Papi and Popeye. "You think I look like Popeye the Sailor Man?"

She bobbed her head.

"I don't even like spinach."

"But it makes you strong."

"Do you want to be strong?"

She bobbed her head again.

"Why don't you go ask Nana to make you some spinach for lunch then? Tell her I'm hungry, too, and I'll join you."

Surprisingly Nika threw her arms around his neck and kissed him on the cheek. Then she ran off toward the kitchen in the clumsy way of four-year-olds that made you wonder why they didn't fall flat on their faces.

Ernest went back to work but made time for lunch with Neeti and Nika that afternoon, which turned out to be a superb feta and spinach quiche. He had lunch with them every day for the rest of the week.

Later that month in what should have been one of the most challenging decisions of his life but turned out to be one of the easiest, he sold his company to Microsoft, then an up-and-coming startup. With plenty of free time and nothing to do, he took up gardening as a hobby so Neeti would always have fresh vegetables with which to cook.

Neeti and Nika became the focus of his new and simple life, a life he never knew he wanted but one he would come to cherish...

Ahead of him the beam of the flashlight caught a pair of bare feet disappearing into a side tunnel.

The thing that took Scooter?

Adrenaline surged through his veins like quicksilver. He lowered the flashlight to the ground and unsheathed the Bowie knife. He disengaged the Colt's manual safety with his thumb. He held both weapons raised before him like he might a knife and fork before digging into a good meal.

He waited and listened.

He heard thunder crash and bang far above, bassy and muffled, but nothing else.

Nevertheless, he knew the thing was there, just ahead and around the corner, and it knew he was there, too. The flashlight had given him away.

As quietly as he could Ernest pulled himself forward with his elbows. He stopped just before the two tunnels met.

He still heard nothing, but he smelled a pungent, sour body odor.

If he had ammunition to spare, he would have blindly aimed the pistol around the corner and fired off two or three shots. But he only had two rounds—

Movement. Fast. Something coming at him.

Hands seized his head.

He shoved the barrel of the Colt against rock-hard flesh and squeezed the trigger. The blast was deafening, followed by a reverberating echo.

The creature smashed the pistol from his grip, and in the next instant the hands were back, only now around his throat.

Ernest stabbed the thing with the Bowie knife. He felt the blade deflect off bone. He yanked it free and stabbed again and again.

The hands squeezed tighter, strangling him. He couldn't breathe. He stabbed the thing a final time, dropped the knife, and gripped hairy and impossibly thick wrists, trying to pry the hands from his throat.

Spangles of light danced in the blackness. Ernest gasped and choked. He pressed his hand into a broad, waxy face. He dragged his fingernails over a protuberance that felt like an elongated tumor and then over a bony eye cavity. He dug his fingers deep, clawing at the eyeball. The creature grunted and jerked its head.

Yet still it refused to release his throat.

Ernest felt his consciousness fading, slipping further and further away.

Before the abyss swallowed him, he thought, *I'm sorry, Scooter. God help you.*

PART 4
HOMO DENISOVA

CHAPTER 19
LANA DAO

Nika watched in terror as the repulsive creature stepped toward her. She aimed her phone's flashlight directly at its brutal face, hoping to frighten it away. It squinted but otherwise seemed undeterred.

And then, suddenly and swiftly, the Asian woman was on her feet. She raised what appeared to be a rock and said, "No!"

The creature glowered at her, then at the rock, which was small enough to fit neatly in her palm. It said something, a butchering of vowels and consonants that might have been primitive words. It continued toward Nika.

She scuttled backward in a crab crawl. "Go away!" she shrieked, wild with panic.

The woman moved between the creature and Nika, still holding the rock aloft as if it were a magical talisman. "No!" she said again.

The beast growled more words while baring large and yellow teeth. Hatred burned within its deep-set, gimlet eyes as it stepped to its right to get around the woman. She matched it with a step to her left.

"No!" She pressed the tip of the rock to her opposite wrist like she was about to cut herself. "No!"

Its brow furrowed. The muscles in its jaw and biceps bunched as it balled its hands in a very human-like expression of rage. Its scowl was almost a smile—maybe a sneer. With a murderous glance at Nika and a nasty snort, it turned, lowered itself to its hands and knees, and scuttled from the room.

Nika released her breath and dropped to her butt. Her arms and legs felt like cooked noodles, and her heart was beating so quickly it seemed to rattle her entire body.

The woman kept looking at the hole through which the creature had departed until she seemed satisfied it wasn't coming back. She sat back down, folded her arms protectively across her chest, brought her knees to them, and rocked back and forth while staring at the ground in front of her.

Nika watched her in silence and gratitude and concern. Finally she said, "Do you speak English?"

The woman kept rocking.

As her fear-fogged mind cleared, Nika recalled that the woman did indeed speak English. She had called the creature a "long-lost cousin."

"Hello?" Nika said.

The woman turned her head sidelong. Her eyes gleamed wetly in the backsplash of the phone's flashlight, yet there was nothing in them. They were uncannily doll-like.

And then she spoke: "Are there others?"

Nika blinked. "Others?"

"Are they dead?"

"Who are you talking about?"

"The rescue team."

Nika shook her head in confusion. "I'm not... There's no rescue team. I don't know who you are."

The woman's eyes remained vacant and lifeless. Then a single tear slid down her left cheek. She looked back at the ground in front of her.

Nika wanted to cry, too, but she wouldn't let herself. She worried that might not stop. "Who are you?" Her voice was scratchy and hushed, almost unrecognizable. "What's your name?"

The woman didn't reply.

"I'm Nika."

The woman mumbled something.

"Hana?" Nika said.

"Lana," said the woman. "My name is Lana Dao. My name is *Lana Dao.*" She rested her forehead against the tops of her knees and squeezed her eyes shut. Her shoulders shook.

"Hey? It's okay. Don't cry." Nika found it bizarre that she was the one offering comfort when her sanity felt as though it were being held together by fraying threads. "Don't cry, please don't cry—"

A spine-chilling sound erupted from somewhere behind her.

Nika whipped around and saw what she had missed during her frenetic scramble into the room. Another woman, Caucasian and young—a girl, really—sat against a far wall wearing tattered clothing. Her face was dirty and deathly pale. Her mouth was a lipless black circle, and the sound coming out of it was a moaning wail punctuated by the flat, hard slaps of her open hands repeatedly clapping against the sides of her head.

The woman named Lana went to the girl. She gripped her wrists and said something in a quiet, cooing tone. A few moments later they wrapped their arms around each other and rocked silently together.

I'm at the bottom of the rabbit hole, Nika thought desperately. Not one filled with cute animals and a chaotic tea party but rather sadistic, bloodthirsty creatures and a couple of very crazy people.

Can you blame them, NC? Living like this for however long they've been imprisoned? Subjected to... God only knows what. Can you blame them?

\#

Sometime later the two women ceased rocking. Lana spoke softly to the girl, and then she fell silent. A little after that she began to snore.

Nika couldn't sleep. She was wet, cold, miserable, and wired with fear. She had reluctantly turned off her phone's flashlight to save what little battery remained, and the subterranean room was abyssal black. She couldn't even see her hand when she held it in front of her face.

Far above, the storm had yet to let up. The rain falling through a ventilation shaft, like the one in the other room, splattered the ground with an incessant patter. It smelled fresh and clean, which only exaggerated how sweaty and dirty she felt. Under different circumstances, she might have stripped off her clothing and stood beneath the rain to take a tropical shower. Not now. No way. Not with the David Lee Roth monster lurking somewhere down here. For all she knew it might be crouched in the small entrance shaft, watching her, fantasizing about what it wanted to do to her if it got her alone.

Nika didn't let herself dwell on that.

She listened.

The *tat tat tat* of the rain.

A peal of thunder.

A split-second flash of lightning during which she glanced toward the entrance hole.

Nothing there.

Nika wondered about Claude. Had he escaped the creatures?

Had he reached the village? Were he and Mr. Thang somewhere where they could get cell reception? Were they calling the police at that very moment? Was help on its way? She wished that were all true. Yet she couldn't stop thinking of the more likely alternative. Claude was dead. The things had caught him, killed him, and cut off his head, just as they'd done to the person with the zebra shirt. But why? If they were brain eaters, why not just take the brains? Did they keep human heads as trophies? Did they use the skulls as soup bowls...?

Flowers and clouds. Green valleys and ice cream. Think about nice things, NC. That bicycle you got for your fifth birthday. It was turquoise, wasn't it? With a white saddle seat and rainbow streamers dangling from the end of the swept-back handlebars. There was a big front basket, too, remember that? You used to stuff your entire collection of Beanie Babies into it. And the rubber tires. You've never forgotten how that rubber smelled. You can almost smell it now, can't you? And the chrome-plated wheels that you spent an entire afternoon decorating with spoke beads. And those stupid training wheels that you were so embarrassed by and begged Popeye to take off even before you were ready...

Popeye.

Nika's heart sank. He had crawled down into these tunnels with nothing but a flashlight and a knife. He had crawled into the creatures' *home*. He didn't know better. He couldn't have. But he must have encountered them. And they would have—

Flowers and clouds and sugar and spice and everything nice and stop thinking about skulls and brains and all that shit because Popeye's okay, he has to be, he can't be dead—

"Why are you here?"

Nika jumped at Lana Dao's voice.

Why am I here? she thought. *What kind of stupid question is that?*

She said, "They attacked me. They brought me down here."

"They didn't pick you off a busy street corner. Why were you in the jungle in the first place?"

"I came with my grandfather and a friend. My grandfather..." She shook her head even though she knew the woman couldn't see her. "It doesn't matter, does it?" She swallowed tightly. "What do they want with us? That thing, that...*thing*...tried to... You called it a long-lost cousin."

The woman didn't reply.

"What did you mean?"

No reply.

"You don't believe they're human, do you?"

Nothing.

"What do you know about them? Can't you tell me? I'm terrified right now. I don't know what's happening. I need to know *something*. Please?"

Nothing.

Nika was suddenly furious at the woman. She might not know much about their captors, but she had evidently been down here for some time, so she had to know something. Why was she being so mute and stubborn? Popeye and Claude might be dead, and she was likely going to be raped and maybe killed, as well, and this infuriating woman wouldn't tell her a damn thing—

"Once upon a time," said Lana Dao, her voice disembodied in the blackness, "long, long ago, humans evolved from a genus of apes called Australopithecus."

Nika blinked. "Excuse me?"

"I've been composing an article for *Nature* or *Science* in my head. It's the only thing that's kept me sane...or somewhat sane." She cackled, a wretched sound filled not with mirth but a good dose of madness. "Oh fuck... Oh fuckity fuck fuck fuck." A loud exhale. "Anyway, I've worked it over so many times I have it memorized. Would you like to hear the start?"

"Yes, I would."

A long pause followed. Nika wasn't sure if the woman had fallen asleep again or what. But then she said, "That's how it starts: Once upon a time, long, long ago, humans evolved from a genus of apes called Australopithecus."

Nika said, "It's a good hook."

"Well, eventually those humans set out from… Sorry, no, I shouldn't have used 'well'. This will be a scientific paper, after all. Let me revise." She cleared her throat and giggled. "Ready?"

"Ready."

"*Eventually* those humans set out from East Africa and colonized most of Europe, Asia, and Oceania. Humans in the forests of Europe and western Asia evolved into *Homo neanderthalensis* (Neander Valley Man). Humans farther east evolved into *Homo erectus* (Upright Man). And the humans in the jungles of southeast Asia and Indonesia evolved into *Homo denisova* (Denisova Cave Man), *Homo soloensis* (Solo Valley Man), and *Homo floresiensis* (Island of Flores Man). While all of this was happening, our own species, still minding its own business back in East Africa, evolved into what scientists pretentiously named *Homo sapiens*, or Wise Man. Keep going?"

"Yes, please."

"Okey dokey little pokey. Due to the different climates in which these species lived," she continued in a weird kind of serenading yet professorial cadence, "they developed differences in their genetic code as well as in their cognitive and social abilities. Some were bulky and cold-resistant. Some were dwarves no taller than chimpanzees. Some were violent hunters while others were harmless foragers. Some formed language, controlled fire, and crafted jewelry and rock art. But at the very least all of them stood erect, used stone tools, and fell under the umbrella of the genus *Homo*. In other words, all of them were human beings. And for about two million years many of these different species of human beings lived concurrently together on the planet.

"That's something modern humans tend to forget. For most of our history we've been the only branch of our family tree still around so we find it hard to believe, or even to conceive, that other groups of humans once walked alongside us. But they did, just as leopards walk alongside lions and Shih Tzus alongside Great Danes. So what happened to them?

"There are two competing theories. The first suggests that when *Homo sapiens* began encountering their archaic cousins, they interbred with them to such an extent that they absorbed their populations into their own. Reproductive imperialism, you might say. The second suggests that *Homo sapiens* committed the first and greatest act of mass genocide in history—or prehistory. This perhaps is the more plausible of the two theories as we're not exactly the most tolerant of species, are we? How many wars over race and territory were waged in the last century alone? And there is scant evidence to believe that early *Homo sapiens* were any less racist or territorial or murderous—or any less human—than we are today.

"The bottom line is that it wasn't long after *Homo sapiens* spread from East Africa into the Arabian Peninsula and across Eurasia that the native human populations went extinct. The reign of *Homo neanderthalensis*, which once roamed from Portugal and the British Isles to Siberia, ended some 40,000 years ago. Our most mysterious relatives, *Homo denisova*, which are responsible for up to five or six percent of DNA in many living Asians, lasted the longest, exiting the evolutionary stage as recently as 10,000 years ago—or, at least, that's the current scientific dogma.

"Because here's the rub, little pokey: What if a few die-hard bands of Denisovans held on? What if they developed sophisticated cultural practices to stay hidden, such as living in remote territories where even the ever-expanding modern human population didn't encroach? The balance between isolation and survival would be difficult but not impossible. Ironically, the biggest threat to their existence would come from within their own biology since eventually, inevitably, generations of inbreeding would lead to infertility. The surviving bands would dwindle to just a handful. Groups once consisting of around fifty members would be reduced to large families of a dozen or so. The writing would be on the wall. Genetic isolation would no longer be feasible. If they were to survive, they would once again have to mate with their mortal enemy, *Homo sapiens*.

"How might this have played out? Well, one of the few remaining bands of Denisovans—Sorry! I did the 'well' thing again. One of the few remaining bands of Denisovans—a family that had retreated to, say, the deepest jungles of Vietnam, a family that had found refuge in, say, some long-abandoned tunnels—might resort to snatching a modern female human from a nearby village if the opportunity arose, or perhaps a female university professor and her female graduate student on a field trip into their territory. Or a pretty young girl who, for reasons known only to her, ventured with her grandfather into the secluded, primordial woods that they call home. The family of Denisovans, desperate for a new generation of offspring, might keep these hated females imprisoned underground while they attempted to impregnate them. They would feed and clothe them to keep them alive and healthy, but yes, they would ultimately impregnate them, and the women would be forced to live out their days like vermin kept in a dark, dank cage, keenly aware that something human but not Sapiens was growing inside their wombs..."

A self-satisfied sigh punctured the vile spell that Nika had fallen under.

Lana Dao said, "That was the first time I spoke any of that out loud, and it's just as good as it was inside my head. What do you think? Maybe I should turn it into a novel instead. Could be a best seller, no?" She laughed once more, that mad, terrible cackle.

Nika could no longer hold back her tears. She began to cry, and just as she'd feared, she found she couldn't stop.

\#

After Lana Dao had outlined Nika's dire predicament and even bleaker potential fate, Nika had somehow drifted off to sleep. She awoke to the sound of Lana once again speaking to the girl in cosseting tones.

"So you're a university professor, huh?" Nika said.

For several long seconds no reply came from the blackness. But then Lana said, "Yes, I am. Or I was. Are you still what you were when you're stripped of what made you what you had been?"

"Why was it afraid of that rock?"

"It wasn't afraid of it."

"I'm pretty sure it was."

"You don't know anything."

"No, I don't. Why did you hold the rock up like you did if it wasn't afraid of it?"

"You ask a lot of questions."

"What else am I supposed to do? I can't just sit here. I'll go —" Nika almost said *insane* before catching herself. If Lana Dao wasn't insane already, she was well on her way to getting there. Nevertheless, there was no debate that the graduate student had flown away with the fairies a long time ago. "Can't you just talk to me?"

"All right, little pokey," said the woman challengingly, almost provokingly. "Do you know how Sapiens wiped out Neanderthals and all the other species of humans?"

Nika didn't but said, "We were smarter than them, I guess."

"Smarter? Maybe, or maybe not. Neanderthals had larger brains than Sapiens. And what would 'smarter' have meant 50,000 years ago? Both species made tools and clothing. Both could turn a flint stone into a spear point. Both knew which mushrooms and plants they could eat and which ones made them sick. Both knew how to hunt large game."

Nika said, "I'm not really an expert on this stuff…"

"Then it's a good thing that I am. Sapiens had language."

"Neanderthals didn't have a language?"

"They could vocalize. They could make a sound that meant a cave bear was spotted nearby. They could make other sounds signaling the presence of a nearby herd of bison or woolly mammoths. They could make a whole range of sounds. But that's not a language, is it? Sapiens, on the other hand, developed advanced linguistic skills that allowed them to talk in detail about their environment. Rather than just announcing the presence of a nearby cave bear, the member of their group who spotted it could elaborate, describing the bear as old and injured. They could also suggest that acting quickly could allow them to catch up to it before nightfall made tracking impossible."

Nika said, "Language let them plan and organize their attacks on the Neanderthals?"

Lana said, "It would let them do that, yes, but Neanderthals were physically stronger and more robust than Sapiens, so while better planning and organization would help Sapiens in a battle, it wasn't a guarantee for success. Certainly it wasn't what allowed them to extinguish the entire Neanderthal race within a span of a few thousand years. If you ask me, what likely contributed to that was Sapiens' ability not only to communicate with each other about their environment but also about the members of their own band. For example, who was mating with whom, who was brave and who was cowardly, who was a liar and opportunist and who was honest and fair, and most importantly, who was trustworthy. In other words, they gossiped."

"Gossip wiped out the Neanderthals?"

"Today gossip is often dismissed as unimportant and even uncouth in certain circles. Yet it remains a ubiquitous part of our daily interactions, doesn't it? Office employees don't gather at the water cooler to discuss sales figures. They want to hear the juicy details about the affair one of their colleagues is having, the bad blood between two others, or how the new guy only got his job because of his father's connections. Gossip isn't simply a frivolous pastime; it's deeply ingrained in our nature, stemming from our evolutionary past when it played a crucial role in fostering cooperation within larger populations.

"The Neanderthal tribe members would have built bonds similar to chimpanzees today: through physical contact, sharing, and affection. Guiding them would be the alpha male, the strongest member resolving disputes and making decisions on hunting, foraging, and relocation to maintain social order. However, this hierarchical structure could only function effectively within smaller groups of fifty members or fewer. Beyond that, intimacy and trust would diminish, leading to the tribe's fragmentation into smaller groups, where intimacy and trust could be rebuilt.

"This scenario didn't apply to Sapiens. Once they developed the cognitive ability to gossip about others in their band, they were able to form more meaningful bonds with each other, essential for maintaining stability in larger populations. As a consequence, if fifty Sapiens encountered a fertile valley inhabited by fifty less organized but stronger Neanderthals, the outcome of the ensuing battle would always be uncertain. But if 150 Sapiens marched into that valley, the smaller Neanderthal population would be slaughtered every single time."

Although Nika was listening to Lana Dao with interest, she was pretty sure the woman had forgotten what Nika's question had been in the first place, and so she said, "What does language have to do with the rock you were holding?"

"Do you have somewhere else you need to be, little pokey?"

"My name's not 'little pokey.'"

"You sound like a little pokey to me, and Sapiens' advanced linguistic skills are indeed related to my rock. The advent of language had another ace up its sleeve. It facilitated cerebral changes that enabled Sapiens to construct narratives about themselves, their lives, and their identities. This led to a level of sophistication and self-awareness unparalleled in any other species of human. And it was this heightened self-awareness that allowed Sapiens to conceive the entirely new and novel idea of *felo de se*."

"What's that?" Nika asked.

"Self-murder."

"Suicide?"

"Correct! Neanderthals, like Sapiens, were hunters and gatherers, primarily killing prey animals for meat and skins. But they also resorted to killing fellow members of their tribe if necessary. Unlike Sapiens, though, they never reached the level of sophistication and self-awareness to think that they could kill not only animals and fellow clansmen but also themselves. This realization holds profound implications because for a Sapiens to entertain the notion of self-inflicted harm, to think 'I can kill myself,' they first must have a grasp of who this 'self' is, and what will result from 'killing' it. If you've ever tried to imagine what it was like before you were born or what it will be like after you die—to imagine what it would be like to cease to exist—you will understand what a philosophical pretzel these questions present.

"So my point in all this, little pokey—yes, I do have a point, and yes, I have rambled, but it's rather refreshing to speak to someone who can still listen and understand intelligently—is that when George raped me—"

Nika frowned. "George?"

"The Denisovan you met earlier. He needs a name, and George is the name of a colleague that I despise. Now please let me finish while I can keep my train of thought. After George raped me..." Her voice changed slightly, hardened. "I won't talk about that. Only that it happened again and again. But at some point, when I determined that I was with child, I was..." Silence. Then quietly, almost a hiss: "I was repulsed. I was beyond repulsed. And in that moment I resolved to do something I never believed I was capable of. I found two rocks and used one to sharpen the edge of the other, which I used to cut my wrist. Clearly my attempt was unsuccessful, and when I regained consciousness, my wrist was bandaged, with Denny watching over me.

"Denny's the only Denisovan in this tribe that I don't loathe. He's a teenager who brings us our food. I believe he's half Sapiens from a mother imprisoned here long before us. You'll meet him, you'll see. In any event, after that, after my suicide attempt, George was different around me. Not frightened as you incorrectly observed. Cautious, I would say. He would watch me from the shadows of the entrance to this room, sometimes for hours. One day weeks later he approached me. His intention was clear. I shouted at him. I grabbed my rock to throw it at him. And his demeanor changed instantly. He turned around and left. I assume now that he thought I was threatening to kill myself —and his unborn child—and that was an incomprehensible power to him, an act beyond his realm of reasoning, something he could neither challenge nor fight. He never returned...until today."

There was another stretch during which neither of them spoke, and the only sound was the driving rain. The impenetrable darkness became unbearable, almost suffocating. Finally Nika said, "I think I should get myself a sharp rock, too."

CHAPTER 20

DENNY

Nika turned on her phone and started searching the small room. She found no rocks, only a few clumps of hard dirt that broke apart when she toed them with her shoe. She discovered nothing embedded in the walls either. "There aren't any rocks in here," she complained.

"That's too bad," said Lana Dao.

Nika liked it better when she couldn't see the woman. Her lips were pulled wide in a horrible rictus, and it was very likely she had been smiling like that the entire time that she had been talking about early humans and the advent of language and George raping her.

"Where did you find your rocks?" Nika asked.

"In the other room."

"What other room?"

"Where we go potty potty, little totty."

Nika hadn't given any consideration as to where the two women relieved themselves down here, and the idea of a dirt room filled with feces sickened her.

"It's not as bad as you might think," said Lana as if reading her thoughts. "Every now and then Denny collects our waste in a basket and burns it in their fire."

"What fire?"

"The Denisovans live in a room much larger than this one. Actually it's not really a room at all; it's a naturally formed cavern. They keep a large fire there. I've never seen it go out."

"You've been there?" Nika asked, surprised.

"What else do you think I do with my time?"

"I mean, they let you walk around with them?"

"Of course not. I remain hidden. They never see me, but I can see them."

"What do they do?"

"Sleep, eat, cook. Mend their clothing. Skin hides. Groom each other. It's not terribly exciting. Every morning most of them leave with spears and traps and baskets through a tunnel. They come back by midafternoon carrying fruits, berries, roots, nuts, and whatever animals they catch. Usually squirrels and lizards and frogs. But sometimes they'll have a monkey or wild boar. Once they returned with a black bear and her two cubs. They were very happy that day."

Nika's mind was buzzing. "When you say *most* of them leave, how many remain behind?"

"Three or four."

"Three or four! That's it? And you've never tried to escape?"

"Escape? Ha! How would I do that? Three or four Denisovans would still remain between me and the exit, and even the weakest in their tribe is much stronger than I am."

Nika's enthusiasm dampened. She couldn't fight her way past one Denisovan, let alone three. She said, "What about at nighttime? When they're all asleep? Would it be possible to slip out past them then?"

Lana said, "Why don't you give it a try and tell me how that works out for you?"

"What's that supposed to mean?"

"There is no escape from here, little totty. Go have a look. You'll see what I mean." Her strained rictus teetered on the edge of mad laughter. "Just don't get caught."

#

The deluge of laughter never came. Lana Dao had settled back into the role of a docile, introverted prisoner, rocking on her tailbone, saying nothing. Nika used the quiet to convince herself she was really going to go through with her plan to leave the room and spy on the Denisovans. Before she lost her nerve, she stood up and said, "Can I borrow your rock?"

The woman didn't reply.

"Lana? Can I borrow your rock?"

"Why?"

"I'm going to check out the cavern you mentioned."

"I don't think so."

Nika had expected this response. "Please? I promise I'll give it back to you."

She didn't answer.

"Lana?"

"If they catch you, they'll take it from you."

"They're not going to catch me. I'm going to stay hidden like you did."

"This rock is mine. Mine, mine, *mine*. You can't have it."

"Can I have the other one?"

She looked up. "Which one?"

"The one you used to sharpen that one."

"That's Karen's." Her expression darkened. "You can't have it either."

Nika glanced at the crazy girl sleeping in a fetal position against the wall. She knew arguing with Lana Dao would get her nowhere, and she wasn't going to fight the woman for her rock. Realizing she was going to have to leave without any way to scare off the one named George if it discovered her, she turned to the tunnel entrance—and froze with fright.

A Denisovan was crouched in the small opening, looking directly at her. It held a torch in one hand and a crudely carved wooden bowl in the other.

"Oh, hello, Denny," said Lana Dao pleasantly.

Denny, Nika thought, recalling Lana's earlier words: *Denny's the only Denisovan in this tribe that I don't loathe. He's a teenager who brings us our food.*

Her fear ebbed a little as she studied the creature, which didn't look anything like George. It was much slimmer, smooth-faced—and dressed absurdly. A steel army helmet covered its head. The band that once might have held cigarettes or a small bottle of insect repellent now displayed a variety of talons and claws. Black feathers decorated the chinstrap that dangled unused from one side. A tattered and sun-bleached olive-green fatigue shirt was unbuttoned down the front and appeared to be inside-out. The legs of a pair of matching pants were torn off at the knees, revealing hairless calves and mud-caked feet.

"Say hello, little totty," said Lana Dao, standing.

The creature's dark eyes went from Nika to Lana and then back to Nika. Unlike George's, there was no hatred in them, only what appeared to be curiosity and perhaps a spark of cleverness. If it had a sloped forehead and beetle brow, they were hidden beneath the helmet. Its visible features, while unusually wide, wouldn't have drawn a second glance on a busy San Francisco street.

Lana said, "Go on then. Say hello."

Nika worked some saliva into her dry mouth.

"What's wrong, little totty? You're being rude."

"Hello…" She cleared her throat and said with more confidence, "Hello."

Lana cackled, drawing the creature's attention again. "Hello! Why not greet him with *konnichiwa* or *bonjour* or *ciao*. He's fluent in those languages, too, of course!" She opened her arms wide.

The Denisovan—Denny—crouch-walked into the room and stood upright. It placed the torch in a fissure in the wall, which seemed to have been fashioned for just that purpose, and then went to Lana Dao, moving with a loping stride. It set the bowl by her feet—it was filled with chunks of meat—and wrapped its short arms around her upper body. They remained in an awkward embrace for several long seconds. Then Lana patted it on the back, and it patted her on the back, and they stepped apart.

Nika stared at them in amazement.

Lana said, "Your turn."

"I'm not hugging a caveboy," she said as a worrisome giddiness tickled up her throat. She pushed it back down.

"Why not?"

"Can't I just shake its hand?"

"*His* hand. And, no, you cannot. He doesn't understand our language, and he doesn't understand our cultural gestures. Shaking his hand would be as odd to him as if you tried to shake his foot."

"But he understands hugging?"

"It's a form of social bonding and comfort used by all our evolutionary relatives. Chimps, bonobos, gorillas, orangutans all hug. Denisovans are no exception."

Nika exhaled heavily. *Don't flake out, NC. This is really happening, so it's best to just go with it.*

Trying not to make a face, she held her arms open. Denny quickly came over and wrapped her in a hug, which was surprisingly gentle. She wrinkled her nose at a queer combination of musky body odor and pungent woodsmoke.

And then she heard it—him—sniffing her.

"Stop it," she said, stiffening.

He kept sniffing her.

"Stop!"

She broke apart. He backed away, appearing uncertain.

"What's wrong?" asked Lana.

"He was sniffing me."

"He probably likes the smell of your shampoo."

"Well...I don't like being sniffed." *Not in a house, not with a mouse, not here or there, not anywhere, I do not like being sniffed, Sam-I-Am.*

The suppressed giddiness finally escaped her lips, a bitter and brash sound.

Stop it, she thought. *Stop it before you lose it.*

"Denny?" Lana sat down and patted the ground next to her.

The Denisovan went back to her and sat obediently where she had indicated.

Nika said, "He knows his name?"

"Of course. Would you like to eat now?"

She looked at the bowl. "What is it?"

Lana pulled some meat from a bone and tasted it. "Rabbit, I think."

Although Nika was famished—her last proper meal had been at Happy Jack's with Popeye—she said, "No, thank you."

"You're not hungry?"

Nika pictured the pair of grubby hands that had butchered the rabbit. "Not really." She looked at Denny, who was watching her closely. "Can you tell him to stop looking at me like that?"

"Like what?"

"Like I'm an alien."

Lana stuck another strip of meat in her mouth and sucked grease from her fingers. "He finds you interesting."

"He's creeping me out."

"Maybe you remind him of his mother?"

Nika didn't want to think about any of that interbreeding stuff and said, "How long is he going to hang around for?"

"Quit being so rude, little pokey. Come sit with us even if you don't want to eat."

Nika hesitated—*best to just go with it*—and then went over and sat down across from Denny and Lana. Denny made a pinched, nasally sound and patted his chest.

She said, "What does that mean?"

Lana shrugged. "No idea." She shook the graduate student's ankle. "Food?"

The girl opened her eyes and then closed them again without replying.

Nika said, "Why's he wearing army clothes?"

Lana said, "Guess he likes them."

"George wore caveman clothes."

"Would you stop calling them that? And George wouldn't fit into our clothing. None of the adults would. Not the males anyway. They're too thick in the shoulders and chest."

"Where did he get them from?"

"The clothes? How should I know? The tunnels around here are likely littered with relics from the war. There's a tank in the cavern."

"A tank?"

"A tank. Bang, bang, you're dead. A tank, yes. It fell through the ceiling."

Crazy, Nika thought, saying nothing. *You really are crazy, lady. Or half-crazy.*

She returned her attention to Denny, whose gaze had fallen on her phone. She had all but forgotten it was in her hand. She was about to power it off as the torch made the LED light redundant, but then she changed her mind. The bright white light had been aimed at the ground all this time, and now she inched it toward Denny. He made a high-pitched sound and scuttled backward.

"Stop that," said Lana.

"Why's he scared of it?"

"Why do you think?"

"George wasn't scared of it."

"George isn't scared of much."

"He's scared of your rock."

"Cautious. He's cautious of it."

Denny was still staring at the cone of white light as if weary it would come after him again.

"Hey," Nika said curtly.

He looked at her tentatively, and she felt a cruel urge to aim the light at his face. Her sudden animosity surprised her, and she forced a smile.

He smiled back, showing straight teeth.

She patted her chest as he had done earlier.

He patted his chest.

She clapped a hand against her thigh.

He clapped a hand against his thigh.

"He loves to imitate," said Lana as she picked through the bowl of meat.

"Monkey see, monkey do."

"He's not a monkey."

Nika made her eyes go as big and round as possible.

Denny did the same.

That made her laugh.

He emitted a sound that was more like a mewl.

She thumbed her nose and stuck her tongue out.

He threw his head back and yowled.

"Is he laughing?" Nika asked.

"He's likely never seen a fool before," Lana retorted.

Nika opened her camera app and snapped a photo of the laughing Denisovan. She showed him the screen. He leaned forward and barked something that had the rising intonation of a question.

"That's you, Einstein."

Acting on a whim, she got up and plopped down next to him.

"What are you doing?" demanded Lana.

"Taking a selfie with him." She raised the phone. "Say cheese!"

He hooted something.

She snapped the picture and showed it to him.

He stared at it for several long seconds. Then he took off his helmet, revealing for the first time his flattened skull and jutting brow ridge, which instantly and dramatically transformed his face, pushing it outward like a warped reflection in a funhouse mirror. Nika shuddered in disgust. The fact that he had looked so human—so Sapiens, as Lana would say—made his differences even more abhorrent, almost like deformities.

When the miniature version of himself also didn't take off his helmet, he frowned at her.

"It's still you, silly."

He grabbed her phone.

"Hey!" she said, holding on to it. "Let go!"

He tried pulling it from her grip.

"Stop that! Let go!" She tugged the phone free.

The screen timed out and went black.

Denny yelped in alarm. In the next instance he was on his feet.

"Hey, hey, hey," said Lana, getting up, too. "It's okay, Denny. It's okay, sweetie. You're okay. You're still here."

Grunting repeatedly to himself, he snatched the torch from the fissure and scrambled out of the room. The amber glow from the flames faded, and the darkness returned.

Lana's voice, filled with an undercurrent of anger, pieced it: "Good going, little pokey."

"Why did he freak?"

"Last I checked, prehistoric humans hadn't invented photography. So congratulations. You just introduced 21st-century technology to the Stone Age."

CHAPTER 21
ESCAPE PLAN

Nika crouched at the threshold of the room. She hadn't stepped a foot outside it, but her heart was already racing inside her chest. She checked her phone—five percent battery left—and realized this was likely her only chance to navigate the tunnels with light.

You can do this, NC. Go have a peek. See what you're up against. Otherwise you're just going to be sitting around here in the dark all day with two rabbit-eating lunatics to keep you company.

She activated the phone's flashlight and duckwalked into the tunnel. Going left would lead to the feces room. She went right, the way she had first come. Occasionally her elbows brushed the walls and the top of her head knocked against the ceiling, but the tunnel seemed as though it had been dug for somebody of her size. George, who was extremely wide and thick in the shoulders and chest, would have found it a tight squeeze.

George. Was she really calling the creature that? It was such an inappropriately human name for something of its nature. "Denny" suited Denny, but George was more of a…Throgg or Grom or Brok.

Nika recalled the abhorrent thing chasing her through this tunnel not too long ago. It had felt like a nightmare—disjointed, unfathomable, unreal. Her mind hadn't caught up to the reality of the situation. One moment she had been about to get high from THC-laced gummy bears with Claude in a rather enchanting jungle thunderstorm, and the next moment a creature from hell was smashing her head into the ground, and in the *next* moment, her next conscious moment at any rate, she was somewhere deep underground where another creature from hell wanted to rape her.

Nevertheless, thanks to Lana Dao's detailed explanations, she knew the reality of her situation, and that made it less of a nightmare that didn't make sense and just more of a really shitty spot to be in.

Nika had read books about philosophers during her stint in prison. She preferred the ancient Greeks to the modern Europeans because the Greeks' philosophies were more visual and easier to understand. But the Europeans tended to have great one-liners, like Nietzsche's "God is dead" and Descartes' "I think therefore I am." There was another one by a French guy that went something like, "Humans can become accustomed to anything."

And he couldn't have been more correct. A few hours ago, if someone had told her that cavemen existed in the jungles of Vietnam, she would have dismissed them outright. But now, having encountered two face-to-face, she couldn't imagine any other truth.

After about thirty meters of duckwalking—it had seemed much farther when George had been pursuing her—Nika passed the room in which she had woken. She didn't realize how lucky she had been then to choose to go left instead of right. Left had led her to Lana Dao and her magic rock. Right would have taken her straight into the arms of the Denisovan tribe.

She powered off her phone and stuck it in her pocket. She didn't know how far ahead the cavern with the fire was, but she didn't want to risk announcing her presence.

Pressing onward through the now total darkness, she ignored the stiffness in her knees and back, as well as the voice in her head telling her to turn around. She wasn't sure how much farther she went—judging distance proved difficult when you couldn't see—but eventually she heard a throaty yet shrill wail. She froze, her mouth bone dry. A few moments later she heard another wail, although it was deeper, more of a bark. She forced herself to keep moving.

A light source she couldn't yet see lit the darkness ahead of her. Blacks faded into grays, and grays shifted into browns. She could once again make out the contours of the passageway which, she realized thankfully, had expanded so that she was able to walk upright. The ground angled downward steeply, and she took shorter steps while trailing a hand along the clay wall. Every few feet she stopped to listen. There were no more zoo-like noises, but she knew the creatures were close. Soon she smelled smoke and heard the crackling and popping of what sounded like a very large fire.

The tunnel ended, and Nika emerged on a high ledge where the air was warmer than it had been moments before. She lowered herself to all fours, craning her neck to look up at the rocky dome of a vast cavern. Stalactites protruded like canines from the arched ceiling, their wet surfaces reflecting the faint glow of the fire she couldn't yet see. In the center of the inverted bowl, the jungle floor had collapsed. Rain poured through the jagged hole, and vegetation overgrew the rocky rim, dangling like tentacles searching for a meal.

The last time Nika had checked her phone it was a little past eight a.m. It wasn't much later now, yet the storm kept the morning sky devoid of sunlight.

Abruptly a sharp cry rang out. Several barks responded. Nika flattened herself to her chest. She couldn't move. She didn't *want* to move. The hard ground pressing against her ribcage was reassuring. The creatures couldn't see her if she stayed as she was. She could still turn around and crawl back to her cell like a good little prisoner. She could still find a rock to keep George at bay. Living in darkness, sleeping on dirt, eating frogs and lizards, and relieving herself in a foul space that would make a public restroom seem like a palace would be hellish. But she would be alive.

On the other hand, if she peeked over the ledge and they saw her...

Nika pictured Lana Dao rocking back and forth to keep her madness at bay, her maniacal energy mirrored in her manic grin, her once rational mind broken and irreparable, her spirit destroyed.

And then Lana Dao's face became her own.

I'm not going back, she thought, a determination that filled her with relief but also raw terror. *Not now, not ever. I can't. I have to find a way out of here.*

Nika inched forward until she could see the cavern floor—and what she saw left her breathless.

Directly below the skylight in the ceiling, resting on a large mound of earth and jumbled rocks, was the army tank that Lana Dao had mentioned. She had been right; it really had fallen through the ceiling! Its treads angled upward on the rubble as if it were about to crest a summit, with the cannon mounted atop the turret pointing skyward. A small lake surrounded its collapsed pedestal, the surface rippling from the relentless assault of the rain.

Other smaller pools dotted the uneven ground, calm and shimmering in the light of a huge bonfire that blazed in a corner. Ringed by boulders, its yellow-orange flames whooshed fifteen feet high. Clouds of gray smoke billowed up on the warm air currents, dispersing through the skylight into the stormy morning.

Nika took all of this in at once, but her focus was fixed on the dozen or so black-maned Denisovans going about their daily business. One was smoking hunks of meat over a small fire separate from the bonfire, while another was lining a pit with what might have been heated stones. Another was scraping the flesh, fat, and hair from a hide. Others crouched around a pile of stones, making either weapons or tools. A few were still sleeping. A single toddler in an area fenced off by interwoven branches banged a bone against the ground. The only female Nika saw wore a skirt fashioned from strips of fur. She sat by herself tearing a cured hide with her teeth, presumably to sew a waterskin like the others stacked next to her.

The rhythmic clacking of stone on stone and the crackling bonfire, filling the air with the acrid smell of woodsmoke, combined to give the primitive scene an eerily sublime quality, reminiscent of a museum gallery depicting the dawn of human history. However, while paleontologists often portray our ancestors as noble savages, that wasn't the case with this Denisovan tribe. They might be organized, they might have developed the use of crude technology, and there might be a division of labor, but they were far more savage than noble. That was evident from the countless skulls adorning the hull of the army tank. Some belonged to large animals, some to small ones, and some were unmistakably human. Most gruesome was a very new addition: the decapitated head of the fake Ranger, his features frozen in an expression of horror.

Nika's emotions bounced between awe, disgust, and desperation—but mostly desperation. Lana Dao had been right. There was no way out of here. She saw only one other tunnel on the far side of the cavern, about ten feet from the ground and accessible by a dirt ramp. It would be impossible for her to reach it from her position without being seen.

Slow down, calm down, she told herself. *You can't reach it now, no. But remember what Lana said. Some—no, most—of the Denisovans will be leaving soon to hunt and forage. Surely they won't be deterred by the rain. And if only two of them remain behind, even three, you might have a chance...*

Just then a Denisovan dressed unlike the others emerged from somewhere directly below the ledge that Nika was on. She could only see his back as he made his way to the center of the cavern. Draped around his shoulders was the stripped body and expansive wingspan of a large bird, maybe a vulture.

When he reached the tank, he raised an arm in the air. Dangling from his fists by stringy optic nerves was a pair of eyeballs. He tilted his head back and issued a haunting, mournful sound that echoed throughout the vast cavern. The other Denisovans stopped what they were doing and got to their feet. They became either excited or anxious and began to chatter and make other noises.

The Denisovan wearing the vulture cape lowered his fist and turned around. His face was painted white with black charcoal around his eyes and a red ocher around his mouth, giving it the appearance of a grinning wound.

Despite the barbaric makeup, Nika had no trouble recognizing George.

#

As he returned the way he had come, Nika once again flattened herself against the ground in case he looked up and saw her. She heard the other Denisovans following him, and she realized there must be a tunnel she hadn't seen directly beneath her. When the last of the sounds subsided, she peeked over the lip of the ledge.

The cavern was deserted.

Go! Go! Go! she told herself. *Go while you have a chance!*

She hesitated. What if the tunnel on the other side of the cavern, the one she figured led to the exit, actually led to more tunnels and dead ends? What if the tunnel below her was the way out? Had the entire tribe just gone aboveground to hunt and forage?

The pounding of drums disrupted her thoughts. They beat out a resounding, urgent rhythm that reverberated from the tunnel beneath her.

Nika was confused. Some sort of ceremony? A morning ritual? George had held eyeballs in his hand. Whose eyeballs were they? Her stomach churned with dread. *Claude's? Popeye's?* She looked at the army tank. The fake Ranger's eyeballs weren't missing, which she took as a good sign.

The eyes belonged to an animal, that's all. Maybe the rabbit that Lana Dao had eaten for breakfast.

Regardless, none of that mattered, did it? She knew which tunnel to take, and she couldn't afford to waste any more time.

She looked down to the cavern floor forty feet below. The wall was steep and vertical, but bamboo spikes stuck out of the rock in two rows at regular intervals, forming a primitive ladder of sorts.

Oh, boy, Nika thought, but got moving.

With her weight on her forearms, she carefully maneuvered her lower body over the edge of the ledge until she found a set of bamboo spikes with her feet. Gripping the highest spikes with her hands, she aligned herself vertically with the rock face. Slowly and methodically, using the spikes as hand- and footholds, she descended.

About halfway down, one of her feet slipped. She gasped, hanging by her arms until her foot found the spike again.

How the hell does Denny do this carrying both a torch and a bowl of food?

The inane question preoccupied her for the rest of the descent, and when her feet finally touched solid ground once more, she had concluded that he must make two trips, the first carrying the bowl, the second carrying the torch.

Great! Good work, Sherlock! Now hurry!

Nika dashed across the cavern, euphoria filling her as the beat of the drums faded behind her.

I did it! I'm going to make it!

As she passed a ten-foot-tall stalagmite, her hope plummeted. A female Denisovan, previously hidden out of sight, was leaning against the rock formation, breastfeeding the toddler that had been in the primitive crib earlier. Her riot of hag-like hair was streaked with gray and festooned with feathers. Her eyes widened in surprise. She dumped the toddler on the ground and raised an alarm of shrill shrieks as she gave chase.

Nika ran faster and didn't slow when she reached the dirt ramp, but she tripped while ducking to enter the tunnel. Her forearms and knees took the brunt of the fall. Her chin also struck the ground, sending shooting pain through her face.

The old hag seized her ankles and dragged her away from the tunnel.

"Let me go!" she cried, kicking her legs.

It did no good; the creature's grip was like a vice.

Nika clawed at the dirt, leaving furrows in the ramp. She flipped over onto her back, finally freeing her legs. She kicked the hag in the face. The creature fell away, cupping her nose.

Yet behind her, racing across the chamber, led by George, came the other Denisovans, all of them roaring with excitement and frenzy.

No! Nika sobbed, knowing she was doomed.

Still, she scrambled back up the dirt ramp, tears blurring her vision. Before she reached the tunnel, her head snapped backward.

She screamed.

Was yanked to her feet by her hair.

Was spun about.

Was face-to-face with George.

His red mouth twisted into a sneer that was as much a smile because his black-rimmed eyes gleamed with delight.

"*Please!*" she blurted.

George swung her around to face the mob of Denisovans gathered at the bottom of the ramp. They screeched like monkeys, thrusting their arms in the air.

George released her hair. Her legs, jellied with fear, buckled beneath her. She collapsed to the ground. Then his hands were on her again, tugging her back up—no…tugging her poncho up. He yanked it over her head and stuck his thick fingers into the waistband of her jeans.

"No!" she shrieked, flailing, as he turned her upside down and tried to peel her pants up her thighs.

She kept screaming as he shook her like a thug shaking somebody down to get money from their pockets—only what fell out of her pocket was not money but Claude's baggie of gummy bears.

One of the Denisovans snatched it up.

George dropped Nika on her head and took the baggie from the Denisovan. Curled on her side, frozen with terror, she watched as he held the baggie up in front of his face. The other Denisovans went still and quiet except for the heavy wheeze of their breathing.

George shook the baggie. In the half-light and dancing shadows of the bonfire, the gummy bears glimmered like jewels. He sniffed the baggie and frowned. He poked the plastic with a dirty black fingernail and seemed perplexed when the miniature bears didn't respond. He glanced down at Nika, his eyes narrowed with suspicion and low cunning. Then he snorted and tore the baggie open. Some of the gummy bears fell to the ground. The Denisovans gasped collectively. But when the gummy bears didn't attempt to run away, George plucked a red one from the baggie. He held it between his index finger and thumb. Then he held it to his nose and sniffed. Finally he stuck it in his mouth and chewed. His brow furrowed, but then he ate a green one, then an orange one, then a yellow one.

The other Denisovans watched in rapture.

\#

Over the next half hour George ate the rest of the gummy bears one by one, clearly savoring the textures and flavors. He was obviously getting high, too. After about twenty minutes—and forty or so gummy bears—he had to sit on the ground. It took him twenty more minutes to eat the remaining dozen because he had totally slowed down. When he accidentally dropped a yellow gummy, he stared at it for a good two minutes before lifting his very heavy hand to pick it up and place it in his mouth.

Some of the Denisovans appeared agitated by his odd behavior, but they didn't intervene. When the baggie was empty, George watched the rain washing over the rusted army tank for a long time—then fell flat on his back, his arms splayed. Two Denisovans wearing strips of monkey fur around their foreheads like bandanas rushed to his side and sat him up. He shoved them angrily aside. On his second attempt he got to his feet and started across the chamber.

As the rest of the Denisovans fell into step behind him, Nika prayed they would forget about her. But then the two that had helped George to sit up appeared on either side of her, took her by the arms, and hiked her to her feet.

"No!" she cried, digging her heels into the ground as they frog marched her forward. "Please! Let me go!"

They lifted her higher and carried her between them.

George entered the tunnel at the base of the rock face that she had climbed down. The other Denisovans followed. Nika's escorts lowered her back to her feet and they entered last.

The passage was large enough they could continue three abreast without crouching. Niches cut into the walls held burning torches that had scorched the rock around them black. After twenty feet the passageway emptied into a room roughly the size of a classroom. It was blisteringly hot and filled with smoke. George stood facing a small fire that a Denisovan was feeding with weeds. A body lay at his feet. Nika thought its face was decorated with red paint until she realized it wasn't ocher but blood, spilling from the empty eye sockets.

The fire tender tossed a large branch onto the fire, causing the flames to whoosh higher and sparks to explode. George began swaying back and forth. The movement might have been a reaction to the mind-bending amount of THC he'd ingested... but then again, maybe not, as other Denisovans joined him. Those remaining on the sidelines slapped their thighs in unison, while two others pounded skins stretched taut over hollow logs, creating an offbeat, woeful tempo.

Then George began to dance, flapping his arms like wings. The others stomped and leaped and twirled. The fire tender threw more weeds on the flames. The drums quickened into a deafening din, prompting the dancers to move faster and faster until they were blurs darting between the shadows and the smoke.

Time seemed to slow down—or speed up—Nika wasn't sure. Her lungs burned and her eyes watered. Sweat dripped down her face. Her mind spun dizzyingly. Breathing and even thinking became difficult as drowsiness overwhelmed her.

How long did she stand there for, lost to the smoke and the pulsing, primitive rhythm? Minutes? Hours? Distantly she realized that her escorts had left her to join the dancing. She forced herself to turn around to leave—and collapsed to the ground, unconscious.

CHAPTER 22
THE RESCUE

"Sucky-fucky, ten dolla."

The woman's long black hair fell over her shoulders and framed her large breasts. The top three buttons of her silk blouse were undone, and she ran a painted fingernail up and down between her cleavage.

Ernest grinned. "No, thanks, sweetheart."

Cowboy said, "You nuts, Soup? Why not?"

"Listen to handsome fren," the prostitute in the doorway told Ernest. "Sucky-fucky, twenty dolla, you and fren both, good deal."

"Maybe we'll come back," Ernest said, wrapping his arm around Cowboy's back and leading him away.

"Sorry, ma'am," Cowboy called gaily over his shoulder. Then: "Fuck, Soup, you see those tits?"

"It's too early for that. Let's have some fun first."

They'd landed in Thailand earlier in the afternoon for their much anticipated seven-day vacation. After a military officer briefed them on the dos and don'ts while in Bangkok, they checked into a cheap hotel, showered, and changed from their fatigues and spit-polished boots into civilian clothing. Cowboy, of course, went full Texan, with his leather Stetson, a denim shirt, bell-bottom jeans held up by a black belt with a huge silver buckle, and scuffed cowboy boots. Ernest was dressed no less conspicuously in a brown suede jacket with tassels, a Rolling Stones T-shirt, tight red corduroy pants, and showy Italian shoes. Their fashion screamed American G.I.s on R & R.

They wandered the seedy, bustling streets of Patpong, Bangkok's red-light district, drinking cans of warm beer. After an hour or so they came to a fun-looking club blaring Motown soul where a half dozen giggling, beckoning bar girls stood out front. They found a table inside next to a group of pretty hostesses groping drunk Japanese businessmen.

Looking at all the topless girls gyrating on a colorfully lit stage to Marvin Gaye's "I'll Be Doggone," mouthing lyrics they likely didn't understand, Cowboy said, "You know we're getting the clap, don't you?"

"No shit," Ernest said. "But don't worry too much about that. Doc's got pills that will fix us up when we get back. Just enjoy yourself."

"Damn right I will. Bang-cock—right? Yee-haw!"

Ernest ordered a pitcher of beer from a scantily clad waitress and then said, "Don't take this the wrong way, Cowboy, but what about Kelly?" Kelly was his wife with whom he had a young daughter.

"Aw, fuck, man."

He said, "Just asking."

"I love Kel. I love her to death, okay? But she's back in the World, you know? We're in-country, and there are different rules here. I mean, fuck…I can shove my gun into a gook's mouth and blow his brains out the back of his head if I don't believe what he's telling me about the VC, and that's okay 'cause nobody will say nothing. Sarge can drag a sixteen-year-old by the hair behind her family's hut and fuck her six ways to Sunday, and that's okay, too, because he's the Sarge. We can torch a village 'cause maybe some dink might have a cousin that went off to fight with Charlie, we leave them with nothing but the clothes on their backs, and that's all fine and dandy because, hell, we got the guns and the bombs. Vietnam's fucked, man. The whole country's fucked. The shit we've done and seen…and you tell me, after sweating it out in the jungle for months and months, crawling through boobytrapped tunnels, getting shot at more times than I can count…you tell me I should be thinking about my wife who's nine thousand miles away?" He lit a Marlboro and exhaled a stream of smoke. "I'll take care of her, don't you worry about that. When I get back to the World, I'll be the best damn husband there is, but right now, I'm not there, I got a week's pass outta hell, and I'm going to enjoy myself 'cause if I get shot next month, if I'm lying on my death bed, I don't want to die thinking I was stroking my cock while you were banging the shit out of little miss big tits over there…okay, Soup?"

\#

"…okay, Soup? You hear me? Time to get up. Wakey, wakey, sucky-fucky."

Ernest opened his eyes and saw Cowboy hunched over him in a dark tunnel. For a moment he was sure he was back in the war, but Cowboy wouldn't be nonchalant about the bloody, gaping wound in his chest if that were the case.

Ernest sat up, shoving a heavy, smelly body off him…and it all came back. He grabbed his flashlight, which was next to him on the ground, still powered on, and aimed the beam at the creature that had attacked him. It had rolled onto its back so its mishappen face was visible—and all at once Ernest thought he understood.

The creature wasn't a creature at all. It was some unfortunate man born to a mother exposed to napalm or other chemical agents. Due to his birth defects, he became a target of mockery, and so one day he wandered into the jungle to live the life of a hermit. Or maybe he went there with an equally disfigured young girl, and over the decades they raised several generations of oddball outcasts that had lived happily ever after underground.

"It ain't what you're thinking, Soup," said Cowboy. "This ain't *The Hills Have Eyes*, and those ain't genetic mutations. Ugly sucker, for sure. But he's *supposed* to be like that."

Ernest looked again at the creature. Cowboy was right—or, at least, *Ernest* was right, since Cowboy was nothing but a figment of his own imagination. The creature wasn't disfigured; it was simply different. Human but not human. An extant hominin species that somehow nobody knew about.

Ernest touched the hard, bony brow and experienced a swell of resentment. He studied the lifeless brown eyes set deep in large sockets, the retreating chin and straggly beard, the barrel-like torso covered with blood from a bullet hole in its shoulder, and the half dozen knife wounds in its abdomen.

"Looks like some kind of Neanderthal man," he said.

Cowboy laughed. "Fuck you know about Neanderthals, pal?"

"Not much, but that's what it looks like to me."

"What's a Neanderthal doing living in Vietnam? Don't they know they're supposed to be extinct?"

"Remember the rock apes?"

"That ain't no rock ape. I saw one up close and personal, and that ain't one."

"What did it look like?"

"I told you a thousand times already."

"Tell me again."

"Strong like him. Muscular. Flat head and big brow like him, too. But it was covered in reddish-brown hair. It was an ape.

Definitely an ape."

"Or that's what you thought back then because it made more sense to believe that than to believe in a living Neanderthal."

Ernest looked at the hominin a final time and realized he didn't really care what it was. According to Claude, there were more of them, and they had taken Scooter prisoner.

He picked up his Bowie knife and wiped the blade on the creature's fur leggings. The blood had already dried and wouldn't come off. He stuck it in the sheath on his belt and searched for the Colt Mustang, finding it beneath the prone body.

"So what's the plan, Soup?" asked Cowboy. "We going hunting for old time's sake?"

"We're finding my granddaughter."

"And if they've done something to her?"

"If they've done something to her," he said tightly, "then they've made a very bad mistake."

#

The passageway continued for a considerable distance, gradually sloping downward, before arriving at something Ernest had never seen in all his time as a tunnel rat: a cathedral-like cavern so vast that, despite a roaring bonfire, much of its walls and ceiling disappeared into darkness. What he could see of the shadowy space bristled wetly with fang-like stalagmites and stalactites, resembling a giant, hungry mouth.

In the center, resting on a tongue of rocks, was a long-digesting meal: an M551 Sheridan light tank, corroded, washed-out, but intact. Introduced during the Vietnam War as an airborne assault vehicle, it was designed to land safely by parachute in remote locations—but certainly not in a seventy-foot-deep sinkhole.

"Woo-wee," said Cowboy, shimmying up on his elbows next to Ernest to take in the view. "Wouldn't want to be the poor sucker driving that when the jungle floor gave out. And hey, there's your old Ranger friend."

Ernest saw the drunk—or at least his head—sitting atop the turret at the base of the tank's 152 mm cannon. Next to it was another recently severed head. Below them, on the hull, a graveyard of skulls was on display, including at least two large tiger skulls and numerous human ones.

The cavern clearly served as a central living area for the creatures. Animal hides used for bedding were scattered about the ground, some with furs for blankets and grass and leaves for pillows. Along the walls, hunting weapons and traps hung from hooks made from wooden stakes and animal bones. Shelves carved into the rock held stone tools and skin containers. In one corner, a simple hearth was surrounded by a variety of clay pots, charred wood, a spit for roasting meat, and several shallow pits lined with stones for baking.

Ernest felt as though he had been whisked back in time 50,000 years, and he couldn't deny a certain feeling of superiority.

We've gone to the moon and back, and these poor fuckers, whatever they are, never evolved beyond the Paleolithic Era.

"Where is everyone?" asked Cowboy.

"Look over there," he said, pointing to the far wall. "That another tunnel?"

Ernest turned off the flashlight and slipped it into the waistband of his pants, freeing both hands to carry the Colt and the Bowie knife. He started down a ramp to the chamber's floor, glad to be able to walk at full height. The air was warm and filled with the musk of smoke and animal hides. As he crossed the enormous room the only sounds other than his footsteps were the rain splashing over the old tank and the crackling bonfire.

Until something cried out.

Ernest dropped to a knee and listened.

He heard nothing more. But a few moments later he spotted one of the hominins, a female, step from the thick shadows beyond the hearth. It held a struggling infant in its arms. The infant cried out again, and the creature set it on the ground to crawl around on its own.

Ernest moved stealthily toward them, using the stalagmites as cover. When he was within two dozen feet, he waited until the female's back was turned and quickly closed the distance between them. The infant saw him and stared curiously. The female began to turn. He smashed the butt of the Colt against the back of its head. It staggered and then fell to its side.

The blow should have knocked it out cold. However, it glared up at him. Then its lips curled back from its teeth. Hissing, it leaped forward, its hands reaching for his throat.

Ernest stepped to the side and cracked the butt of the pistol against its head a second time. Again, it fell to the ground but seemed uninjured.

"Christ," he said, realizing it had one hell of a thick skull.

In the next instance it charged. Its speed surprised him, and it crashed into his chest, pushing him backward. Then its teeth were gnashing at his face. Shoving it away from him with the hand holding the Colt, he thrust the Bowie knife into the underside of its jaw. It stiffened and spasmed, and then it became dead weight. He lowered his arm to let its lifeless body slide off the six-inch blade.

The infant began to cry—or maybe it had been crying throughout the brief struggle. Either way, it was making a bloody racket.

Ernest tore a strip of fur from the hominin's skirt and used it to gag the menace. It was red-faced, teary-eyed, and clearly not happy, but at least it was quiet.

"Goddamn," said Cowboy. "You almost got beat up by a girl,

man."

"Thanks for helping out."

"I would have loved to, Soup, but I'm not really here."

And Ernest realized that Cowboy *wasn't* there. The cavern was empty except for him. He was talking to himself again.

He hurried the rest of the way to the tunnel. When he reached it, he hesitated. Spikes protruded from the rockface, leading into the darkness above him.

To where? A lookout spot? But there were no predators down here to look out for, and he doubted the primitive humans cared much for a good view.

Another tunnel then?

That was more likely, but he had to check the one in front of him first.

It was spacious enough to walk upright. Torches lined the walls, some burned out, the others flickering on their last flames. The stench of smoke grew sharper until he emerged in a small room where the embers of a fire glowed, casting enough light for him to see a dozen shapes lying on the ground, many of them snoring.

Yet it was the shape just in front of him that commanded his attention.

Scooter.

Gripped with cold terror, he knelt next to her, expecting the worst.

But her pulse was steady and strong.

"Scooter," he whispered, patting her warm cheek. "*Scooter?*"

She mumbled something unintelligible.

A nearby hominin snorted.

He patted her cheek harder. "Scooter! Wake up. *Wake up.*"

She opened her eyes. They were distant, unfocused. "Papi?"

"Quiet," he told her. "We need to get out of here."

The hominin that had snorted now stirred, slowly sitting up.

Ernest didn't move, but it looked directly at him.

For several long moments it didn't react. Then it threw back its head and hollered.

The other hominins woke up. Seeing Ernest, they filled the room with a cacophony of agitated shouts.

"Get up, Scooter," he said urgently. "Right now."

Together they rose to their feet, but there was nowhere to go. If they turned their backs to flee, they were both dead.

\#

The hominins organized themselves into a circle around Ernest and Nika. They appeared wary of Ernest, their glances darting between him and a creature that appeared to be their leader. It stood in front of the fire, a black silhouette with a painted face and an intimidating cape of feathers.

Slapping its chest, it barked out something that sounded like a challenge.

The other hominins went quiet.

"*Papi...*" Scooter hissed, her voice tight with terror.

"Stay where you are," he told her.

He stepped forward.

The leader's eyes, wide and white, sized Ernest up. It glanced at the Bowie knife but ignored the Colt.

Ernest tossed the knife on the ground between them.

The hominins on the sidelines oohed and awed.

The leader cocked its head and looked at the weapon sidelong, reptilian-like.

"Go on," Ernest said. "Take it."

The leader obviously didn't understand English, but it nonetheless bent down and picked up the knife by the handle. It examined the sharp blade with its finger and snarled when it cut itself. Then, with an exalted cry, it thrust the weapon over its head.

The others cheered.

Buoyed with confidence, holding the knife at chin level, it moved cautiously toward Ernest, who it seemed to believe was unarmed.

Ernest waited until the leader was close enough that he couldn't miss. Then he raised the Colt, aimed the barrel at the center of its malformed forehead, and squeezed the trigger.

The blast, amplified tenfold in the underground space, almost blew Ernest's eardrums. The leader's head flew back. When the afterimage from the muzzle flash faded out, Ernest was pleased to see the fucking thing lying motionless on its back.

Chaos erupted.

Pant-hooting like a troop of panicked chimps, the creatures ran from the room, giving Ernest a wide berth as if the slightest contact would mean instant death.

When they were alone, Nika threw her arms around Ernest's neck and sobbed into his shoulder, "*Oh, Papi, thank God, thank God, thank God...*"

He patted her back reassuringly even as he was thinking, *What now?*

CHAPTER 23
A LONG WAY TO THE TOP

Nika thought she and Popeye were alone in the room until she noticed movement in a dark corner. Denny stepped out from the shadows.

Popeye broke from their embrace and aimed the gun at him.

"No!" she said, grabbing his arm. "Don't shoot him! He's okay."

Popeye glared at her. "Okay? Its one of *them*, Scooter."

"No, he's not. I mean, yes, he is. But he's half-human, too."

"What the hell are you talking about?"

She shook her head. It was too much to explain right then. "Just don't shoot him. He's not a threat. I promise."

"What's with the uniform?"

"I told you, he's half-human. Maybe he understands that and likes dressing like us, I don't know. But trust me, Papi. He's okay."

Popeye hesitated, then lowered the gun. "Lucky for it, the gun's not loaded anyway."

"What?" she said, alarmed.

"I fired the last round into the bird man. The pistol's useless."

"How are we going to get out of here then?"

"Not that way clearly," he said, looking at the torch-lit tunnel that led back to the cavern.

Panic gripped her. "We're *trapped*?"

"Depends," he said, "on whether the tunnel over there leads out of here or not."

Nika squinted in the direction that he was pointing. Beyond the fire, she made out a small hole in the rock wall only slightly darker than the shadows surrounding it. "I'm not climbing into that! It's tiny!"

"We don't have a choice, Scooter. If we return to the cavern, we're done."

"They're scared of the gun. They don't know it's out of bullets. Maybe you won't even have to fire it. Just wave it around. Lana had a rock— Oh, no. *Lana Dao*. We can't leave her!"

Popeye frowned. "Who?"

"They're keeping two other women as prisoners down here. A university professor and a graduate student."

"I didn't see them."

"They're in a tunnel high up in the cavern. We can't leave them, Papi. They're both crazy, they've gone mad, but we can't leave them behind."

"We can't do anything for them, Scooter. We have to move. Those hominins are going to work up the nerve to come back in here sooner or later."

"Hominins?"

"The creatures."

"They're Denisovans."

"What the hell is a Denisovan?"

"Like a Neanderthal."

Popeye scoffed. "That's a hominin."

Nika pictured the poor women sitting in the dark with only

each other for company. "We can't leave them," she repeated stubbornly.

"Yes, we can," he snapped. "I'm not arguing with you. We'll send help back for them later." He retrieved his knife, which was next to George's body, and went to the small hole in the wall. He looked back at her. "Dammit, Scooter, *get over here.*"

Nika knew her grandfather was right. Even if they returned to the prison room without the tribe of Denisovans killing them (they would make woefully easy targets while climbing the rock face), who was to say Lana Dao and the girl would willingly come with them? They were so far gone, they might both prefer to remain where they were rather than attempt a dangerous escape.

Reluctantly Nika joined Popeye. He produced a flashlight from the waistband of his pants and turned it on. Crouching before the dog-sized tunnel, he aimed the beam into the cavity and said, "The Viet Cong always dug back doors so they wouldn't be trapped underground. I'm hoping this is one of them."

"And if it isn't?"

"I haven't seen any other tunnels. And I doubt there was an exit in the one where they were holding you."

She said, "What if I get stuck?"

"You won't. Anywhere I can fit, you can, too."

Lying prone, Popeye used his elbows to drag himself into the hole, which was just wide enough to accept his shoulders. When his boots disappeared, Nika looked back at Denny, who stood next to the smoldering fire with his arms wrapped across his chest in a self-hug. She waved goodbye. He didn't imitate the gesture; he simply watched her with an unreadable expression.

Nika lowered herself to her belly and followed her grandfather into the unknown.

\#

The tunnel was too small for her to crawl on her hands and knees, so instead she used her forearms and toes, similar to how a cadet might navigate an obstacle course in boot camp. It wasn't pitch black; some of the light from Popeye's flashlight spilled around him as he led the way. Even so, the experience was claustrophobic and terrifying. The crumbling walls and ceiling brushed against her back and shoulders only occasionally, like a shy date, but they were always *there*, always within inches of her, supporting an unfathomable weight of earth and rock that could crush her at any moment.

Nika didn't want to think about that, or the possibility of getting stuck, or reaching a dead end, or a dozen other worst-case scenarios—but they were the only things she *could* think about. Her mind was in overdrive, and she couldn't shut it off. So she employed a trick she had used often in prison to pass the monotonous hours of each day: she went back to her childhood and rebuilt memories she had thought were long forgotten.

The first one that came to her was of a birthday party at Chuck E. Cheese's. She tried to remember the friends she had invited, and discovered it was easier to recall the ones she hadn't. The food they'd eaten (pizza, chicken wings, and baskets of French fries); the games they'd played (whack-a-mole, skee-ball, and claw machines); the presents she'd unwrapped (the only boy she'd invited gave her a pack of Hot Wheels cars), the loot bags handed out at the end of the party (she'd traded some scratch-and-sniff stickers with her best friend for a strip of temporary tattoos that she had put all over her face). And, of course, the animatronic Pizza Time Theatre Band with the big Cheese himself on vocals, a chicken on backup, a purple monster playing the keyboard, and some kind of dog guitarist.

Nika kept reminiscing, filling her head with a memory of a

Halloween when she had dressed as a mermaid (and gave every box of raisins from her stash of candy to Popeye); an Easter when she had thrown a temper tantrum because she couldn't find her Easter basket (it had been her own fault as she'd greedily collected the trails of chocolate eggs scattered throughout the house, not realizing one of them would have led her to the basket); and a Christmas when the biggest present she had ever seen had been waiting for her beneath the tree (what turned out to be, anticlimactically, a play kitchen set).

That was the same Christmas when she had nearly died.

She had been in the backyard, working on an "igloo," which was just a large drift of snow that had built up against the side of Nana's garden shed. She'd burrowed a tunnel into its base and hollowed out a room big enough for her to sit upright in. When she finished packing the snow that formed the ceiling so it wouldn't collapse on her, she crawled into the tunnel to leave—and *that* collapsed on her.

She had always thought snow was light, but the snow she was pinned beneath felt as heavy as cement. She couldn't move an inch, nor could she see. She yelled for help. The cocoon of snow muffled her voice, and she didn't think anybody would hear her unless they were standing right outside the igloo, and there was a slim chance of that. Nana was in the kitchen preparing lunch, and Popeye was working in his office.

The snow pressing against her face quickly chilled her nose and cheeks. Her fingers and toes turned so cold they began to itch, despite the fact she wore a pair of wool-knit gloves beneath her mittens and two pairs of socks in her sturdy winter boots.

She yelled for help again and was alarmed to discover that her voice was little more than a rasp. In fact, it had become hard to even breathe. She was pretty sure she was dying, and she was relieved that it didn't hurt. It was just like going to sleep, and she realized she wasn't even scared. She would just have to wait with her parents in heaven for a while until Nana and Popeye could join them...

"Papi?" she said. The soles of his boots were right in front of her face. "Do you remember my igloo? It collapsed on me when I was a kid during Christmas."

"What about it?"

"You dug me out."

"Somebody had to."

"How did you know I was buried?"

A pause. "Do you really want to talk about that now?"

"How?"

"Your grandmother was keeping an eye on you. She knew you were playing in the igloo. When she looked out the kitchen window and could no longer see the tunnel you'd made, she came running into my office as though her dress were on fire and said that you did it again."

Nika frowned. "Did what again?"

"You'd only been with us for a little while then and you'd already stuck a safety pin in a wall socket, suffocated yourself with a plastic bag, fell asleep underneath my car..."

"The plastic bag was supposed to be a mask. I was copying someone I saw on TV who had used a paper bag. I was four. How was I supposed to know the difference? And I was under your car because I was looking for the place where your feet came through the floor like in the Flintstones. I don't know why I went to sleep."

"You used to fall asleep in all sorts of ridiculous places. Anyway, that's what your grandmother meant when she said you did it again. You're the reason her hair turned gray, did you know that? But I guess all those antics pale in comparison to getting yourself kidnapped by a tribe of... what did you call them?"

"Denisovans. Lana Dao, the professor, told me that. She thinks they're dying off because of inbreeding so now they're breeding with humans."

"She sounds like a crackpot to me."

"No, she's smart, even if she is crazy. Papi?"

"I'm right here."

"I'm..." Nika hesitated. Apologizing had never been her strong suit, particularly with her grandfather. "I'm sorry I messed everything up."

"Messed what up?"

"My life. I should never have dropped out of Stanford. You were right. You're always right. I should have listened to you."

"I'm not always right, Scooter," he said. "But *you're* right. Dropping out was a mistake. But when you get knocked down—"

"You gotta get back up, yeah, yeah. So I'm going to. When we get back to the States, I'm going to reenroll in Stanford. Finish my degree."

"I think that's a wonderful idea. You won't mind being older than everyone else?"

"There were older people in some of my classes before. They're called 'mature students' these days. They were the ones who always raised their hands, the ones who wanted to be there. Everybody else was just waiting for the bell to ring. I want to be like them—studious. If prison taught me anything, it's that I enjoy learning. So maybe there's been a silver lining to all the Ari stuff, after all..."

Popeye stopped abruptly.

"What's wrong?" she asked, concerned. The childhood memories and conversation about her future had been effective distractions. Yet she was once again keenly aware of the gravity of their situation.

"There's water ahead."

Water? she thought, confused. Had the tunnel flooded? But if that were the case, wouldn't water be running past her? She said, "Can't you crawl through it?"

Popeye said over his shoulder, "We're going to have to swim, Scooter."

"Swim?"

"We used to blow tear gas and other shit into the tunnels to smoke Charlie out. They countered by digging water traps, which worked like a P-trap beneath a sink, preventing the gas from reaching deeper into the tunnels. We just came to one of those water traps."

Nika suddenly realized what he was saying. "You mean, we're going to have to swim *underwater*?"

"It won't be far."

"No way," she said, shaking her head. "I can't. No way."

"I'll leave the flashlight for you.'"

"I can't, Papi. I really—"

"The trap's a good sign. It means the exit isn't much farther ahead."

"I just can't—"

"There's no going back, Scooter," he said sternly. "So you can and you will. I'll be right on the other side waiting for you. Take a deep breath, and you'll be fine. Okay?"

She couldn't reply. Paralysis had squeezed the breath from her lungs. But she watched as he disappeared into the pool of water before him, leaving behind only ripples on the ink-black surface. And then those were gone, too.

#

You can do it, she told herself. *You're a good swimmer. You have to do it.*

Nika stuck her hand into the water. It was cool but not cold. She imagined some weird species of cave animal living down there where no sunlight had ever touched. Maybe a blind fish with sharp teeth, or a poisonous salamander, or something even worse that nobody had ever heard of...

Go on! Get it over with!

She picked up the flashlight from where Popeye had left it on the ground, closed her eyes, and waded headfirst into the water. When she was fully submerged, she kicked her legs to propel herself forward. The top of her head bumped the ceiling of the passage, and she opened her eyes to navigate better.

She could see only blackness.

The flashlight wasn't waterproof.

Nika banged her head again, harder. She rolled and pushed herself away from the earth with her hands and feet. She flipped back over—and realized she no longer knew up from down.

Panicked, she instinctively swam up—or what she thought was up—and touched the earth again.

Was that the ceiling or the floor?

She pushed off it.

Which way had she been going? She had no idea. She'd lost all sense of space and direction.

Her pulse raced despite the mantra running through her mind to keep calm. Her lungs ached. She was already out of breath! She kicked wildly until she found the wall or ceiling again. She kept kicking while pulling herself along it with her hands.

It went on and on and on.

Her chest felt as though it were about to burst open. She forced down a scream and thought, *You need to turn around. You're not going to make it. You're going to drown—*

Her hand broke through the surface. Her head punched through next. She coughed up water she hadn't even realized she'd swallowed. Popeye was there, saying something to her, but she couldn't stop coughing. He dragged her onto solid ground and slapped her on the back.

Gradually the coughs subsided. She breathed deeply until her lungs no longer burned.

"You made it, Scooter," he told her. "You're fine. You're fine now."

#

"I dropped… I dropped…the flashlight. It wasn't waterproof."

"Was supposed to be," Ernest said. "Chinese junk. Hold on." He dug through his pockets until he found his Zippo lighter. He clicked the spark button a few times before a small flame ignited. "Good thing I took up smoking again."

Dripping wet, Nika looked miserable. "I'm—I'm cold. I can't stop—shivering."

"Then we should get going. The movement will warm you up." He raised the lighter higher to reveal more of the tunnel, which was much larger on this side of the water trap. "We can probably stand up."

"Does that mean we're almost at the exit?"

"We're near the surface. Listen, you can hear the storm above us."

They got to their feet—Ernest had to crouch only slightly—and he led the way down the passageway. After twenty feet they came to a side room. He stuck his head into it and whistled, impressed. Arranged neatly on the ground were the dismantled pieces of a 105-mm field artillery howitzer, including its big black rubber wheels. Against one wall, stacked neatly, were unused shells, fuses, and propellant charges.

"What's that?" asked Nika, squeezing beside him to have a look.

"A goddamn 105 field gun."

"A what?"

"A howitzer. Charlie used them to shoot down our helicopters. Bastards must have taken it apart and carried it down here piece by piece."

"Why would they do that?"

"For maintenance maybe. Or to hide it if they knew we were patrolling the area. One of the reasons they always got the jump on us was because we never knew where they kept their big guns. They'd rain rockets and mortars down on us during the night, and when we went looking for them in the morning, we could never find them."

"Guess you should have been looking underground."

"Thanks, Scooter," he said dryly.

They continued down the tunnel until it ended abruptly at a dirt wall.

"A dead end!" said Nika.

"No, it's not," Ernest told her, pointing at a square in the ceiling. "See that? It's a trapdoor to the surface. Now, move back the way we came."

"Move back?"

"It's boobytrapped."

#

Holding the Zippo lighter high, Ernest gingerly fingered a trip-release wire that was tied to a hook in the bottom of the trapdoor. He followed it to a small wooden stake protruding from the wall. He pried away the dirt next to the spike with his fingers until they brushed a hard, cold object.

His mouth was suddenly dry. He steadied his breathing. Then he continued to scrape away the dirt until he could see most of the buried grenade and where the trip-release wire was fastened to the exposed safety pin.

Holding the pin in place, he removed the grenade from the dirt and—

Nika screamed.

He snapped his head toward her. She was five meters away, facing away from him. And then she said, "Oh, it's just *you*."

"Who?" he demanded, his heart pounding from the scare.

"Denny! He followed us."

She held open her arms. The hominin in the army fatigues and helmet emerged from the darkness and wrapped his arms around her.

"What the hell are you doing?" he demanded.

"This is how they say hello," she said.

Cursing to himself—she'd nearly caused him to drop the grenade—Ernest removed the trip wire from the pin and reattached the safety clip over the safety lever, rendering the grenade harmless. He stuck it in his pocket and pressed upward on the underside of the trapdoor.

It didn't budge.

He wasn't surprised; it was likely covered with more than fifty years of dirt and debris.

He pressed again, harder, and after a few tries the wood cover finally lifted free. He set it aside and tilted his head up at the rain falling on his face.

"You did it!" cried Nika, joining him. She looked up through the square hole and laughed. "I don't think I've ever been so happy to see rain before in my life!"

"Give me your foot and I'll boost you up."

"What about Denny?"

They both turned to look at the hominin. His wide, deep-socketed eyes regarded them anxiously.

Ernest said, "What about him?"

"Is he coming with us?"

"Coming with us? To *Saigon*?"

Nika shrugged. "Why not?"

"Because he's not human!"

"Technically, he is. Or scientifically, he is. Whatever. Lana Dao said he's our distant cousin."

"He's not a pet, Scooter. You can't keep him."

"I don't want to *keep* him. But if he wants to come with us, then we should let him. I don't think he's very happy here with the other Denisovans."

Ernest wanted to shake some sense into her, but what he wanted even more was to get back to the boat. "For the love of God, fine. I don't give a damn."

He gave her the Zippo to hold and then made a stirrup with his hands. She stepped into it, and he helped boost her through the trapdoor. He impatiently waved the hominin over and lifted it out the same way, too.

Looking through the trapdoor, Nika extended her arms, attempting to pull him up, but they quickly realized it was impossible.

He said, "You're going to have to go find something for me to stand on. A log or—"

"Hold on," she said, disappearing.

A few moments later the hominin took her place and stuck its arm down. Ernest hesitated, then reached up, and they clasped each other around the wrists.

With surprising ease, it lifted him up through the trap door and set him down on the muddy ground.

"And you wanted to leave him behind," said Nika, grinning.

#

A mass of black and gray storm clouds smudged out the morning sky and cast the jungle in murky, filtered light. If they hadn't already been soaked to the skin, they would have been drenched very quickly by the deluge.

While Ernest was getting his bearings, lightning flashed overhead and thunder boomed, and somewhere not too far away what sounded like a large branch or even a tree crashed to the ground. "This way," he said and started through the tangle of vegetation. "Watch where you step."

Nika called through the storm, "Where are we going?"

"The boat!" he called back.

"How do you know it's this way?"

"Listen! You can hear the river ahead of us."

A short distance later, beyond the thinning foliage, the river came into view. They were somewhere north of the NVA base camp, so he followed the river south. Roughly fifteen minutes later they arrived at the partly collapsed dock. The fishing boat was thrashing up and down at the end of its rope in the current.

When Nika and the hominin caught up with him, Ernest said,

"I want you to wait for me here, Scooter. I shouldn't be too long."

She wiped the rain from her face. "Where are you going?"

"To get your friend."

"My friend?" Her eyes widened. "*Claude?* He's alive?"

"Last time I saw him, yes."

She slapped him on the chest. "Papi! Why didn't you tell me Claude was alive? I thought he was *dead!*"

"I didn't know that. He told me that he ran away when you two were attacked. He stepped on an old boobytrap from the war, and one of his feet is no good, so I'm assuming he's still where I left him. I told him to stay put. But he might have tried to walk back to the village during the night. I won't know until I check."

"I'll come with you."

"No, you won't." He pointed at the hominin. "It's buddies might be up here looking for us. So I want you to get in the boat. If you hear one of them, or God forbid see one, you cut the rope. The current will do the rest." He took the Bowie knife from the sheath and handed it to her.

She frowned at it. "If they're looking for us, you're going to need that."

"Christ, Scooter! Do you have to argue with everything I say? If I run into them, the knife's not likely to do me much good. Now take it."

Reluctantly she did. "But you and Claude will be stuck here."

"No, we won't. The drunk from the restaurant came in a canoe." He waved to the bank a little way downriver. "I saw it over there in the mangroves when I was looking for you earlier."

He walked carefully along the solid side of the dock to where the rope was tied, gripped it in both hands, and pulled the boat toward him, hand over hand. Nika leaped into the bow. The hominin remained on the dock.

"Come on," she said, holding out her hand. "It's just a boat."

It moaned, a tentative, frightened sound.

"I told you we shouldn't have brought it," Ernest griped.

"It's not an *it*. It's a *him*."

"Not to me it isn't."

"Come on, Denny," she said. "It's okay."

Still moaning, the creature climbed aboard and sat down hesitantly on the rocking deck.

"Remember, Scooter," he told her as she sat down with her back against the front seat. "If you hear one of them, you cut the rope. Don't worry about me."

She pulled her knees to her chest and hugged them. "Just hurry back."

CHAPTER 24

THE CHASE

"Where are you, sport?"

Claude's white Reebok shoe, as well as his inside-out bloody sock, lay on the ground beneath some ferns. But the Frenchman was nowhere in sight. It seemed he had decided to return to the village on foot, after all—on *one* foot, which would have been difficult. In fact, in the storm, without a crutch of some sort, it would have been damn near impossible.

"Ernie?"

Shielding his eyes from the sheets of rain with his hand, Ernest looked up. Claude was twenty feet above him in a tree, straddling one of the highest branches that would support his weight.

"It's still 'Ernest' to you," he called up. "What the hell are you doing up there?"

"I figured I would be safer here than down there if they came looking for me."

He worked his way down from his roost, a slow and methodical process because of his injured foot.

When he reached the lowest limb, Ernest helped him to the ground and said, "How are you holding up?"

Claude gripped Ernest's shoulder, balancing on one foot. The bandage around the other one was mostly red with blood. "It really hurts," he said, his face gaunt and pale. "I didn't sleep all night."

"Give me your arm. We'll be out of here soon enough."

Claude hooked his arm around Ernest's neck, and they moved awkwardly together through the jungle. It took a little time to coordinate their gait before they got into a rhythm. Even so, the mud was slippery, and in places the undergrowth was impassable, forcing them to make numerous detours.

When they finally reached the perimeter of the NVA base camp, Claude was panting from the effort. Ernest eased him down onto a rock on top of a bunker and said, "Don't go anywhere."

\#

Ernest entered the derelict base, keeping low while darting from one abandoned hut to the next. Through the slashing rain, just ahead, he saw his tent. It was flattened to the ground, and he wasn't sure that was because of the storm.

When he got closer, he stopped beneath a tree to scout the area. To his left was the kitchen pit with the trapdoor at the bottom. It crossed his mind to toss the grenade in his pocket down the hole to collapse the entrance. He didn't. The hardened clay would likely survive the blast. And more, if the hominins were already aboveground, then they would know exactly where he was.

He didn't see anything suspicious, so he continued to the tent. The black Nike bag with Cowboy's remains was where he had left it, zipped closed and undisturbed.

To his dismay, however, fresh footprints crisscrossed the mud in every direction.

#

"Where did you go?" demanded Claude, looking just as tired and frightened as when Ernest left him. He frowned at the Nike bag strapped over Ernest's shoulder. "You went all the way back just for that—?"

"Quiet," Ernest hissed. "They're here."

"Here? *Where?*"

"Aboveground. They're looking for us."

His already pale face turned alabaster white. He scanned the rain-washed jungle as if expecting the hominins to leap out at any moment.

Ernest helped him to his feet, and they got on their way, only this time they were moving as quickly as if they were in a three-legged race. Cutting through the NVA base camp would have been the easiest route, but it was too exposed. Instead, Ernest decided to head directly east to the river and then follow it north to the boat—

From somewhere nearby a cry cut through the storm. Several answered it.

Ernest didn't know if the hominins had discovered his tracks, or whether they were simply coordinating their hunt. He said, "Faster."

"Tryin'," Claude panted.

The river appeared before them, and they went north, plowing recklessly through thickets of snarled undergrowth and splashing through deep puddles. Miraculously they remained on their feet—until Ernest caught his boot on a root. He stumbled. Claude lost his balance and put weight on his bad foot. He shrieked in pain, falling over.

From behind them the jungle erupted with hoots and hollers,

much closer than before.

"Shit," Ernest said, picking up Claude and pushing forward in their frustratingly clumsy way.

"How much...farther?" Claude gasped between breaths.

"Just...'head," Ernest replied, ducking as branches brushed past his face.

And while he believed that was true, he didn't think they were going to make it. They were moving too slowly. The hominins sounded as though they were right behind them. Nika would have heard them by now, and he prayed that she had listened to him and cut the rope—

Through a break in the mangroves, he glimpsed the rushing river again.

And the fishing boat.

Still tied to the dock.

"Keep going," he told Claude. "I'm gonna...slow 'em down."

"*What?*"

He slipped Claude's arm from around his neck. Propelled by his momentum, the Frenchman hopped forward on one foot and latched onto a tree branch. He glanced back over his shoulder, his eyes wide with terror.

"Go!" Ernest barked and then turned to face their pursuers.

\#

A bare-chested hominin wearing a fur bandana and holding a wood club burst through the vegetation. When it saw Ernest standing his ground two dozen feet away, it slid to a stop in a defensive crouch. Under its prominent brow, its sunken eyes shifted towards the Colt that Ernest aimed at it.

"Remember this, do you?" Ernest said.

A moment later another creature appeared, then another and another. Seven arrived in total, carrying various weapons: clubs, stone axes, spears. All of them sized up Ernest and the pistol in his hand. They had fallen quiet so the only sounds were the droning rain and the roaring river.

The one wearing the bandana barked something and stepped forward. When it didn't mysteriously fall down dead like its leader had earlier, it took another, more confident step. Its eyes never left the Colt.

"You want it?" Ernest said. "Take it."

He lobbed the gun at the creature's feet. It leaped backward with an alarmed yelp. The others chattered anxiously. But it recovered its composure quickly and plucked the pistol from the ground. Gripping it by the barrel it turned it one way and then the other, experimenting with its weight. Then it threw its head back and let out a shrill, triumphant cry.

"Like it, huh?" Ernest said. "Then you can have this, too."

He produced the grenade from his shirt pocket and held it out. With slow, unthreatening movements, he depressed the striker lever, pulled the pin, and hurled it toward them. It landed where the pistol had. This time, however, Bandana didn't leap away but swiftly scooped up its prize.

Ernest ran like hell.

#

Nika spotted movement in the vegetation along the riverbank a moment before Claude appeared, wild-eyed and muddy, lurching from tree to tree, dragging one shoeless foot. When he reached the dock and there were no more trees to support him, he fell to his hands and knees. There was more movement behind him. Nika expected to see Popeye, but instead a barrel-chested Denisovan burst from a cluster of tree ferns.

"Claude!" she shouted.

Before he could turn around, the Denisovan jumped onto his back. He was one of the two with the monkey-fur bandanas that had carried her through the cavern. Snarling in rage, he grabbed Claude's hair and slammed his face into the dock. He yanked Claude's head up again. In the brief moment before the Denisovan slammed it down, Claude looked directly at Nika, although his eyes were unfocused and frighteningly lifeless. Blood gushed from his nose and covered his lips and chin.

Nika was already scrambling out of the boat. She rushed down the dock as the Denisovan, trumpeting almost gleefully, slammed Claude's face into the wood planks a third time.

He didn't look up as she approached, but at the last moment he saw her—and the knife—as she plunged it into the soft flesh between his neck and shoulder. His squeal abruptly ceased. His surprised expression quickly turned to stone. He tugged the knife free and got to his feet. He looked at the bloody blade and then at her, baring his teeth and hissing. He pressed the flat side of the blade against her cheek, turning her head to the side. He sniffed her. His lips brushed her ear as he said something. It wasn't any word she understood, but she had no doubt it held some sort of sinister meaning. He tugged the end of her hair downward, tilting her chin up and exposing her throat. The blade left her cheek and the tip pressed into the underside of her jaw.

Nika's mind screamed at her to do something, but her trembling body remained mulishly unresponsive, paralyzed by the knowledge that she was moments away from dying—

She suddenly flew backward and landed hard on her tailbone. At the same time Denny lunged past her and seized the other Denisovan around his throat. They struggled back and forth like two stiff dancers before the Denisovan reached over Denny's shoulder and plunged the knife into Denny's back. Denny wailed, his knees gave out. Yet he never released his grip on the

Denisovan's throat, and they tumbled off the dock into the river together, disappearing beneath the rapids. Nika thought she saw an arm break through the surface some distance downriver, but it vanished just as quickly and didn't reappear.

Her heart went out to Denny, but she set her feelings aside for the moment and said, "Claude? Claude! Are you okay?"

He groaned.

She brushed his wet bangs from his forehead. "What can I do?"

A sharp explosion rocked the jungle. It sounded like a gunshot, only much louder. And then she realized what it was: a grenade detonating.

"Papi!" she blurted.

Claude struggled to sit up. "The boat..." he said.

"*Where's Popeye?*"

"He was right behind me. Need to go." He crawled past her.

Nika froze with indecision. They couldn't leave Popeye behind! But was he alive or dead? Had he blown the Denisovans up? Had he blown *himself* up—?

Another smaller Denisovan emerged from the tree ferns, his long black hair plastered to his skull from the rain, a dark hide cape trailing from his shoulders. He charged toward her, his eyes blazing, a spear held high in one hand.

Nika shot to her feet and ran to the end of the dock where Claude was climbing into the violently swaying boat. All she could think was, *We don't have the knife! We can't cut the rope! We're trapped!* And then a powerful hand gripped her shoulder, spinning her around.

She delivered a knee to the Denisovan's groin. Grunting, he shoved her to the dock. The impact punched the breath from her lungs. The back of her head struck the wooden planks. A black wave washed over her, but she didn't pass out. The Denisovan held his spear in both hands, poised to drive the tip through her chest.

She squeezed her eyes shut. When the anticipated pain never came, however, she opened them again and she saw Popeye behind the Denisovan, his arms coiled around the creature's head. With a forceful twist, he snapped the Denisovan's neck, letting the nearly lifeless body collapse onto the dock at his feet.

Glowering down at her, he said, "What did I tell you about cutting the goddamn rope, Scooter?"

CHAPTER 25
GOODBYE

Mr. Thang drove them to a hospital in Cu Chi where Claude was given a cold compress for his broken nose and had his foot properly cleaned, stitched up, and bandaged. He filled the doctor's prescription for antibiotics and painkillers at the hospital pharmacy and slept soundly during the rest of the drive to Saigon. Ernest informed Mr. Thang that he had achieved his purpose for venturing into the Ho Bo Woods. To explain Claude's injuries, he said the Frenchman had accidentally stepped in a punji pit while exploring the jungle and had banged his face while hobbling through the storm on his way back to their camp. He didn't mention the hominins or any other part of their ordeal not because Mr. Thang wouldn't believe him, but simply because it all seemed too exhausting to talk about.

Mr. Thang clearly suspected Ernest was keeping something from him, but he was too much of a gentleman to pry, and when he dropped them off at Claude's townhouse on a quiet street in Tan Chann Hiep, he simply told Ernest that he was glad his friend would be getting the burial that he deserved and bid them farewell.

The townhouse was small and tackily furnished with two beat-up sofas, a blue armchair, and a dated yellow moped all crowded into a living room the size of Ernest's study. Claude went straight to his bedroom and passed out on a Japanese-style floor futon. Nika told Ernest that she would stay the night to keep an eye on him, and Ernest took a taxi back to the Reverie.

It was early evening when he reached the hotel. He soaked in a hot bath, dressed in clean clothes, and waited until eight p.m.—what would be six a.m. in San Francisco—before calling his lawyer's personal number. They spoke for nearly three hours. After the call, Ernest removed the backing of the framed photograph of him and Neeti on their honeymoon in Italy to retrieve the folded piece of paper he kept there. He purchased a greeting card from the hotel gift shop and then took a taxi back to Claude's townhouse. It was almost midnight by then. Nika was sprawled out like a rag doll on one of the ratty sofas.

Ernest lingered at the threshold between the kitchen and living room for a long while.

"I'm going to miss her, Cowboy," he said quietly.

"At least you were there to see her grow up, Soup. I would have given the world to have been around for my daughter."

"You're going home now. I've arranged everything."

"And it's about doggone time, ain't it?"

Ernest didn't take his eyes off Nika. "I should have been a better role model to her. She might have had the sense not to get involved with that IT shithead."

"Everybody makes mistakes, Soup. But she's a good girl. Is she a little stubborn? Sure is. A little headstrong and fearless? She's those things, too. You always said she got all that from Palak, but that's not exactly true, is it? Because you know who else is stubborn and headstrong and fearless? That's right, pal. You. She looks up to you, Soup, and a lot more than you know. Which means you did something right along the way. So don't be so quick to criticize yourself. You raised her well, or well enough, and she's going to be just fine going forward…"

Ernest finally turned away from the living room. The kitchen, of course, was empty except for him. He placed the envelope with the greeting card on the round table and left the townhouse, closing the door quietly behind him.

#

Nika woke feeling stiff and sore all over but refreshed. The hands on the wall clock above the TV were both pointing to 12. When she laid down on the sofa it had been eight p.m., and she was certain she had been asleep for more than four hours. She got up and pulled back a heavy curtain from a sliding glass door, revealing a small brick patio. It was bright outside, and she realized it was twelve noon the next day; she had slept for sixteen hours straight.

Yawning, she checked in on Claude and found him snoring loudly on the futon. In the kitchen she opened the refrigerator. It was just as barren as it had been the night before. Then, she had eaten an entire block of cheese and a small container of hummus. Now, she grabbed the only edible thing left: pickled cucumbers in a jar. It had never been opened, and she couldn't twist the lid loose. She gave up and set the jar on the kitchen table—next to a red envelope with her name on it.

Curious, she picked it up and found a greeting card adorned with flowers inside. She opened the card and read a message in Popeye's familiar script:

I'm not good at these things, Scooter, so forgive me if I keep it brief. By the time you read this, I'll likely be on my way back to the tunnels with the police to find the two women you mentioned. If we run into those things, I guess we'll deal with them one way or another. But I suspect if there are any left, they'll be long gone. They seem to have a knack for staying under the radar. I'm not going to mention you or Claude to the police. But the discovery of another species of humans is going to be one hell of a big news story, and it's probably going to come to light that the two of you were involved. Which is why I've left the name and number of my lawyer with the front desk at the Reverie. You can trust him. He knows everything, and he'll take care of you, as will my estate. You won't be seeing me again. I'm sick. Late-stage cancer. Doctors say I have less than six months left. You remember what your grandmother was like in her final few months, and I'm not going to go through that. We all have a beginning, and we all have an end. My end is now, on my terms, and that's how I want it.

Your loving grandfather,

P

Through burning tears, Nika read the letter again, praying she had misunderstood something, knowing she hadn't.

A folded piece of lined paper was taped to the inside of the card. She peeled it free and opened it.

Drawn in purple crayon was a stick figure of a man with a sailor's cap on his head, a pipe sticking out of his smiling mouth, and a can of spinach in his outstretched, three-fingered hand.

Below it was a single word:

POPƎYƎ

BEFORE YOU GO...

**Love survival horror with tension,
mystery, and shocking twists?**

Don't stop now.

Next stop: a crumbling mansion in Barcelona's Gothic Quarter. Nine rooms, nine trials, and one contract that feeds on your darkest secrets. Welcome to *The No-End House*. Escape is optional. Survival isn't guaranteed.

ABOUT THE AUTHOR

Jeremy Bates

USA TODAY and #1 Amazon bestselling author Jeremy Bates has written over twenty novels and novellas, with more than one million copies sold worldwide. His work has been translated into multiple languages—including Russian, Czech, German, Arabic, Taiwanese, and Portuguese—and optioned for film and television by major studios. Midwest Book Review compares his storytelling to Stephen King and Joe Lansdale, calling him a "master of the art."

Bates is a KDP Select All-Star and winner of both the Australian Shadows Award and Arthur Ellis Award. He was also a finalist in the Goodreads Choice Awards—the only major book honors chosen entirely by readers.

His latest novel, The No-End House, is a standalone horror story set in Barcelona's Gothic Quarter, where two strangers face nine nightmarish rooms in a sinister house. Publishing through Kensington in July 2025, it's a chilling tale of survival and escape.

Visit Jeremy's website to claim your free copy of Black Canyon, winner of the Lou Allin Memorial Award.

Made in the USA
Las Vegas, NV
13 October 2025